What people are saying about …

In the Arms of Immortals

"Garrett tackles one of history's most perplexing questions: Where is God when evil seems to triumph? A powerful and moving novel that depicts a turning point in history: the moment where superstition and faith collided. Highly recommended!"

Siri Mitchell, author of *Love's Pursuit*

"*In the Arms of Immortals* paints a breathtaking portrait of life and death, of hope and despair, of unspeakable joy and indescribable sorrow. Ginger Garrett skillfully transports her readers from modern times to fourteenth-century Sicily in an intricately crafted illustration of God's lifesaving power. This book has it all—detailed research, flesh-and-blood characters, and a captivating tale that kept me enthralled from beginning to end."

Virginia Smith, author of *Age before Beauty* and the rest of the Sister-to-Sister series

IN THE ARMS OF IMMORTALS

IN THE ARMS OF IMMORTALS

GINGER GARRETT

David C Cook

transforming lives together

IN THE ARMS OF IMMORTALS
Published by David C. Cook
4050 Lee Vance View
Colorado Springs, CO 80918 U.S.A.

David C. Cook Distribution Canada
55 Woodslee Avenue, Paris, Ontario, Canada N3L 3E5

David C. Cook U.K., Kingsway Communications
Eastbourne, East Sussex BN23 6NT, England

David C. Cook and the graphic circle C logo
are registered trademarks of Cook Communications Ministries.

The Web site addresses recommended throughout this book are offered as a
resource to you. These Web sites are not intended in any way to be or imply an
endorsement on the part of David C. Cook, nor do we vouch for their content.

This story is a work of fiction. All characters and events are the product of the author's
imagination. Any resemblance to any person, living or dead, is coincidental.

LCCN 2009929973
ISBN 978-0-7814-4888-8
eISBN 978-0-7814-0344-3

© 2009 Ginger Garrett
Ginger Garrett is represented by MacGregor Literary.
Visit Ginger at her Web site: www.gingergarrett.com

The Team: Andrea Christian, Ramona Tucker, Jaci Schneider, and Karen Athen
Cover Design: John Hamilton Design
Cover Photo: © HarperPoint

Printed in the United States of America
First Edition 2009

1 2 3 4 5 6 7 8 9 10

062509

For Mishael …
and every reader who has wrestled with the question of "Why?"
but contented themselves with the question of "How?"

ACKNOWLEDGMENTS

For my friends at Cook, including Terry Behimer, Dan Rich, Don Pape, Jaci Schneider, Karen Athen, Amy Kiechlin, Douglas Mann, Amy Quicksall, Mike Kennedy, and the entire team for *Immortals*. Thank you for believing in me. Working with you is such an honor, and I look forward to many years together. And for John and Nannette Hamilton, who designed the cover, thank you for your incredible artistry!

Chip MacGregor, my favorite literary agent. You're simply wonderful at keeping me focused and productive, which leaves my high school teachers in awe of you.

My editor, Ramona Tucker, who has the rare gift of making a writer feel completely at ease when being informed of a manuscript's fumbles and foibles. Thank you for being an editor who is selfless, encouraging, and astute.

I am blessed that so many friends and family members contribute to my ability to function as a writer while still being a mom, daughter, friend, and neighbor. The more I open my heart to you all, the richer my life becomes, and only then do I grow as a writer. I owe most of my gratitude to my husband, Mitch. He loves me, and that's good medicine for anything that ails me.

For my kids, who roll their eyes and pretend to gag when readers think I'm cool. Thank you for reminding me that all that really matters is what's for dinner and where the clean underwear is.

What in me is dark
Illumine, what is low raise and support;
That to the highth of this great Argument
I may assert Eternal Providence,
And justify the ways of God to men.
—*Milton,* Paradise Lost

Chapter One

Thirty thousand dollars bought her the right to avoid being scalded alive.

Mariskka Curtis did not miss the shoddy built-in shower that had been in her old apartment. Now she owned a penthouse, and one of her first decisions as a new millionaire was to have a high-end luxury shower installed.

"For thirty grand, it should make my breakfast, too," Mariskka said to no one.

At least the bathroom was warm, making goose bumps and bad leg shaves a thing of the past. The maid had lit the fireplace in the master bath an hour ago and brought a fresh carafe of coffee up. The milk still needed to be frothed, but Mariskka didn't mind that.

She pumped the handle six times and the milk bubbled up. She poured coffee into her monogrammed cup, then the foamy milk over the coffee. Mariskka inhaled, surprised that coffee could still bring her so much pleasure.

Rolling her neck to get the morning kinks out, she swung open the shower door and sat inside. The shower began as a slow warm mist around her feet, giving her a few minutes to finish her coffee before the gentle raindrops started from the shower head and the dawn lights bounced pink off the shower glass.

Later this morning she was scheduled for an appearance on yet another talk show to dazzle America with her rags-to-riches tale. She hated the hollow feeling in her stomach that came from lying. She had stolen her best-selling manuscript from a patient's room. The patient, Bridget, had been a famous editor and left it behind when she died. Mariskka stole it on impulse, thinking it might be valuable if sold on eBay. Only later, when packing the editor's belongings, had Mariskka seen the business cards thrown in the bottom of her bags. One was for an agent. Mariskka had contacted the agent, passing the manuscript off as her own. It couldn't hurt anyone, she had thought. Mariskka had also stolen Bridget's watch, but only because she intended to return it to the family. Only later did she realize Bridget had no family.

When the agent sold that manuscript in a seven-figure deal, it was as if God answered her prayers. Mariskka made a pile of easy money. She bought things she never dreamed of owning. She even donated some of it, paying hospice bills that threatened to bankrupt families and sent worn-out caregivers on vacations. Good things had happened to plenty of people because of her decision to steal.

As the mist rose, she finished her coffee and waited for the overhead shower to turn on. Hard rock blared suddenly through the shower speakers, and she dropped her coffee cup in surprise.

It shattered at her feet. Instinctively she yanked her feet out of the scalding puddle. Losing her balance in the mist, she hit her head on the imported tile and blacked out.

The smoke stung Mariskka's eyes.

She blinked, trying to clear her mind, groping in the darkness for the shower door. The shower had stopped, and the music was dead. She wondered if the building had lost electricity.

She crawled over something sharp and jagged. The lights must have shattered above. It was too dark to see anything; as she pushed back the shower door, she wished she had windows in her bath.

Something was coming.

She felt the vibrations through her legs, shaking her to her stomach. Straining to hear above her thundering heart, she heard a heavy scraping against her hardwood floors, the sound of a sharp tool being dragged over the floors, catching every second or so, bumping over a seam. Heavy footfalls shook the floor, and metal screeched together with each step. She thought of the armored boots she had seen on medieval knights in museums.

Something slammed against the door, making the wood split.

It hit again.

"There is no Blood here," someone said.

"God help me," she whispered.

When she said the word *God,* the thing outside the door shrieked like an animal. A sword pierced through the door, creating a jagged seam as the intruder jerked it back and forth in the split wood. Light streamed in from her bedroom windows, but she could see nothing except a sword sawing its way through the door.

They should be testing the microphones for the television hosts right now, she thought. Amber-Marie Gates, her publicist, was going to be furious when Mariskka didn't arrive on time. Or when she didn't arrive at all.… Mariskka's mind was gone, traveling down more familiar tracks, unable to process her death.

Then the door burst apart, and she was showered with wood fragments. A figure too large to pass through the door frame stood twisting its head in different directions, staring at her. The glowing blue dawn outlined its frame. Morning sun rays shot up from behind its head and between its flexed arms, illuminating dust particles spinning down and turning the shifting light into a kaleidoscope.

Metal wings reflected the light at their sharp ice-pick tips; below these, the shoulders of a man were layered with scales. Each finger was tipped with dozens of iron claws, all pointing backward. Once it grabbed her, she wouldn't get free without tearing herself to shreds. It was built for death.

"There is no Blood here," he said.

"What?" she screamed.

"You have no Christ."

A tail with an iron tip, long and scalpel sharp, rose behind him as he pointed his sword at her. He turned his shoulder to come through the door. As he thrust his wings against the frame, cracks ran up the walls above the door.

He lifted his sword, aiming for her neck. She wondered if her lips would still be moving after death, the way Anne Boleyn's had.

He spun back around, his sword in motion.

❧

A shower of sparks was burning her.

She remembered lights like this.

She was a child at Disneyland, watching the magical parade of lights. A green, scaled dragon floated past her as she sat on the sidewalk, full of lemonade and ice cream. When the dragon swung its head in her direction, with its blind paper eyes and red paper streamers coming from its mouth to look like fire, Mariskka vomited right between her shoes. No one noticed, not even her mom, who had taken the wide white pills so she could get through the day, one of their last together. Mariskka wanted her to take the pills so she wouldn't be in pain, so she wouldn't groan in the night, but the pills made her dull and distant. Either way, Mariskka lost her mother a little more each day.

She stood, grabbing her mother's hand, pulling at her to run. Her mother laughed, tipsy from the combination of opiates and Disney princesses, swinging her around in a dance, not understanding the panic in her daughter's eyes. Mariskka struggled to get free, to see where the dragon went, but it was gone. She would lie awake for years after that, wondering where it was now. The eyes had only been paper, but she knew. It had seen her. It had seen something inside her.

Mariskka was still remembering herself as a little girl when she noticed her impending death had been delayed. Another creature was here, holding a sword, blocking the iron-winged monster from killing her. He had gold-and-straw-colored dreadlocks that ran down his back and the body of a linebacker. Judging from how close his head was to her ceiling, Mariskka guessed he was about eight feet tall.

The man picked up the dark iron-angel by the neck and slammed it against the wall. Plaster rained down.

"She is ours," the iron-angel said. "We can take her."

"Not yet," the new creature said.

A dark stain spread underneath the iron-angel on the tile floor. The stain shimmered as teeth began to appear, ringing the edges.

The new creature yelled over his shoulders, "Cover your eyes!"

Mariskka stared at the stain, which was devouring the iron-angel as it moved up it his legs.

The new one screamed again, "Mariskka! Now!"

Mariskka obeyed.

She heard the sound of an animal screaming in pain, and then all was quiet.

She looked up to see the new creature staring down at her. His nose was inches from her face, and his dreadlocks fell forward, tickling her cheeks. *If he were human,* she thought, *he would be beautiful.* But he could not be real, not with his strange eyes that were like big gold saucers and canine teeth that peeked out from his lips. His breath smelled of meat, too. She collapsed, losing all control over limb and thought.

His arms slipped behind her knees and under her neck, lifting her without effort. He carried her to the bed and laid her down, drawing the curtains and stepping back into the shadows. He sat in a chair, resting one arm on the armrest, watching her. A thick, numbing sensation started in her toes and poured slowly into her body. She felt it filling her, working its way through her abdomen, then her arms. When it got to her eyes, they closed and she slept.

Chapter Two

When Mariskka woke, it was dark in the room. Her stomach contracted with enough force to jerk her to a sitting position, and she grabbed for the nightstand lamp, knocking it over. She yanked it to her lap and fumbled for the on switch.

It lit neatly.

He was gone.

She yanked the shade off the lamp and swung it in all directions. Nothing was there, nothing was out of place. She checked the clock. 5:45 a.m.

She checked it again and watched until it read 5:46.

A laugh started low in her throat, then burst out, making her throw her head back and laugh. She grabbed the bottle of prescription sleeping pills from the nightstand and kissed it with a loud smack. The package insert had said, *Warning: visual and auditory hallucinations have been reported.*

It had worked—and far better than she had hoped.

She was a little humiliated that using a sleeping pill was the only way she could come up with a creative idea for a sequel. But once again, no one had been hurt. There was no right or wrong in publishing. There were only sales figures. Even Mariskka knew that. And she needed a sequel, fast, or everyone would know she was a liar. And a thief.

She groaned then, thinking of the talk show. She had to be out of here in fifteen minutes, and she was not a fifteen-minute kind of girl in the morning.

Mariskka missed a step on the stairs and slid the rest of the way down, a dry scream stuck in her throat. A huge man wearing sunglasses sat at her kitchen table; a book with massive iron hinges lay open in front of him. Words swirled around the page with a hum. Mariskka had the terrible feeling she should know him.

Another man stood by him. His back was turned to her, but she recognized the yellow dreadlocks flowing down his back. He spoke in coarse whispers that sounded like a lion's huff.

She landed at the bottom of the stairs, her head hitting an iron baluster with a crack, making the men turn.

"Get her up, Mbube."

The man with the dreadlocks walked toward her.

She began kicking, scrambling to stand and run back up the stairs. He extended a clawed hand, catching her by the back of the neck. Lifting her gently, he brought her to the kitchen table and deposited her in a chair. The men stared at her. If they were going to hurt her, they didn't seem in a hurry.

"Would you like coffee?" the one with sunglasses asked.

"I don't drink coffee," she replied.

They looked at each other.

The one in glasses got up and poured coffee into her favorite mug, pressing the button for frothed milk. He was making it just the way she liked it. Handing it to her, he turned and opened the pantry, retrieving a vegan protein bar. She had bought it when she first believed money changed people, but she never ate it. Money was no match for her bad habits.

"Don't skip breakfast today," he said. "You'll need your energy."

"Get out of my house." Mariskka said.

"You stole my book," the one in glasses said.

"Who are you?" Mariskka asked. She had a very bad feeling she already knew.

"I am the Scribe," he replied.

"And him?" Mariskka asked.

"I Mbube," her dreadlocked man said. "I yours."

"You're my what?" she asked. She was flipping through the stolen manuscript in her mind, trying to remember what the whole point of that story had been. If it even had one. She had never really made it past the fourth chapter. She had gotten a headache from all the storylines.

"Wait!" she said. "You're an angel, my guardian angel,"

"Your name is not written in the Book of Life. You are under no one's protection," the Scribe replied.

"Everyone has guardian angels," she said.

The Scribe leaned over her, blocking all the light behind him. "Did you even read the manuscript you stole?"

"It was confusing."

"Believers have angels, Mariskka, children have angels—but you are adrift. A passerby may help you, but no one walks with you. You rejected God long ago."

"Don't use that tone with me. You never walked a mile in my shoes!" she said.

"My dear," the Scribe said, his voice turning soft and kind, "we would have carried you if only you believed."

She wanted them gone.

They smelled of her past, of the baking hot cement at Disney, the stale hospice gelatin and turpentine odor of capsules and medicine bottles. Mariskka remembered throwing open her mother's bedroom door and shaking her mother by the shoulders, trying to force her to sit up. "Wake up!" Mariskka had screamed. "You don't get to sleep through this!"

Her mother had swatted her away, missing Mariskka by a yard. She looked like a windmill, cranking her arms in circles. Mariskka let her fall back into bed and return to her snoring.

Mariskka had crawled in, under the covers. Wrapping her arms around her mother, she tried not to cry as she fell asleep too. She had been only nine. And there had been no one to help her. She was alone when her mother died. She had always been alone.

"Get out," Mariskka said to the men. They didn't move.

Jumping up, she went to the closet to get her fire safety box, a relic from her mother's estate that didn't lock. She yanked out the plastic bag she had stuffed the original manuscript into.

Dragging the bag to the fireplace, she started the gas flames.

Flames were soon eating the bag, the plastic melting in noxious, warping shreds. The paper inside caught, the words disappearing into black, burning patches that glowed red at the edges.

"Get out," Mariskka said again.

"What is done cannot be undone," the Scribe said.

"She have no Blood of Christ!" Mbube shouted. "No one protect her!"

"You can," the Scribe replied.

Reaching for his book, the Scribe stroked its spine. He whispered something to it, and the iron clasps released, the book opening. Pages began turning front to back, back to front, fast and repeating, like cards being shuffled.

"What do you want from me?" Mariskka asked.

"I am the Scribe, the first writer. My books lie open before the throne of God and someday will be the only witness of your people and their time in this world. I will tell you a story of your own," he said.

"You want me to watch a story and write it down, like Bridget?" Mariskka asked.

Mbube shook his head, not looking her in the eyes. "You not write this one. You live it," he said.

Sounds began rising from the pages, filling the kitchen, with shadows floating in the air. She heard women's voices and horses on cobbled streets. Men were laughing as if they shared a secret, and somewhere, far down another land, a child was calling for its mother.

"No," Mariskka yelled. "No, I burned the book! You can't do this!"

"You now enter our story as a wandering, lost woman," the Scribe said, "dirty and unpleasant to be near. If you try to speak, they will not comprehend you. They will think you mad. The kindest among them will pity you. The rest of them, well, how little work there is for the Devil when men walk the earth!"

Chapter Three

Blood Month had begun. Panthea Campaigna watched the sun-burned peasants drive the lean cattle up the cobbled streets as horses with braided manes and genteel riders picked their way through the hungry, tired masses. Roasted chestnuts were for sale on every corner of the piazza, the carts surrounded by begging children and lazy old men who eyed her boldly and gave her harmless, toothless grins.

The shops surrounding the piazza, with its church tucked neatly in the center, were swarming with nobles and commoners alike, though the peasants knew better than to look upon what their labour had bought the ruling classes. She would have to shop later, much later perhaps. She had to reach the church and return home before it was too late. She would not spend her lifetime regretting how a wasted moment at market had cost her everything. Not that she wholly believed it would work, though she had brought plenty of money. She had generally avoided God when she could. Kneeling in church ruined her fine skirts and humiliated her. The common people looked at her, which she hated.

Lazarro, the village priest, had once said churches were quiet because God was always listening. Everything depended on it now. The negotiation would be straightforward.

Winter was not yet in the air, which was still perfumed by roasting meats, drying herbs, and stalks of dried flax bundled and laid in carts. A few ambitious boys ran from cart to cart, asking for a bronze token to separate the pith from the fiber. The sun was the only true monarch here in Sicily, and even in October it reigned in splendor, sending warmth to the stones and cheer for the final harvest festival. Free wine would flow tonight, the vineyards celebrating the last grape harvest of the year. She wanted so badly to stop; this was the last of the good milk, too, before cows were fed fermented grain, not fresh, and threw off tainted-tasting milk. October was the end of every good thing, she groaned to herself.

This was her city: the sound of carts meant she would have bread for the winter, the scent of herbs meant her foods would be seasoned. Everything seemed well enough, she thought. It was a good omen of God's mood.

The number of cows in the square surprised her, though. The peasants brought only the cattle to slaughter that they had not the grain to feed over the winter. This year, there were more cattle than she had seen in previous times, the caked mud around their hooves telling of their long journey. Sicily had colours of soil that surprised the traders from Europe: yellows, greens, reds. The cows, each hoof banded in mud like the rings of a magical coloured tree, lumbered on. The mud fell as they walked, ruining the stone streets swept clean for tonight, distressing the shopkeepers. Mud would be tracked in everywhere. But all the merchants held their tongues. Cows for slaughter meant peasants who would soon be the best kind of customers: drunk and unaccustomed to heavy pockets. They would spend wildly, buying in a frenzy, shoveling the money at the shopkeepers for a taste of another life.

This would be a good week for the shopkeepers, Panthea saw. There would be much blood running from the butcher's shop by morning.

She would not think of another's misfortunes. She would think of the vegetables and fruits that would store well for the cold, calm months ahead, when no man would break ground and four hours of Sicilian sun would not grow gardens. Blood Month was the final month of the harvest year, when workers assessed their state and claimed their wages, when all reaped what they had sown, and the butcher Del Grasso worked late into the night at his killing.

It was a bittersweet time, for she loved the festivals, the bargains, the stories spilled over ale in her father's manor, the commotion that kept her mind from feeling the emptiness at her hearth. Her mother had loved these festivals too. They would have shared a pie and paid a minstrel for a song. Her mother had usually demanded the fee back at the end of the song, claiming the minstrel had no right to charge for such a poor voice. The minstrels would laugh and play her a new song, one the others would not think to ask for. These second songs were always best. It had given Panthea a taste for secrets.

A pregnant dog darted in between the cattle moving up the main path. She could see its ribs, every one of them, though its belly was full almost to the ground. The cattle stopped moving, their heads pulling back when they felt something at their feet. They blocked her entrance to the church, unsure what was underfoot.

Panthea called to the peasant to move his animals. He faced her with a sneer, then, seeing her finery with the blue crest, pasted a smile on his face and bowed his head. She made a clucking sound, and the dog worked its way back to her hand.

"Come on, girl," she crooned. The brown fur across the dog's head was so soft, sweeter than any of her own furs. It was a shame such an animal had no home, no one to stroke this sweet fur and feed it.

She would save them all if her father allowed her. "If I allowed you one," he said, "I'd have to allow them all, wouldn't I? Yes! Well, no, I can't, even if you have your mother's charms."

Pulling a bronze token from her skirt, she bought a cold meat pie. Rosetta, the baker's wife, was pushing a heavy rolling stand of pies through the crowds, though Rosetta was great with child too, Panthea realized. Rosetta had a strained bodice and a jealous eye as the street dog was given a rich pie. The dog ate with wolfish big bites, then licked the ground and sniffed round for more.

Panthea was about to buy another pie for it when a procession pressed through the crowd, peasants and cattle pushing to either side. Women sang and played tambourines, dancing in slow circles underneath flowing black veils. They looked like the whirlpools Panthea sometimes saw in the inky blue sea that was only a moment's walk from where she stood. Men carrying a wooden pallet came next; a body was shrouded with linen, overlaid with flowers, and bundled with herbs.

The children in the piazza ran to the men, calling down blessings on the fallen soul and offering prayers for which they were paid by coins tossed in the air. The family of the dead one came last, a woman with tears in her eyes, surrounded by many friends and family who bore her gently behind the procession. Sicilians believed in God and honour, and believed no man could die well without both. This coffin was exquisite; Marzcana had spent many hours in the carvings. It was an honour for the dead man to rest in this piece; the family had done well by him. God and memories were honoured.

To Sicilians, the manner of burial was as important as baptism; indeed, Lazarro taught, was not a body welcomed to earth with cleansing waters and prayers, in the best fashion a family could afford? In the same way, each must be offered back to God, washed by women's hands, blessed by a priest.

The volcano above them rumbled, lightning striking down from a cloud to its steaming core. Peasants crossed themselves and struck the cows, driving them faster. Panthea pushed a token to the pie maker Rosetta, asking her to feed the dog another cold pie. Rosetta's fingers grabbed it too quickly.

"Take care of this dog," Panthea said. "If you need more money, I will be in the church."

Panthea ran for the church, pushing with both hands against the heavy doors weighted with iron handles.

Inside, candles flickered at the altar, reflecting off the gold painted on the columns and the stained-glass images surrounding her. She was alone in this swirling sea of illumined faces and fiery streaks of colour. The Virgin sat enthroned above her, cradling the infant Jesus on her lap. The archangels Gabriel and Michael flanked her, their stone eyes moving in the shifting light.

She worshipped here, of course, part of the daily crowd that attended and understood nothing of the Latin service (it was enough that God understood, Lazarro promised), but she had never been alone before God. She did not know what to say to Him. She felt she was a child again, meeting knights of great legend returning from Jerusalem. They had all towered above her, with stories of marvels seen in distant lands, and red valleys of scars that fascinated her. She longed to push her fingers in to discover their depth and ask their meaning. They had praised her for her beauty and sent her away. She was only a girl.

Kneeling, her eyes darting to either side, Panthea wondered how this was done. With a deep breath to shake off the embarrassment, she stretched out her arms above her. She had seen a saint doing that in a painting.

"I am afraid!" she called. "Will You delay it?"

She peeked up.

No one answered.

"Do not give me to that man," she whispered. "Delay my father's decision, please."

Panthea emptied her pockets into the collection box, pausing between each coin to let the sound fully carry.

Michael and Gabriel stared from the cold stone, unmoved.

She dropped her face in her hands. "I am not what this man thinks I am," she whispered, surprised to feel her palms wet from tears.

Something rustled in the shadows beyond the altar. She wiped her face, holding her breath. It was wrong of her to be here without Lazarro to speak on her behalf. God might get angry at her impropriety. She remembered what Lazarro had said about those with pride.

God brought disaster on them.

❧

Slipping from between the thick doors, Panthea ran down the lane toward the sea. A fog was coming in as the sun was setting.

It would be a dark night, without stars.

Turning the corner to fetch her waiting horse, Fidato, she was run over by a pile of children pulling a stick behind them, the end of which was being clung to tightly by a woman. The woman looked delirious with fear, and when she tried to speak, such horrible sounds came out that the children scolded her to be silent. It didn't appear she understood them, which only made them shout louder. Panthea hoped they were leading her to Lazarro. Only a priest would touch this wretch. If she was still on the streets by nightfall, she would be sore abused. She wore such odd clothes, and her hair was curled in fat waves. She could not have been a woman from this city.

The outcast stopped in front of a shop that sold paper goods from the city of Amalfi. Tears streamed down her face and grated sobs shook her shoulders, making strangers stop and point. The children shouted at her to keep moving, that Romano the shopkeeper would beat any beggar standing too long in the doorway, but the woman would not be moved. Like the others around her, Panthea craned her neck to see what was causing such a reaction from the strange woman.

Seeing no one was observing her, Panthea reached for something set too close to the crowd, unattended among the bottles and jars.

When she saw what the woman looked upon, Panthea grinned with the others and made her way to her horse. The woman had only been staring at a calendar, which proclaimed it to be Anno Domini 1347.

The woman was surely mad.

Panthea's horse moved quickly on the rough paths, picked clean often by her father's servants. Even one piece of volcanic rock could hurt Fidato, and she worried often for this. She did not like taking him out at dusk for this reason.

On any other night, she would tend to his feet herself, but there would be no time tonight, so he must not step on anything sharp. She would miss the nightly ritual of grooming him. A brush in her hand was as good as a prayer book, she thought. Only when she stood before Fidato did she sense a world bigger than herself. He had comforted her many nights, his mane soaking up her tears, his heart reminding her own to beat. He was a pristine white, perfect Andalusian, and no horse was his equal, save one. That horse had been bought by her father for someone else, the man who caused her such fear.

She loved Fidato, just as he was, not even minding the way his tail tangled endlessly, no matter how many times she reminded it to lie straight. She loved him deeply because it was so easy. Panthea knew Fidato loved her back, too. He was always kind, always long-suffering, always gentle. Panthea had heard of Saint Paul's commands to practice those ideals and thus please the Lord.

"You see, you're a good Christian, Fidato," she said, noting she would have to bring him an extra sweet after the feast. It would all be over then. Surely she would have a lighter heart. Father could not do this to her. Not tonight. She needed time to convince him that she did not need a husband.

She marked the setting sun, thankful she had stolen cinnamon at market today for her father. He was often unwell, fits of sweats and shaking seizing him. No one could communicate with him when he was having a fit. Of course, Panthea had relied on the priest for the first diagnosis. Only God sent illness, only God could cure illness. Lazarro had examined her father's urine, tasted his blood, and consulted his charts before declaring him to have a classic case of an abundance of bile poisoning. Cinnamon on the tongue was good for this, he said, as well as more frequent confession. Her father applied both, with somewhat mixed results. His breath was better, but he sinned and sweated every day just the same.

In her worst moments, Panthea was tempted to call upon Gio, the herbalist who lived close to the volcano. Panthea would have to walk—she could not take Fidato up that road. The path was sharp and dangerous, and only the poor or desperate would bother. Gio did not charge the peasants, but the noblemen could be expected to pay twice the fair fee. That did not surprise Panthea. Everyone hated the rich. The rich only hated being poor.

Her servants whispered that Gio was a witch. Panthea considered this likely although she had never met Gio and had no real opinion of her. She had heard tell of miraculous cures and fires that burned bones until there was only black ash, which Gio gathered up as if it were manna. Gio did not attend church, and Lazarro had been urged many times to stone her.

No, Panthea should not bother with a woman like that. Besides, the Church controlled all healing arts and Panthea had just made a significant donation. She was in good favour. Even if God refused her own plea, He might still answer a prayer for her father. Everyone in the village looked up to him.

She rose higher on the winding road that would bring her home in a few more steps. Had God heard her in the church? When would she know if she had been delivered? She was stupid, she thought, to leave so much money. God had made no promises. She had much to learn if she would ever become as great in business as her father.

Fidato slowed, choosing his steps with care, and Panthea saw he was disturbed by little bursts of fur fleeing on the path. The rabbits who lived here had never bothered him before; why would they run from him tonight? There were rabbits and other little animals everywhere underfoot, running up, away from the sea, up toward the volcano.

A blast from a ram's horn signaled a ship arriving in the port below, startling her. She caught her breath and leaned far to the right in her saddle, peering over the edge of the path. Ships arrived in port every day in their season. This one was late but still welcome. Yes, any ship arriving would delay her father's decision. This must be God's answer.

She saw the outline of a ship cutting through the fog. The masts were stripped bare, so that the wood beams showed. The ship was like a skeleton with one blinking yellow eye that shifted and roamed.

Someone on board was holding a candle box, staggering from side to side in the winds.

It moved through the fog, scraping over the rocks just beneath the waterline. The ship would not be able to make its return journey, not without repairs and weeks spent in the harbour. Had this captain never sailed into Sicily before? Why was there no crew, only this man with a lamp? It was impossible that he had made the journey alone in that ship.

A greater answer there could not be. This would have the whole village swarming. Her father would smell the money in the air. Strange affairs made excited people, and excited people spent more. Her father would be too busy making money to finish the marriage contract he had begun with her enemy.

Panthea wished again for her mother, the second time today. Her mother would know what to do. Her mother would have secured a better marriage.

Her father believed she would be utterly lost unless she submitted to a man. To Armando. Panthea bit her lip, hard, to stop those thoughts. If God had crafted her, He should understand. The alliance was not fit. Panthea was not what Armando hoped for. Worse, Armando was not what she hoped for.

Fidato stopped.

Swinging his head from side to side, he flung the red tassels draped across his neck in all directions, and Panthea fell to the ground. He stepped over her, caging her in with his legs. Snorting, twisting his head, and biting at the air as if he were chasing a fly, he kept her there.

Panthea panicked. Fidato had never lost his mind before. He was a proper horse for a baron's daughter, a gentleman and a smart one at that. But now he was rearing back on two legs and clawing at the air. His two hooves on the ground danced to keep his balance; he almost stepped on her. Panthea searched wildly but could see nothing on the path to fear—no snakes, no sharp stones, no angry sea birds. The little rabbits were all gone by now, and had not Fidato seen enough of those, nibbling the straw in his stable? He didn't mind them.

A hoof smashed down, missing her by a finger's width. Scrambling out on all fours from under him, she tried to escape. He swung around, turning on her, biting her on the ankles. He wouldn't let her stand up without getting bitten; he advanced too quickly. She scrambled backward like a crab into the crevice of the rocks behind her. He nipped at her until there was nothing of her outside the hiding place. She crushed herself into the hole, her legs so closely drawn to her chest that it was hard to breathe.

Fidato turned and screamed, blocking her from escape.

"What have you eaten, Fidato?" she yelled at him. "Something drives you mad!" A sound from lower down the path made her seal her mouth with tight lips.

It wasn't Fidato she was afraid of now. It was *him*. He was tearing up the path.

Chapter Four

Gio picked her way down the devil's ladder, a prickly, steep path under the belly of the volcano. Mists were the only thing that sprang from the black ashes and glass rocks up here. Long ago, the Greeks had believed it to be the workshop of Vulcan, the god of fire. Vulcan punished them when he was angry. Gio understood their superstition; she had not finished her work but had to abandon the effort before she was singed by falling ash. She was angry to be interrupted and wished she could blame someone, too, even if it was superstition.

She would not sleep well now. The singes would be forgotten, but that old hunger would find her in her bed, dead asleep, compelling her to rise and work again. How she envied Lazarus, who had been raised only once. This was the curse of her kind: Hunger for her work was relentless. Few would understand how that hunger could hurt, how resistance to it made panic rise in her throat, fearing that one day it would call, and she would be too old to obey. When she had still had the courage to attend Mass, ignoring the whispers and stares, she had heard the great church painters of Europe called blessed with talent. She did not think they felt that way, but she would never know. Men avoided speaking to her, and men of the Church most of all. Gio had once wept at the thought, but today she kept moving down the path.

Planting her feet in the mist, Gio knew just where to step. She knew this mountain better than she had ever known a man. She knew how it settled and rose, the soft crevices where green things grew hidden and the stubborn rock outposts that jutted onto the path without regard for anyone else. She knew how to pick around those, how to press and dig and find its secrets. The villagers feared the volcano, its red fire and the spirits it loosed among them. Gio was content that the people stayed away. Up here, she was as far away as the moon.

Others, the Romans who had been here before, had built great temples to the volcano, honouring it as a god. Their worship was just as silly as the peasants' fear, she thought. Not everything green was noble. The roiling sulfur clouds, the rivers of mud, and the glass shards that belched forth were proof of nature's obscenities.

But below the volcano, Sicily had the sea and trees that were like stout women with big bosoms, making everyone smile just to look upon them. Children snuggled beneath those trees in summer and peeled oranges, and old women stopped for a rest under them while walking home from the market. Sicily was in every way a woman like them. She gave the fishermen big lusty catches that danced in the nets and flashed silver-sparkled fins each morning; her trees gathered the weary to her bosom when sleepiness and heat overcame them; her stones and earth kept them warm at night with silent compassion. Women and Sicily understood each other.

Sicily seemed the origin of all things good, and all things life, and all things worth tasting, whether from glass, plate, or lips. Sicily had her passions, her turns of thought as sudden as storms that swept in from the sea with no warning, untraceable to any event or misplaced word. She could rage from the volcano, singeing them all, or she could push her wide, fleshy arm through the sea and sweep it up into the village, splashing cold water onto their delicate pastries and oak barrels of vinegar.

But everyone loved her. Sicily charmed the men and gave herself to no one. She was Europe's most savage and beautiful courtier. All who came here by land or sea pledged their love at once to her. Other Italians loved her, too, but the women knew the others were jealous. Sicily was the sister who had a certain magic. She was Italian, true, but not all Italians were Sicilians.

Gio's sack cut into her shoulder; she readjusted it, wincing at the weight of the stones. She spied a cluster of wild garlic, the last that would grow here until spring. She could not come down empty-handed. Nature had her cycles, and so did shame. Shame was followed by secrets, and secrets were followed always by more lies— lies that bloomed into hollow days.

No one in town would break bread with her. Even those who sought her help drew a deep breath before crossing her threshold. Many nights she sat outside, hoping to hear the sounds of the town below. She listened for laughter or arguments over beer or impatient mothers and their squawking children. Gio's heart twisted and stung most when she heard the sounds of family. She would never have one herself.

"Not for you! Not for you!"

Her hand already extended to yank the garlic bulbs up, she saw the Old Man just as she heard his screech. That was his name—the Old Man, a wanderer (some whispered an infidel or Turk) and he had long found work and shelter in the town.

"Did Lazarro send you to raid my garden again?" she yelled back, yanking the bulbs up and stuffing them in her sack.

He scowled and she saw how his eyes never opened now at all, even to reveal the spoiled, filmy irises, and how his whiskers grew more coarse and longer every month. Either his razor had dulled beyond repair, or his hand was now unsteady.

"As if Sicily could belong to one woman, *signora!*" he shouted.

"Get along, Old Man. The garlic is mine."

He raised his walking stick in her direction and swung. "I will bash your head in, you witch! No one would blame the blind Old Man!"

She jumped out of his way and continued down the path, making way for him to stagger up to her former spot.

"*Buona fortuna!*" she called behind her. "I see a patch of purslane your crooked old nose missed! My soup bowl will be full tonight! And lamb besides, and new wine, and bread! How good my dinner will be after a long walk on my mountain!"

She hoped he would find the garlic bulbs she had left. They were the best ones and a pity if wasted.

The sound of his riding was unmistakable. He wore heavy boots with iron spurs, lodged into iron stirrups. Great gold clasps held the blue velvet blanket on his horse; the blanket was trimmed in black velvet ravens with a thick black stripe down the side and Panthea's father's matching coat of arms on the neck. The man wore black leggings, reinforced at the knee with black leather patches, a blue velvet cloak draped across his shoulders, and an iron belt with his sword sheathed inside. It made a slight clank as he rode.

His horse's shoes were quite different from Fidato's. They covered the hoof and extended in gilded bullions up the sides so the legs appeared to flash as he rode. Panthea's father had insisted on spending a sickening sum on this finery. The finery was a waste, but Panthea knew women were wiser than men in this, too. Women wanted to live on their money, men wanted to live through it. *Foolishness,* she thought.

Still, the horse, Nero, was one of the finest she had known, a magnificent black charger, one of the best bred horses for the knights of conquest.

"Fidato?"

The knight Armando recognized her horse's call. He got down with a fluid swing, grasping Fidato's harness. Stroking his muzzle, Armando calmed the animal and placed his hands along its neck. "Your heart is beating so fast, Fidato! What has scared you? Where is Panthea?"

Fidato began sauntering to the castle, leaving Panthea exposed. She stood and brushed herself off, refusing to look at Armando.

"I was resting," she said and began walking home.

"Of course," he replied, following her. "I, too, sleep here, sitting in the rocks. I find more comforts here than in the straw bed your father provides me in the root cellar."

"There are other accommodations in the village," Panthea replied. "Why, you could even marry. Isn't that a lovely idea? Some poor wench with horsey eyes would think herself blessed."

"Don't hope for so much," he said.

"Aye, that's what I'd tell her, too!"

"Panthea," he said.

She kept walking.

"Panthea!" he yelled.

She turned and raised an eyebrow.

"Take Nero," he said. "I'll lead Fidato in and look over him. He must have had a fright."

"Yes, you were upwind."

"Panthea." He sounded disappointed.

She resumed her walk.

"Take Nero," he said, "or take me."

She walked back, glaring at his open palm extended to help her onto the horse. She would not move until he backed away. He sighed, stepping back, and she mounted the horse. It was good, she thought. Fidato would get groomed, and she would have a chance to ride the magnificent charger. Best of all, Armando would be delayed coming inside to the feast.

"Did you know a ship has arrived?" she asked. "Perhaps it brings a new suitor for me, one with great fortunes and many servants."

"I am your servant, Panthea. I do the work of a hundred men for you."

She dug her heels into his horse, which lurched up the path. She hoped it kicked plenty of dust upon him.

He was so wrong about her. They all were.

❧

Gio added the purslane to her soup kettle hung over the fire. Pulling down a rough-edged plate from a shelf, she ripped apart the coarse bread and set the largest hunk on the plate. Scooping a ladle of wine from the crock, she indulged herself in a taste before pouring it into a bowl next to the plate. Stacked stones on the outer edges of the fire were keeping a thin slab of roasted lamb warm. She pulled some free. It was the last addition to the meal. Gio marveled at her good fortune. She had such food in a time when women like her—indeed, any woman without a family—knew daily hunger. Invalids, or the very old, starved to death.

As if in proof, skeletons hung above her from the rafters, surrounded by greasy tapers hanging by their fraying wicks, plus her collection of shark jaws, bulbs of drying garlic, amulets, beads, and dried viper flesh to protect against the evil eye and jealous lovers.

Her hut, thatched together with stone, timber, and mud—all of it bartered for or offered as gifts by peasants—was like a wild animal's den. It had her scent, the smell of the trees and smoke, herbs and old leather satchels. No one was welcome inside, unless the person was too sick to remember afterward. This sanctuary was immodest in its way. It told too much of her story, too many of her tales.

Gio pulled out a copy of a religious tract, written in useless Latin, and ran her fingers along the brown woodcut images, finding the telltale splinter marks in each where the artist had moved his chisel too fast as he got near the delicate center. Edges, the beginning of a work, were easy to do for anyone. Few could draw near the heart of a matter, whether in image or in life, and remain composed.

Gio fished around for her magnifying glass, which she suspected had been stolen by the peasant who offered it to her as payment. She loved it anyway, and her hand seized on it somewhere under a pile of gemstones she meant to grind later. After looking at woodcuts, she loved to look at her map and dream of other lives she might have lived. With her glass, she could follow her world until it faded along the bottom of the scroll into an unknown land called Antarcta. It was a Greek map, of a round world no less, a world where the sea led you south, and south again, until you found a new land called Antarctos. In Antarctos, you lived upside down, and all natural laws were reversed.

She would like to visit such a world.

Sighing, she pulled a stick from her hair, dropping her black braids down. She brushed them out, weaving her spider-quick fingers through them to undo the pattern. Her hair felt like cool water running down her neck and shoulders. This was pleasure even the poorest woman in Sicily could have. Saint Paul had been right when he said long hair was a woman's *splendore*. He had not known that for some it would be the only one.

She brushed away snarls and entanglements, brushing until each strand lay peacefully against the next. Lying down on her pile of sheepskins, feeling her hair fall away from her shoulders, she tucked her hands under her head for a pillow. She wished she could lie here for hours.

Looking up, she admired her collections. There were rows of tinctures, herbs, and spices, all manner of strange talismans and teeth, but on the top shelf, pushed back into the darkness, were her best treasures.

Every holy man in all of Italy knew she had the pigments. No one knew the land like Gio, no one had colours like hers. Bishops sent their monks here for them. First came the plaintive entreaty that these must be given in the name of the Lord, to further His work here on earth. She always refused. Next came the subtle turn, the set of the mouth, the implication that forgiveness would not come easily on her next confession if she didn't sell. Their mouths fell open when she said she didn't go to confession anymore.

Some blushed and apologized, emptying their purses on her threshold, probably as worried about her soul as their mission. She liked them, but she would not sell to them.

Some grew red with anger, demanding that she sell or be beaten. She would open the door a touch, letting them see the dead men swinging inside. Those buyers fled, leaving curses and threats behind.

Precious few would ask to see them, just because they loved them as she did. For these, she would sell, but at a high price.

The money was needed for her other work, caring for the *fiume perse*, the Lost River. They streamed to her door, in winter more than other seasons, needing relief for an abscessed tooth (cumin packed tight into the tooth until it could be pulled), babies who grew thin whose mothers had no milk (fenugreek three times a day, and a stout wine no more than once), or coughs that shook a child until his ribs hurt (mustard plasters and keep him near the fire). Few of these people could afford the priest and his blessing, and few were certain God even saw them, except for judgment. Indeed, His judgment already rested heavily upon them, for they worked until their backs gave out and still starved through the winter.

She did not have to look beyond her door to see the suffering of the world. It was a river, and no man could find its beginning or its end. It simply flowed on, sweeping the weak in, roaring in the ears of those who stood out of reach.

The poor never seemed to fight it. They were born to be dashed to bits. Their children died, their homes burned. Only one thing could stir them to rage: one word that was never spoken, one word that could cause the banks to overflow and their rage to drown the world. Gio had no remedy for the poison it loosed. The poor never questioned why—why some were born to die starving, and why some born to lives troubled only by gluttony and boredom.

She stretched her feet out near the fire and wiggled her dirty toes. They looked like roots, gnarled and clinging to dirt after so many travels up and down the mountain. She did not mind. She was almost thirty, but there was no one to admire her beauty or mention the lack of it. She felt her big stomach pressing up against her breasts. It, too, had lost its maiden shape, but she liked its warmth, liked the feeling of being rounded and soft, of taking up space in this world. She felt undeniable. She knew people saw her. They had to step out of the way to make room for her to pass.

She had been tiny and thin once. Then they had pushed her aside.

She loved the warmth and spread of her body now, the way it was full and pleasing to her alone. Men no longer took liberties with their eyes. She was able to move among them without lewd regard. She found great peace in getting fat. With the silencing of lewd remarks, she heard the voice of wisdom more clearly. She ran her hands down her thick thighs. They were marvelous.

A twig snapped outside her door.

She knew he was outside, straining to hear noises within, eager to steal what he could. She sighed. She was hungry, too, but she had no time left. Tearing off a portion of bread, she stuffed it in her pocket. The market would be open late tonight for the beginning of the Blood Month festivals. She had to sell what she could, and quickly. Free flowing wine made good buyers. Winter was coming, making all of them long for a few more minutes' sleep under warm blankets, and she would have more trouble getting her money out of their pockets. Reaching to the shelves, Gio selected a few remedies that the nobles would be looking for tonight: charms against sickness and charms to win true love, all tied with red wool strings and to be worn in secret, dried bundles of vervain for happiness, lemon balm for excess passion, and St. John's herb for melancholy. The nobles could afford Lazarro, yes, and all believed that God alone sent sickness and God alone healed, but some people had the money to be wrong. They ate the witching herbs, tucked their amulets under their robes, and never missed Mass.

She opened her door, clearing her throat, and left.

The Old Man was out there, in the shadows that began to fall, waiting. He stole from everyone in the village, but Gio was the only one careful to feed him first. Over time, he had stolen less and eaten more from her, and Gio was at peace with that.

She picked her way through the narrow lanes, made pitch-black when clouds flowed over the moon if the torches had not yet been lit. Tonight torchlights graced her path and she could hear the distant sound of the festival in the piazza. Her stomach growled at the thought of enjoying a bowl of pickled *antipasti* or shrimp or even a quick mouthful of her favorite, pistachio sherbet. These lanes, and this food, were all gifts from the Arabs who had built Sicily. Wrenching her body to an awkward angle, she scooted past a shrine mounted against the wall of a home, sticking out into the lane. These shrines had been plastered, hastily, against every available wall when the Normans invaded. Now Sicily belonged to no one but Sicilians.

Gio felt someone sneaking up behind her, but she did not turn. If an enemy ever struck her down from behind, it was all the more to his shame. She held her pace steady, listening for his. The breathing gave him away.

He moved quickly and almost without sound, except for his breathing, as he was really rather large for his work. He was sensitive about that. He had been born for another life, and this is why she hated him.

"Gio."

"Lazarro," she said, waiting for him to catch up. Springing up, the cursed thing still alive in her heart drank in his scent, tried to force her to speak kindly to him or extend her hand.

Forcing the feeling away with a shake of her head, it disappeared, carrying the moment to the secret place of the dead, where her memories were covered with the bitter salt of tears, and her heart waited to see if dead things would grow.

His steps were muffled by the long brown robe he wore. Truthfully, it probably was his white wool hat that made him struggle for a cooling breath on these warm evenings, giving his presence away. His constant presence in the town, the sight of his swirling brown robes and the white dollop of a hat had led the children to name their morning drink after his order of monks, the capuchins.

"I hear you have stolen purslane from my servant," he snapped, stepping into pace beside her. "He is an old man, Gio. Have pity on him, though you would show it to none else."

There was so little room in the lanes. Focusing on keeping her arms against her sides, Gio was careful not to touch him. She was afraid if she touched him, she would use claws. This hate was a mystery to them both. They were both healers. But she had a wound of the sort never discussed among the healers, a wound that festered with time and kind words and was made angry by happy dreams.

"I cannot steal what your God freely gives me, can I? Those herbs belong to whomever picks them first," Gio replied. "Tell your servant I am not afraid of false witness."

"You should be," he said.

"I am not of your faith anymore, am I? I am not under your law," Gio replied.

"The past should be both your teacher and your law, Gio. Dishonour only brings suffering."

Gio stopped. She hated him when he talked like this, as if he knew anything of suffering.

"Should you not remember? Can you not try harder, Gio? Sicily is full of eyes, even among blind old men."

"Why have you come? To punish me a second time?" Gio asked. "Be on your way, dog. I want no talk from you tonight."

"I did not find you to punish you. I came because I know your secret. It is not worth dying for," Lazarro said.

"Which secret is this? That my herbs cure better than your prayers?"

"The villagers say you do evil upon the volcano … that you stir up its anger."

"You forgive sins and promise paradise. At least I do not charge the poor for my lies." Gio walked faster. It was no use talking to him.

"I know what you do up there. I know why your fingers are raw when you return, and you sleep for days. Up there, that is where you free yourself of your pain and guilt. It is not witchcraft. It is worship."

She pushed him against the wall. "Do not blaspheme it, or I'll put a knife to your throat and be free."

She held him against the wall by his arms, surprised at her own strength. She dug her fingers in, hoping to leave a bloody bruise. She wanted to cut through the heavy brown robe and leave a mark, forcing his flesh to bear a memory of her.

"A ship! A ship! One that brings much gold—we have seen it!" A rush of children swept past them, separating Gio and Lazarro, pushing them against opposite walls as the children ran through the lane.

"Come and see!" they cried.

Shutters above them opened, women and nursemaids popping their heads out like hungry baby birds.

Gio allowed herself to be swept along with the children. A ship in port, in this late month, could only bring the most coveted goods. There would be spices and herbs and perhaps minerals and stones for her secret work. Gio wanted first pick. She had to have first pick, especially of the herbs. Too many poor women bore children in winter, even in these lean years, and they would beg her help for their ailing children before the winter was out. Once, Gio had thought her heart would break that she was denied the hope of ever being a mother. She had lived long enough to know that the world broke a woman's heart in many different ways. Burying a child, any child, was a horrid act. Her heart broke each time, and even she, the legendary healer, even she could not heal it.

Chapter Five

"If you cook the prawns now, they will be tough when they are served!" Panthea pinched a servant on the ears. "Did you learn nothing from your mother, or was she a fool too?" she scolded the girl again, relieved to see her cry. The faster they cried, the sooner they learned.

Panthea paced through the kitchen, checking courses, counting plates. She wanted an accurate count of everything. She would recount the plates and goblets later tonight to make sure all were returned. There must be no loss, no abundance of food—only what was necessary for proper appearance and stopping up idle gossiping mouths. She counted the fish, filleted and lifeless on her table, seasoned by an indolent man with bushy eyebrows who cared nothing about her insults. Being a woman, she could not intimidate him, but she could fire him. That would be disaster just before a lean winter. She wondered if he hated her more because she was a woman or because she was his master.

Seeing all the servant keeping their eyes on their work, she stuffed a handful of cooked prawns into a linen and shoved it into her skirt pocket. She grabbed a hunk of cheese as well.

"See that all is accounted for by the end of the evening," she called out. "I want every plate returned in perfect condition, and every morsel of food to be justified. If I hear of any of you stealing the food for yourselves, you'll be gone by morning, and your children will starve this winter."

Looking at them work, she feared for her father. He knew they stole from the kitchen, but he had no will to punish them. She tried to make up for what he lacked.

She left to dress. She would give the cinnamon to her father, along with a lecture about his health, and then go to her room, alone, to eat. Her mouth was already watering.

Gio's lungs were on fire after her run through the streets with the children. She stopped, a hand over her ribs, watching them run on to the water. In summer, they would keep running and jump in.

A broad slice of rock lay at one end of the waterline like an open palm, and the smaller children would stand at the edge, testing the water with their toes before easing into the blue abyss. Below were fish of all colours, treasures from lost ships, and swirling sands that tickled their feet.

The old women swam too, but they were too old to be cautious anymore. With nothing to hold onto for balance, and with frail bones, they could not test the water with their toes and ease in gradually.

So they stood with their arms outstretched, leaned forward, and fell. With no toehold or certainty of the temperature, they simply fell forward, trusting the water to be good. Gio was in awe of them.

The children picked up speed as they ran down the steep descents. Gio feared they would tumble, one after the other, into the smoky mist rising from the water. The butcher, Del Grasso, stepped from his home some distance down, watching them without expression. His home, the farthest out in the village, sat near the water because of his work, the stream of blood flowing down into the water all day, and during this month, the night as well. He stank, continuously, of flesh and blood and fish bones.

Peasants stood in line in front of Del Grasso's home, holding ropes slung low across cow necks, waiting for their turn at slaughter. Some smiled at Gio, those who had found good outcomes with her. Some glared or turned away—those who had received no relief at her door. It did not matter. They stood in line, the *fiume perse* flowing to Del Grasso's door tonight, hungry and fearful. Del Grasso would slaughter what they had tenderly raised and prayed over, and the river coming to his door would turn to blood and find the sea.

The black rocks of the harbour below were hidden by a white fog that crept up to the village. Lightning shot through the night air, illuminating a tall, thin man stepping off the ship. She saw him reach for a writhing snake as thunder crashed overhead, sending the younger children screaming in fear and the older children howling in delight.

Gio stepped back, repulsed, but the children pushed forward, knocking her off balance. She fell to the ground, rolling her shoulder in while trying to protect her hands, causing her cheek to scrape the rough path. Wincing, she touched her cheek, then pulled her hand back to see how much blood it held.

"A curse upon that ship!" she said.

"I have offended you," a man replied.

She lifted her eyes from her bloody palm to see a twisted wood cane with a green and blue iron serpent climbing to the handle, its bulging black pearl eyes shimmering in the moonlight. The serpent's mouth was opened wide to strike, but it had no fangs. Its teeth looked to have been broken long ago.

Standing, but without his hand to lift her, she looked at the man who owned such an odd cane. Long, curling brown hair swept past his shoulders, with eyes that did not seem to move or blink, making her want to wrap her shawl more tightly around herself. His mouth, though, was beautiful. It was everything a mouth should be in a man—succulent, thick lips, parted at the top and bottom by little indentations that made her want to run her fingers, or her own lips, across them and know again what it was to be kissed.

She blushed. It was an awful thought, and she did not welcome it. Once she had known passion and praised God for life. But this sneaking desire made her think of Eve, how she hid naked and trembling in Paradise. This desire, she knew, this kind was wrong. For all women, it changed the way they felt about God—or did it change the way God felt about them? She did not know. She did not like patients who had ruined themselves with it.

"Forgive me," he said. He seemed to take deep pleasure in the words.

"How did you appear before me so fast?" Gio asked.

"You half-wit!" a fish-wife screamed.

Gio flinched, expecting another humiliation. Turning her head away, she saw Del Grasso standing behind her.

Del Grasso was holding a stained saw, crusted blood all over his apron. He looked like a savage, staring in contempt at the visitor. The fish-wife smacked him across the back with her towel. She cursed him for thinking of only violence.

"You're more troll than man!" she yelled as her husband pushed her back into the crowd.

Pushing his way through the crowd, the baron Dario Campaigna extended his hand to the stranger. "Put your tools away, Del Grasso," Dario called. "Please excuse our welcoming party," Dario laughed. "We were at festival when you arrived and had no word a ship was due."

The stranger bowed to Dario but kept his eyes on Del Grasso.

"This is Del Grasso," Dario said, gesturing to the hulking man while pinching his words in a way that let everyone know what an idiot the butcher could be.

"A man of blood," the stranger said. "There is no need to apologize for him. I understand his work."

"Yes, well, and ..." Dario began.

The children held their breath. If Dario used more than twenty words when ten would do, one of them would win an extra share of chestnuts from the others at the festival.

"And work, your work, that is," Dario said. "What has brought you to us in this month? We have not traded since the last harvest was first in, and we rather expected a quiet winter. But we are most glad to receive you, and I now offer you our town. May you walk here as a prince and have everything you desire while among us! We would be most pleased to offer you what comforts we have, and shelter, and food. Of course, I am the baron and banker, Dario Campaigna, and although Sicily belongs to no one truly, the people here consider me a father of sorts. You may find I hold the keys to profitable transactions."

Gio wiped her dirty hand on her skirt. Not a sound was heard that moment, except a cow mooing. Everyone was fighting the urge to kick Dario, except that everyone owed him money and relied on his grace.

"From your lips to God's ears," the stranger replied.

Dario waited, his eyebrows raised and hands extended in welcome.

"Was there a question somewhere in everything you said?" the stranger asked.

Dario laughed loudly, like one who had once been amused and remembered again how to make the noise.

"What do you want here?" Del Grasso asked the stranger. "Where is your crew?"

The children stared at Del Grasso in amazement. The younger ones had never heard him speak.

Dario made wild eyes at Del Grasso before turning with a smile to the stranger.

The stranger held his hands up to stop Dario from saying anything. "My name is Damiano, and I come in service of a distant prince. He has sent me to this town to see if the reports of your prosperity and peace are true. It is said, 'In Sicily, the angels never sleep.' If this is true, if your land is so graced, my prince has a transaction he wishes to conduct. As for the crew, all is well. It is a story for another time."

Gio wondered if she should bunch up the edge of her skirt and wipe Dario's mouth; he was sure to be drooling at the thought of Damiano's purse.

"Yes, well, this is truly a little piece of heaven," Dario responded. "But we should not stand in the street conducting business, my friend. There is a feast at my house tonight, why, yes, this very hour! You must be my guest."

"Is the feast meant for these people?" Damiano asked.

Gio liked seeing Dario in pain, which he was in now. The pain of sharing was the only pain his family ever seemed to suffer.

"Well, but, of course, no," Dario replied, wiping his forehead. "The peasants have worked so hard this summer, and the festival is their one chance to rest. They would not want to trade it for a meal at my humble home."

"Yes, we would!" a boy called from the crowd.

Gio laughed into her hand. The boy was skinny for his age, and bold. She didn't know which had come first.

"Very well," Damiano replied. "I will adjourn to your home, without these good companions." He bowed to the people around him. Gio could tell they liked him. He was a clever man, winning them over by offering someone else's goods.

Dario swallowed, the stone in his throat bobbing hard. Just over his shoulder, Gio saw a woman standing in the door of the little church in the square, almost hidden by the shadows of the old stone arch. She was opening her mouth, pointing at Damiano, and the result was a grotesque howl. Gio wondered if the woman had a severed tongue.

Damiano turned, his eyes kindling when he saw her. "I did not know your town gave shelter to her kind," he said to Dario.

Dario stepped in between Damiano and the awful woman. "A pauper, sir, not going to stay long, not one of us. We've never seen her before today, of course."

"I do not believe in charity toward her kind," Damiano said. He spoke now to the crowd. "You would do well to send her away with blows and curses."

Dario turned to find the butcher and motioned toward the woman. "Del Grasso! Make yourself useful!" Turning and gesturing for Damiano to follow, Dario walked away from the square, in the direction of the manor.

Del Grasso moved toward the old woman, who waved her hands in the air as if in terror, pointing at Damiano's back, spittle flying from her mouth when she tried to speak. Having pity, Gio decided to save her.

⚜

Drowning in food, she had no time to stop to breathe. The shrimp made Panthea's fingers so greasy the food slid from between them as she crammed each bite into her mouth. She had to catch the slippery bits of cheese and prawns before they slid all the way down her chin and ruined her beaded gown. With each swallow her throat popped and burned, gulps of air forced in between bites. She had to eat it all, right now, and then she would paint her face and perfume her breasts and study the portrait of her mother once more. Being a lady was such dirty work.

"Panthea!"

Her father's yelp startled her. She yanked at her bed coverlet, smearing the grease from her face on it, frantically wiping her fingers and running her tongue across her teeth to clean them.

"Panthea!" Dario opened the door without knocking. "Come, my sweet! A noble has come from a distant land—a wealthy noble! Yes, and he is our guest! There is money to be made tonight!"

"Armando already made us wealthy, Father."

"Armando?" Dario replied. "Oh, Armando, of course. Yes, he brought us fortune, but he cost us a fortune, too, always abusing his armor in battle. And his horse has more shoes than the emperor's wife."

"We should move to Florence, or Venice, where the wealthier families are. That is what you must announce tonight," Panthea said. She picked up a brush and worked on her hair. She hoped he did not notice her hands trembling.

He sat on the bed, sniffing the air. Panthea reddened and hoped he did not detect the aroma of food.

"I like it here, Panthea. This is where I loved your mother. I built a life here. You ask me to abandon it too easily, my child."

"Should I not build a life of my own?" Panthea said.

"You know my intentions."

"Do you know what your problem is, Father? You have never asked God for more. You deserve more."

He grew still. "I had your mother, Panthea. I was not a good husband to her. Why, then, would I ask God for anything more?"

"Because she is gone!" Panthea yelled. "You have me to worry on now."

He looked wounded, his tender face bruised, so she softened her tone and tried to smile. "Think of me as an account well overdue and perhaps you will feel my sense of urgency."

"Ahh, Panthea. You have my brains and your mother's face. You will make Armando exquisitely miserable."

Panthea began to speak again, but he held up a finger, grinning.

"Tsk! The feast is ready. You know my will, Panthea. Present me an alternative by tonight or accept my decision. It matters little to me as long as we do not have this same argument again in the morning."

His hand was on the door. "I will not fail you as I failed your mother, Panthea. I will see you married to this good man. I will give you the life I could have had."

"I cannot pay your debts, Father."

"Neither can I, my dear. Neither can I."

He left. Her stomach felt raw and empty, though it was full of fatty foods. Her father concealed his wounds from her, but still he hoped she could heal them. Being the only child of this man made her tense and tired. Though he treated her like a pet, she knew he wanted her to be more of an heir and less like a woman.

Panthea looked at herself in her mirror. Full-length, it was an exquisite trophy her father had bought her mother years ago. Italians were so good at everything, she thought, but especially at admiring beauty.

She looked down at her body. The modest swell of her breasts under her bodice, the hollow of her stomach and curved waist ... *all too thin*, she thought. She turned to see the full, flowing skirt, which hinted at an extravagant bottom. She frowned. The curves were not full enough, even with the extra material the seamstress had added. She was a stick of a woman and she hated herself. Hippocrates was right: Thinking like a man had given her a man's body.

But she would rather be too thin and keep her wits than live a woman's life. Her needlepoint looked wretched, her singing voice had made her tutors wince, and she could barely get through a doorway without her skirts catching on something and tearing. How did other women survive all this without ripping their hair out? Panthea was terrible at being a woman, she knew.

"The essence of women is pleasure," her father had said once. "Women were born for pleasure, and the pleasure of men"; this is what he had said long ago. He would not repeat the words again. When her mother died, her father stopped believing in pleasure.

Turning back to the mirror, rolling her shoulders forward to check her cleavage, she then pushed her shoulders back to set off her bosom at its best angle. It would be difficult to hold this posture all night, but if she could, she would look better.

Thinking of Armando, her posture fell. Panthea could not take a husband who was so easily satisfied. Her poses and practiced witticisms had no observable effect on him. He loved her as she was, and it frightened her.

She wanted to be more, more than just the woman she was. He was pleased to take her in a diminished state. But with more money from her father, and more servants, she could be perfect. She could even conduct her own affairs. She would know how to be a real woman and yet still think the thoughts of a man. Why would Armando accept her now? Marrying her now was a sentence to a life of mediocrity, of settling, of having no good wine on some nights and blowing out candles early to save the wax. To marry now was to face life just as it was, the constant scrape and compromise and secret humiliations. Her mother's early death and her father's eternal penance had taught Panthea that a life can be wasted. She did not want that to happen to her. She did not want that to happen to Armando. She would spend the rest of her years seeing disappointment in his face every morning when he woke.

Though, when no one was present, she let herself sink into a delicious, shameful dream, shameful because it was a typical woman's weakness. She thought of Armando's lips on her hand when he had kissed it in greeting upon his return from the Holy Land. She pressed her hand to her mouth, dreaming that for one moment, she could be as other women were but without consequence. His lips would part as he kissed her, and he would think she was beautiful, and she would believe it. She dreamed of being before him, naked, without pursing her lips or pushing her shoulders back. Panthea dreamed that, in his eyes, she did not have to strive for effect, to create a man's pleasure. Armando would take her in his arms, and they would discover pleasure together.

Foolish fantasies. Panthea shook her head and pinched her cheeks. "It's a wonder I'm not married to a stupid stable hand and mother to ten children. That's what I deserve."

Mariskka was burning alive, swatting at the sparks that were still settling around her.

She was clean. That was the first thing she noticed; how white her flesh was, how she could see pigment and variations of tone. Gone was the grime and the layers of grey unwashed skin.

"Is it over?" she gasped.

"Tell me what you saw, Mariskka," the Scribe asked.

Mbube shook his head.

"That one man scared me. He wasn't human, was he?" she said.

Trying to take it all in was going to burst her, split apart the seams of her mind.

"Describe him," the Scribe said.

Mbube turned his head to stare out the window as the sun rose over Manhattan.

Mariskka decided to try. "There was a blackness all around him, and it was alive. His body was dead, but it moved."

"He called the Destroyer," Mbube said. "He look like man, but not. He much worse. You made anger in him," Mbube said. "Must be careful. He sees light with you."

"Light?"

"You walk in darkness, like him," the Scribe said. "But Mbube is with you."

"Wait ... why is that thing named the Destroyer? What does he destroy?" Mariskka's brain was not moving in a linear direction, not after walking in Sicily seven centuries ago.

The Scribe's face grew red, and his eyes narrowed. Mbube huffed.

"Because you have not read," the Scribe said to Mariskka, "I must pull you out, back and forth, to instruct. You will not survive many trips."

"You don't have to do that," Mariskka said. "Just tell me what to say and I'll say it. I don't need to go back there!"

"I cannot shut a door you opened."

"Yes, you can!"

"Have you ears but cannot hear? You opened this door when you stole that manuscript. No one who walks in darkness will suffer you to live."

"Why?" Mariskka asked.

"You know too much," he said.

"Help me! I said I would believe!" Mariskka yelled.

"In time, yes," the Scribe replied.

She saw him turn the page of the book lying open on the table, and her feet were pulled from below, melting through the floor and time as the darkness hissed at her.

Chapter Six

"Grant me success, my lord. I have served you in distant lands. Now, make my line great."

As Armando knelt before Dario, the hall silenced to hear the reply. Panthea held her breath.

Waving from the floorboards, a hand was signaling another cup being lifted up.

"Father, the beer! You forgot to taste it!" Panthea reached down and grabbed the cup, handing it to her father. Dario sampled the beer, then tapped at the hole with his foot. It was a good keg and should be served.

"The brewer's guild continues to bring honour to their membership," Panthea announced. "We must toast them!"

Her father was the first to stand, though he was already uneven in his balance at this early hour of the feast. She took his arm, whispering to him.

"You should rest, Father. I can conduct the evening."

"No, no," he said, grimacing as he took his chair. The fits were leaving him weaker each time. "Panthea, you must learn to trust yourself in the hands of men. We want what is best for you."

"And you should trust my wishes."

"Panthea, we were both given our riches too young. I fear it has spoiled us for what must come next."

He looked sad, his gaze turning again to his glass. So many nights since her mother had died did he spend searching for answers in his beer. What it promised him, she could not guess, but it was enough that he returned every night.

She loved her father, with his great bald forehead lined like waves of the tide, breaking upon his great bushy eyebrows and wide, sleepy eyes peering out above his spectacles. Everything about him was excessive, and she loved it. His nose was large, and his mouth overly wide, punctuated by enormously long dimples that pinched into his cheeks when he smiled at her. Even his ears were too big for him, sticking out at proud angles and wiggling when he spoke. He had the kindest face ever given a man, and he had never had the heart to use it in being stern with her.

Armando the knight was still kneeling. He would have to stay there all night until signaled to rise, and her father was not a man of details, at least not social ones.

"Father," she asked, "how could this man offer me a better life, when he cannot even raise himself?"

Dario looked at her in confusion, then saw Armando kneeling. "Armando, my son, rise! Armando has served us well, my friends, has he not? Yes, yes!"

Cheers and murmurs of agreement were the people's reply.

"My friends, to me you owe your prosperity, and to Armando, your very lives."

Panthea felt herself growing angry at the fools cheering her father on.

"No good thing have I withheld from you, Armando. You have shared my wealth, my home, and my city, yes, my beloved city. I am an old man now, past my years of strength, and I must appoint another to rise in my place. I have no heir, so I must seek a man worthy of my legacy. A man of honour, of courage, of great strength, of noble heart, of—"

"Father, one moment! Stay this happy news. You forget yourself. I am not yet introduced to our guest," Panthea said, not looking at Armando.

Damiano stood, bowing to Panthea.

He moved with a serpent's selfish grace, surveying her. His green eyes flared with an appetite she did not recognize, and she blushed.

"Let her go, Del Grasso!"

Lazarro yanked the woman free of Del Grasso's grip. Blood was seeping through her sleeves, staining the fabric around her calves.

"What have you done?" Gio yelled at both the men. Lazarro had followed her here because he did not trust her or because he had not finished harassing her.

The mute woman had a wild look in her eyes, and Gio feared she would bite or kick. Forcing a calm smile, Gio held out her hands. The woman looked around at the bloody butcher and the angry priest, then took one faltering step toward Gio. The woman was shaking and crying.

"Can I look at those?" Gio asked, gesturing to her sleeves. Tears streaming down her face, the woman held her arms out, away from her body. The woman looked from side to side, anxiety etched in her face.

"She is frightened of someone," Gio whispered. "Let us be gentle."

Waiting to catch her eye first, Gio smiled, slowly reaching for a sleeve. Lifting the fabric away carefully, she felt sorry when the woman winced and fresh tears came. The fabric was sticking to the wounds in a few spots. Gio had to yank at those.

"These wounds are deep," Lazarro said. "Someone cut her to ribbons."

Del Grasso shook his head. "It is no cut."

"No, he's right," Gio said, trying not to show her surprise that Del Grasso spoke. She didn't recall anyone having heard him speak this many words in one night. "They are scratches, deep scratches, like from an animal claw."

"How did this happen?" she asked the woman, speaking slowly. "What hunts you?"

The woman opened her mouth and groaned, pointing to where the foreign man Damiano had been standing. She grabbed Gio, trying to pull her to the spot, making gestures Gio did not understand.

"We must light fires for the wolves," Lazarro said. He was looking beyond them at the horizon.

Del Grasso turned and stared at him, and Lazarro cleared his throat.

"It is too late," Del Grasso said.

"Yes, well, I will pay some of the children to do it," Lazarro said. "They will be glad for the work."

Gio stroked the woman's cheek. "You're safe now," Gio promised. "There are no wolves here. Is that what frightened you?"

"My child," Lazarro said. "there is nothing to fear here."

"I will mend these wounds," Gio said, challenging Lazarro.

Lazarro was watching Del Grasso. Neither looked at ease.

"Then bring her back to me, Gio. She is deeply troubled."

"She needs a good meal first," Gio replied.

"She needs God more."

Gio took the woman gently by the hand and led her away.

"Don't believe a word this man says about salvation," she said under her breath. "If God intended to save you, wouldn't He have made a start by now?"

⚜

Damiano's eyes captivated her. Their darkness made her mouth moist and reminded her of stolen sweet things, of secrets whispered in moonlit rooms ... how infinite the possibilities of sin were.

Yes, Panthea thought, Brother Lazarro had indeed preached truth to the people: The road to righteousness was narrow. It confined her.

The best she could hope for was to keep one foot in front of the other. There was to be no wondering where else a road could lead. Panthea had been given true love and a real God and found them both too predictable. They never failed, either one, that was true. But they were always there, always dependable, never wavering in course or pitch. This lust, though, was fresh and wild, a dirty, rich feeling that made her knees unsteady.

"Yes, Damiano, our guest!" Her father rose and extended his arms as if to embrace the stranger from this distance. "Damiano was met at the port, was he not, my friends? My daughter had no such pleasure. She is a good daughter, remaining at home to oversee the preparations for our feast. Sir, may I present my daughter, Panthea," he said, gesturing to her. "She has the beauty of her mother, the wit of her father, and the temperament of our volcano!"

The villagers laughed, but only enough to please Dario. They never laughed much at what really amused them. Not when she watched. She was not allowed to see that.

Damiano's eyes still rested upon her. The sounds of the room drifted away as the stinging energy of this stranger took her in an intimacy she had only imagined on her lonely nights of wine and wanderings. She felt him upon her skin, felt his hand moving up her arm, pulling her into his chest, his hot, salty skin, like the sand of a beach for her to run her hands upon, to languidly lie upon and dream new dreams. Dark ones, dreams in a moonless land. Dreams that God did not speak in.

"Thank you for allowing me into your home," Damiano replied. "My lord had prepared me to find Sicily as a place of wonders, but I had not expected to find so great a beauty. A thousand lifetimes, and a man could find no equal to your daughter."

His eyes did not leave her. The darkness made her do a wicked thing.

"Armando, this is Damiano, our guest for the evening," she

said, rising from her seat, gesturing between the men. "Damiano, this is Armando, my knight. No finer warrior could there be found in all of Sicily. My father was intending to pledge me to him tonight, but your visit has surprised us all. Armando could not be pleased to see you."

Armando stood from his seat at the table below Panthea. He was not far from Damiano.

Damiano extended a hand to be kissed. Armando did not look at it. He only nodded.

"You are a man like myself," Damiano said. "You labour in service of another. We go into battle carrying another's flag, and must hope our patron rewards us with our heart's desire. What a life we have been given, my friend."

Armando cleared his throat. "This is too close, sir. I will not discuss my arrangements."

"Well, judging from your clothes, you already receive an honourable share of my host's money. Perhaps, then, you do not fight for money. Tell me, why do you fight? The ways of men's war are always of such interest to me."

"War is not my occupation."

Dario's face was flushing, Panthea saw. Either her father was about to lapse into another fit or he was embarrassed at her provocation.

"Armando fights for my father's name," Panthea answered. "He hopes to claim all this one day as his own, since my father has no male heir. There is a bedroom above us blanketed in blue silk and drenched in Arabian perfumes; he thinks we will soon reside there as man and wife. You must congratulate him."

Armando looked away.

"Ahh," Damiano said. "You fight for love."

Panthea waited. Armando could choose here to embarrass himself or to embarrass her. She wondered which would get a more spectacular reaction from Damiano.

"I do what I am asked," Armando replied. "Please be so good as to excuse me now."

"Well," Damiano said, reaching for a mug, staring at Panthea, "I had not thought to stay, but if war is made for a woman, perhaps I have not given enough consideration to the fairer sex. But then, well, who would want a man such as myself? I have no real home."

"Ah, but your master is very rich, is he not?" Dario asked. "It is a good life, is it not?"

"There is no man richer. His kingdom is as far reaching as the winds."

"A kingdom," Panthea repeated, looking at Armando so her arrow wouldn't miss.

"A kingdom of wind," Armando countered. "I should like to meet your knights, to see how they secure its borders."

"You speak lightly for a knight," Damiano said. "It would not do to bring misfortune on your master. But for myself, I have orders only to conduct my business and leave at once, to another town."

"Must you go so quickly?" Panthea asked. "There are sights in Sicily that would please you."

Her dress slipped off one shoulder and she was slow to take the fabric and slide it back up. She had oiled her chest so well that the dress had no chance of remaining in place, and the shadows worked to her favour. It was important to her that the men of the village understood that while she was unmarried, it was not because she lacked some essential quality.

Damiano lunged up from the table, knocking over his beer and sending crockery tumbling to the floor. Everyone stopped and stared at the guest. Panthea, the colour rising in her cheeks, cast her eyes down, pulling her dress back up over her shoulder.

"Excuse me, sir," Damiano said, bowing to Dario. "I am unsteady after so long a voyage. I meant only to rise and offer a toast. Now I've made for you a mess. Surely you must want me gone."

"Don't jest, my friend! We insist you stay," Dario said. He was beginning to slur his words.

"Please excuse me for a moment," Damiano replied. "I surely need a moment of air, with privacy, mind you, and then I must be a more pleasant companion."

Panthea could not abide it.

Damiano, a prominent guest, was leaving her presence without good reason. Could she pretend to chew and swallow all this food if a guest, and a man at that, esteemed her so poorly? The other guests would have a more intense interest in her, watching her for her reaction. Until she corrected this humiliation, they would have nothing else on their minds. Perhaps if she returned to the feast arm in arm with Damiano, this would satisfy the guests that no insult had been intended.

She rose, smiling, her dimples feeling as stiff as twigs. She held her skirt with one hand and slid backward from the table, bowing her head to them all.

The cool air snapped her out of the worries, blowing through her skirt and bodice. The feast was getting too warm, with the nearby kitchen at fever pitch to feed all those guests. She should conjure an excuse more often to sneak out here during feasts.

Panthea spied Damiano, and ducked into a shadow by the arched doorway into her garden.

"On the first dawn He revealed her to me," Damiano said. Panthea saw no one with him. "I was in awe of her. She was to be my charge, and I would be her guardian. When her time was upon us, I would carry her, watch her in the night, speak His words of love over her. Then you said I could have more. You said I could speak my own words instead of His. I believed, and fell."

A black mist, like a swarm of gnats, spun tighter around him.

"I was not told when she would enter the story," Damiano spat. "I did not know this was her time. I would never have agreed."

The mist snapped and disappeared.

Damiano put his face in his hands. Spinning around, he cursed the night air. "If a guardian stands with her, reveal yourself! If she has given herself to God, what can I do but leave her in peace?"

Panthea held her breath, pressing herself against the wall. She heard no reply.

"If you walk with her, know this: your time with her on earth is over. You will watch her suffer. Tomorrow I begin."

A strong hand clamped her mouth closed, and someone dragged her backward into the castle, her feet leaving lines in the dirt under the arch.

✤

"Let go of me!" Panthea hissed, jerking her face away from his hand.

"You do not know what you are doing," Armando replied. He removed his hand from her face, only to use it to grab her other arm. He was not letting her go. "We don't know who this man is or the prince he serves. Yet you follow him like a puppy."

Armando softened his grip. He had dragged her through the hall into this room as if she were an escaping Turk.

"You're jealous," Panthea said, turning in his arms to see his face. "He fancies me; everyone could feel it. You worry you are no match for him."

Armando stepped back, dropping his grip on her to cross his arms over his chest. "Do you know why you won't admit you love me?" he asked. "Because I know you, Panthea. I knew you when you were a girl and I was just entering your father's service, barely more than a child myself. I knew you then. I know you still. I know you as no other man ever could, and you hate me for it."

"That's rot," Panthea said.

"You hate me because you hate who you are. You want a man to make you forget yourself."

"Lies!" Panthea said.

"You always want more, Panthea, more than any man can give, but you are not greedy—you are frightened, frightened that, alone, you are not enough."

He took liberties she would allow no other man. Shaking her head in disgust, she promised herself to be crueler. She raised a hand to slap him.

Reaching out, he caught her hand, lowering it back to her side. He raised his other hand to her face, running it through her hair, smoothing it down, letting his fingers rest too long against her cheek. She pulled at her restrained hand, so he would know she was not submitting.

She wanted to turn her face into his hand and rest her cheek on his palm. She could smell the sweet herbs he had fed Fidato back at the stables tonight. He was generous with her horse.

"You are enough, Panthea. You are enough for this man."

Looking into his eyes, feeling her stomach flutter, she knew her decision would not be understood, not by Armando. Not by her heart.

She would not let being a woman stop her. She would not fail her mother. She drew a step back. "It is you who are frightened, Armando. You pursue me only because I will not have you. A real man would find another woman."

"Panthea, do you not know who I am and why I have laboured these long years for your father?" He stepped in closer, closing the distance she had created, wrapping his arms around her waist.

She tried to step back again, but his grip tightened.

"I am your Jacob," he whispered in her ear.

Chapter Seven

Dario clattered out into the hall, his unsteady but swift shuffle across the stone floors making it impossible for anyone to ignore him.

"Where has everyone gone?" he called, too loudly. "There is business to attend to, and food, and dancing! Yes!" He spied Damiano. "My friend, do not spend your evening in an empty garden! Come inside and enjoy all I set before you!"

Dario craned his neck to see in the shadows. "Children, come back to the feast!" he called. "Where are you hiding?"

Armando and Panthea stepped into the corridor.

Dario grinned at Armando. "I have made no announcement, Armando. Don't claim your prize just yet!"

Dario braced against the wall, laughing at his own joke. Panthea hated his jokes when he was this far drunk.

Dario shuffled back in, still talking to them all. Never waiting for a reply, he did not notice that none followed.

Resting his back on the stone railing that separated the garden from the Sicilian firs that leaned too far in, Damiano watched Panthea. She was nauseated, having tasted an intimacy with him that she should not have shared. She could say nothing.

Focusing on her, his eyes had the intensity of a dying saint, pinned in pigment forever to the wall of a church. They depressed her, those paintings. Every church she visited had these scenes, or Bible stories, covering every wall, even the ceiling. Even she had no good grasp of the Latin Masses, but the paintings instructed in another tongue. The story spoke of the mighty judgments of God and a Holy Mother who loved her meek Son. Around these three gathered martyrs, saints, and pilgrims. Panthea had yet to see a woman like herself in them. She could not find herself in the Latin or in the ghosts in the pigments. She could not find herself in the Church.

But Damiano had found her. The longer she looked into his eyes, the less she wanted to return to the feast. She did not care what the guests thought.

Panthea stood still, waiting for one of these men to take hold of her.

Armando stepped in front of Panthea, shielding her from Damiano's stare.

"I should like to talk with you further about this transaction you are to conduct," Armando said to him.

"I have a great gift to bestow upon the people of Sicily. Trouble yourself no more with my business," Damiano replied, stepping aside. His eyes found her.

"I remember a tale of a gift made to the Trojans," Armando said, shifting to block her from Damiano. "I will not grant you safe passage through Sicily until you explain your presence."

"Do not test me," Damiano said.

Armando drew his sword.

Panthea, biting her lip, pushed herself against the wall. This was no longer about her.

"You are a man of war, of course," Damiano said, smiling toward Panthea as if she understood some joke. "I talk of gifts and love, and you think only to flash your sword. Would you engage me in a feud?"

"I would engage you to tell the truth," Armando replied. He was holding his ground. Not even his voice changed, Panthea noted. He had probably faced many enemies during his years. Panthea wondered why he had never told her tales of his exploits. He must not relish those stories.

"Yes, a feud between us," Damiano said. "That would please me. Would it please you?"

"No," Armando said.

"Excellent. Let us declare our prize then. A woman."

"No," Armando said.

His voice was changing; Panthea heard it. Armando was losing.

"Panthea is our prize," Damiano said. "If I win, I claim her. If you win, I will tell you the nature of my business."

"No," Armando said.

"But you see, Armando, that's the glorious thing about war. One man cannot stop it, but one man can begin it. I will see you inside. We should enjoy all that Dario has set before us."

Damiano walked over to Panthea, taking her hand for a kiss, pressing it to his mouth. He was hungry too. She did not think she could walk in a straight line after feeling his lips on her flesh.

Armando's arm slipped around her waist, and he pulled her back into the feast.

A servant offered Panthea the bowl first, and when she dipped her fingers in, the water remained clean and pure.

"Oh, that a woman could be so graceful in all her ways!" her servant declared, loudly.

The other women in the room looked at their own hands and hid them, and the men stared blankly at her. Panthea wondered that this trick had been lost on them all. The servant removed the bowl from her and began to pass it down to the other guests.

Only Armando's face changed. He was narrowing his eyes as he looked at her, and a shadow of a smile glimmered. It made her angry. He would never appreciate the amount of work that went into making a memorable impression on the people. He ate as if he were hungry, spoke plain words that he had not weighed for effect, had no sense of his rank or future.

Dario rose. Or rather, he was lifted under the arms by his servants.

"I bid my guests good night and farewell, safe travels on the road home, and may your dinner sit well with you in the morning. I have hosted you all with a joyful heart and must now leave you to conduct business of my home. Peace and merriment be yours in ample contentment, and remember that Dario feeds the poor in the hour of need. Farewell, friends!"

A few of the oldest guests were grateful for the chance to leave now that they were full and the hour was late. They shuffled toward the door. But the others stayed and waited for the dancing to begin.

Representatives from the guilds, heading each table, rose with Dario, preparing to attend him. His lawyer rose, too. Her stomach tightened. She needed more time. Was she wrong to try this tactic? There was nothing else she could do, except this. He should not rush this decision. After all, he had already let her live through her sixteenth birthday without a marriage.

A woman pulled a lyre across her lap, and the musicians gathered round her to begin the tune. Everyone was clapping and flirting as her father and his advisers moved toward the staircase to the upper chamber.

The stolen feast from her bedroom was souring in her stomach. If she didn't work with haste, Armando would have her before morning.

Licking her lips, trying to breathe little bursts of cool air, she turned her face toward the open windows above. She couldn't throw up the great mass of food she had stuffed; it would reveal her deceit. No one had seen her eat. Her pristine hands soiled nothing she touched, while the guests left greasy, gritty stains on their trousers and in the rinsing bowl. She didn't want them to know she was so much like them, so hungry and filthy.

Armando was rising. He would be required to attend her father.

Panthea jumped to her feet. "Come, Damiano, let us walk in the garden. It would aid my digestion."

"Am I mistaken? You did not eat," Armando said. "Not in our presence."

She glared at him.

Damiano was on his feet, walking to Panthea, who was offering her arm to him.

"Come, Armando! I will settle the matter tonight!" Dario called as he was being led upstairs. "By morning you will have your reward!"

Looking between Panthea and Damiano and back again to her father Dario, Armando hesitated. Panthea was pleased to give him this impossible puzzle. Armando had to leave her with Damiano if he planned to claim her in marriage tonight. If he stayed to protect her from Damiano's advances, he might lose her. Panthea wished that Damiano had included her in their little war; he should have, she thought. So far, she was winning and no one had even offered her a prize.

"One would think he does not want his bride! Come, Armando!" Dario laughed, sweeping his arms over the crowd, inviting them into his joke.

Armando still did not move.

"Come, Armando!" Dario commanded, every inch the baron and baker, pushing another man to accept his terms. "If you want the marriage, come now!"

She had never seen this—Armando hesitating where she was concerned. It thrilled her and made her do the second wicked thing of the evening.

She leaned to Armando. "You have not my heart, not yet," she whispered to him. "Go with my father and claim my hand, but my heart is still mine to give away. I do not know what I will do next. I am so new at war."

⚜

"Behold, salvation!"

Gio swung back the thin wooden door, stirring up dust that danced in the air around the fire. The room smelled of seed oil and leather, of smoke and charring meats. Sometimes when the winds outside stilled, Gio could smell all her herbs, too, and name them by their scent. On those nights, she wished she could keep some of them safely elsewhere. Valerian stank like the stockings of a dead man.

Her fire was burning low in the center of the room, her plate licked clean and set at its edge. Wrapping a piece of leather around her hand, she stuck it into the fire, pulling free a blackened bone. Holding it up to the light, she inspected the femur and sighed.

"One more day for you," she said, pushing it back into the fire, making a place for it beneath the hottest embers. The wood snapped and sparked.

A large blanket hung from the ceiling in one corner, hiding something from view. Gio went straight to it, lifting the blanket for the best view, pursing her lips, nodding. It was untouched.

She turned to the mute woman. "What can we call you? Do you have a name?"

The woman made a horrid sound and Gio grimaced.

"Do not do that again! I will call you The Old Woman. We have one called The Old Man. I could marry you off to him, and he'd be thankful for a woman in his bed. He's never had one, I'd guess, and you'd have a companion. He would feed you, though he steals it from me. Would you like that?"

The woman shook her head.

Gio frowned, grabbing the woman, thrusting her hand into her robe, feeling her abdomen. "You could still give him children."

Forcing the woman's mouth open next, Gio peered inside with the greatest of curiosity. "By the saints, you have all your teeth!" Yanking her mouth open wider, Gio pushed her face into the jaws. "What are these little spots of metal you have upon them in the back? Making them stronger, yes? It's barbaric! I must try it."

The woman did not respond. Her body stiffened and she clamped her jaw shut, missing Gio's fingers by a second.

Shrugging, Gio turned to her work. "I have every remedy of Pliny, every remedy of the Arabs, too. Though we've made war with the Turks for so long, their healers have many good tricks. They are more curious, and no Church stops them from their inquiries."

Gio pulled a great brown crock from a dark corner, grunting as she dragged it into the light. "Of course, they are our enemies. Sometimes I fear the cures they tell us of will kill the patient." Gio rummaged about on a worktable until she found a smaller jar and lifted the lid of the crock. Working quickly with a pair of wooden tongs, her hand darted in and out, dropping fat little squirming things into the jar.

"But still, the villages have use for women like me. If my cure fails, they blame me. 'Tis better than blaming God." Gio grabbed for the Old Woman's arm, but the stranger jerked it back.

"Give me your arm."

The Old Woman began to cry and shook her head, tucking her wounded arm under the other.

"I want that arm!" Gio was losing patience.

Gio slapped her hands in front of the newcomer's face. Grabbing the bleeding arm, Gio settled it in her lap and went to work. The Old Woman did not move again.

Taking a knife, Gio sliced away the sleeve up to the shoulder, exposing the length of the arm. Gio used her own dirty sleeve to wipe the arm down, pouring a little vinegar onto it. It did not remove enough of the dirt, so Gio spat right onto the wounds. The Old Woman's mouth opened as if to groan, but when she saw Gio's expression, she closed it again.

Reaching in the jar, humming to herself, Gio retrieved a fat, angry ant, using a pair of wooden tongs to hold it just at its middle section, turning it, watching the snapping jaws in the firelight. Gio felt the woman starting to shrink away and clucked at the woman to be still.

Gio leaned in until she was nose to the wound, lowering the ant into place, hind legs first, positioning it just so. As soon as she dropped the ant's front legs into place over the cut, the ant's jaws snapped shut on the wound, biting with fury. Gio felt the woman jerking from the pain. This woman was an odd one, Gio thought, and not just her clothes.

Taking her knife, Gio sliced away the ant's body, leaving the jaws clamped down over the wound, sealing the jagged edges together. Though Gio was concentrating, she was aware of the other woman taking more of an interest in the medicine. Gio had traded precious blue lapis pigment for this crock of ants. It was good to have them admired.

One by one, she positioned the ants over the wound, letting them bite down to seal it, then slicing off their bodies. The woman had tears running down her face but was blessedly silent.

Pushing back from her work at last, Gio groaned, stretching her back.

"Come, a drink," Gio said.

A twig snapped outside and both women sat up straight, straining to hear. There was no other noise.

"'Tis a man," Gio whispered. "An animal would step on it and keep moving. I keep twigs all around my house for this reason. Is it a man who hunts you, who made those wounds?"

The woman's face was losing all its colour.

Gio stood, pointing to her back wall. "There is a path behind my home, a sharp ascent up to the lands of the volcano; you must take it. Go slow, for at night you will not see the dangers. Unless the volcano is angry, and then you will be able to see but must avoid being burned to death. Follow this path up and around. When your feet begin to bleed, you will know you are halfway to the next village."

The woman shook her head, cowering, resisting Gio's hands that shoved her to the door.

"Without speech, I do not know how you could have made such an enemy." Gio looked at her with suspicion. "Though perhaps you saw something worth killing for."

The woman shook her head. Gio suspected she did not understand much, but she seemed to be ignoring her now. It annoyed Gio. Her ants might have been wasted on this wretch.

"I do not want to die either. Have you thought of that? I won't let you stay here. Get out!"

The woman dug her feet into the dirt floor. Gio's temper flared; how many visitors had come here, thinking to force her into doing their will? She had not even let them past her threshold. This woman she had taken in and given a rare magic to, and she was defying Gio's orders.

Grabbing her leather wrap she plunged her hand into the fire, retrieving the burning femur, swirling it in a red crock at the fire's edge, jabbing it with a thick dripping black wax at the woman. It caught the woman's robes on fire and she panicked, swatting at the flames moving quickly through her soiled robes. Gio watched in satisfied horror as the mute woman tore open the door and ran into the night.

"It worked," Gio said, looking at the crock. She closed the door. "Of course, it could kill her. I should have thought of that."

Smoothing her hair, Panthea waited in the garden, pressing her palm against her cheek where Armando had touched her tonight. For another woman it would be simpler. She closed her eyes and imagined how easy it would be. But God had given her a mind and a will. With her mother gone, who could trust her father to arrange such things? He had stayed in this little village because it kept her memory near, and because it was his nature to be satisfied. Why should Panthea trust his choice for a husband?

Yes, Armando wanted her, but she had seen her father move through his own passions as often as the seasons change. None had lasted. None had brought anything to the family but heartbreak. At least if she married for money, she would not be disappointed. She would have money. Money lasted. Gold would still be gold, even when she was gone and her heirs no longer remembered her name. But to believe that love lasted—this was the foolishness of her kind.

Panthea felt fire burning in her veins at the memory of her mother. Her years had been cut short by an indifferent God, one who demanded their love and obedience, neither of which they could give with consistency, but then He let mothers die no matter how hard their children fought to save them. Had not Panthea prayed? Had she not memorized every Latin prayer and done penance for her mother when she was too weak to walk even to the balcony? Panthea had paid for all her mother's sins, great sins, and sins of no consequence, small sins, all sins, a hundred times over and, still, she died. God would accept no ransom from Panthea for her. Her father had done evil and no one, not even God, ever called him to account.

A troubadour wandered into the garden. He had the blond hair of her northern cousins, and shoulders that were too large for his profession. Panthea wondered who hired him and wondered again why he accepted. Her father had no interest in these songs, and the troubadour looked far too big for this work of plucking tiny strings. Her mother would have loved to trouble him about it.

As the troubadour began his tune, his fingers glided over his lute strings and the soft chords bubbled up through her memories of her mother, quieting the pain. Panthea felt her shoulders soften and took her first deep breath of the day.

Panthea reclined on the bench, reaching for the fan her servants placed outside for her, the one with an ornate ivory handle that burst into a peacock's full plumage. The roses around her were still in bloom, sweetening the night air. Red leaves of October fell like a curtain between her and the guests dancing in the feasting hall. October was magic, a month for conjuring, as distant memories and thoughts of days ahead met side by side, and the people danced in the space between them. Through a thick glass window, Panthea spied as a married couple near her father's age held each other and kissed.

"I have been sent to remind you of such love," the troubadour said to her.

She fanned herself out of embarrassment, looking at him, this stranger, but thinking she knew this voice.

"Speak again, friend. Who has sent you?" Panthea asked.

"Do you not know?" he answered, beginning a new, second tune.

"Answer the lady plainly." Damiano stepped on the porch, and her mother's face was swept away into the darkness of her heart once more.

The troubadour held her gaze, not acknowledging Damiano. His fingers were working this new tune now, a song that made her search her memories once more. She remembered that a lullaby had been sung over her from her cradle days and that wolf bane was tied above to drive spirits away. These were days of songs and sleep, and warm arms that carried her into rooms of wonder. There were flames of candles, and silver spoons to grab at, and her mother's dark curls to bury her face in when it was all too much. He had been there, she realized.

It was not her mother's voice that had sung to her on lonely nights, those nights of feasting when her cries could not fetch her mother and the shadows made frightening shapes against her walls. It was this voice.

"You were my servant once!" she cried.

"I am your servant still," he replied. Something about his expression told her she was right but that it was not the complete truth. He looked too young, too strong, to have served her as a child. He grinned at her while she worked this through in her mind. He was more than a servant, and he had known her since birth, but she could not place him exactly. She knew this: He had once felt familiar somehow, like home, but since she had grown and become bitter, his memory had faded. It was as if her hard heart had sent him away, forced him to keep his distance, even if only in her memories.

Damiano threw a coin, striking him in the shin. "Go on your way," Damiano told the troubadour. "Fine words do not make the riches a true lady requires." Damiano held a hand out to Panthea. "If it is songs you require, Panthea, I will buy a hundred minstrels," he said. "If you were but mine."

"I do not see how your promises are of worth. There is no one else to play for her tonight, and none who knows what soothes her," the troubadour replied. "I will stay."

"Your kind are always underfoot these days, a curse of this age," Damiano said, his hands curling into fists. He had so little restraint. She liked that. Anything could happen with this man.

"Why trouble yourself, Damiano? No harm ever came of a song," Panthea said.

The troubadour sang:

> *To live within the courts built of love*
> *Is better than a feast with wickedness*
> *Better to live just one day with love*
> *Than to give a thousand days to another.*

Damiano clapped once, signaling the end of the performance. The troubadour continued. Damiano took the fan from her hands.

He began fanning her, letting each feather graze her skin slowly, across her shoulders, down her arms.

> *Love will be your light and shield*
> *Love can lead you to the path*
> *that you will walk without fear*
> *Love asks only this:*
> *Yourself, and nothing more.*

She struggled to sit up straight. The troubadour grew red in the face, and Panthea wanted to apologize, though she was doing nothing. She wondered if that was what she should apologize for.

"You remind me of someone too," Panthea said, turning her attention back to Damiano. She wanted him to continue, she wanted to feel these wicked things, but not with this troubadour near. "Perhaps the garden air is magic tonight. It plays tricks on my mind."

"You think we have met once before?" Damiano asked. It seemed of great interest to him. "What do you remember?"

"Oh, it was just a foolish thing to say," Panthea said. "I have been few places but here." She tried to keep him talking until she knew what she should do. "I would like to hear some of your adventures."

Damiano did not look like he wanted to tell those tales.

"Have you had many loves?" Panthea asked. Those would be delicious stories. Besides, she did not know how other girls in the world fared. Perhaps there was more to be gained than she knew to ask for.

"I have had only one love." Damiano sounded offended.

Panthea tried to speak, but he waved her off.

"I have pursued many, though. I have spent my days pursuing young women. I even cared for one once, a girl with your colouring. I showed myself to her, and I think she found me attractive. She made no attempts to keep me away, and I returned night after night, refusing her sleep until she agreed to submit. But her father interfered, sealing the chamber off from me. A priest stood guard over her every night, night upon night, saying his prayers every hour, waiting for me, trembling in fear that I might actually challenge him."

"Why did you not ask her father for her in pledge?"

Damiano grinned and drew her hand to his mouth. He kissed the tips of her fingers, one by one. "Her foolish father had already pledged her to a man far beneath her station. She was destined to spend her life washing, scrubbing, sweating, birthing in dirty rooms alone, the jealous hours pulling at her beauty until she was stretched and worn. She would die having neither beauty nor wealth. It was a terrible thing to watch, Panthea."

His words were burning in her mind.

"What did you do?" she asked.

"Panthea, can I watch as a beautiful girl makes such a mistake?"

"You rescued her?"

"Her betrothed met an unhappy accident late one night returning from the market. It was festival season, so everyone assumed him to be drunk, and his horse was quite powerful. But there was a price."

"For whom?" Panthea asked.

"Her father was with the lad and had only stopped behind to get a stone out of his horse's hoof—this I did not know. How could I? I cannot see all. I cannot see around corners or read minds. People are a constant surprise to me. Who can say what one will do next?"

"What happened to the father?" Panthea felt alarm for the unknown man.

"Oh, I would not harm him. She loved him. Do you believe me?"

The troubadour was listening, Panthea could tell by his face. He looked angry.

"What happened to the father?" she asked.

"He saw me. I was leaning over the boy, only trying to revive him, of course. The sight so terrified him his heart gave out."

"The lad was in such awful condition?"

Damiano looked away.

"You could not save either of them?" Panthea's voice grew higher, straining.

The comment enraged him. "Can I raise the dead?" His hand pulled back to beat her, still holding the fan, but catching himself, he landed the blow with slow care, the feathers prickling her cheek.

"And of the girl? What did you do with her?"

"Nothing. I left her alone. She was too deep in mourning to entertain me further. She clung to the priest for comfort."

Panthea tried to push him away, but he steeled his arms against hers and would not be moved.

"I did not care for that adventure," she said.

"You know nothing about the world beyond your own, Panthea."

"If you want to win your little war with Armando, you should offer better stories. I should not like to visit that one."

"Then let us begin an adventure that pleases you," he said, leaning to her for a kiss.

With flames screaming all around her, burning her face and hands as she clawed through them, Mariskka kept grasping for anything to slow her fall.

She was aware of the muted voices of men, and that she was no longer moving through a dark cloud. She listened with her eyes closed, trying to recognize their voices before she moved.

"No move."

It was Mbube.

"Where am I? Am I in the hospital?" she asked, trying to raise her head. He pushed her forehead back.

"No move. Still 1347."

She groaned, clenching her eyes shut, trying not to burst into tears like she was four. "I want to go home. To my apartment."

"You injured. Too hard to send you back here again."

"I don't want to come back. That's the point."

Mariskka realized that another angel was leaning over her too. This one had broad, heavy wings made of the feathers of a vulture, dark and thick. They looked oily. She stuck her tongue out in disgust. The vulture-angel showed his sharp teeth, clicking them together in anger.

Mbube spoke in another language and the vulture-angel closed his mouth, spreading his wings, glaring at her. Underneath his wings, his feathers were pristine, shimmering with colours she did not know.

"He not look like what he is," Mbube said to her. "He not made beautiful, but he bring healing."

The vulture-feathered one frowned as he heaved Mariskka's burnt thigh onto his lap, beginning his work.

"We must quiet now. He have many places go tonight. He angry at you delay him. He think of hurting children."

Something stank. Mariskka tried to figure out what it was. She looked first at the vulture-angel, accusing, then her eyes moved down to his work. A flap of skin, grey and bubbled, was hanging from her arm. The vulture-angel pressed a hand to her cheek, forcing her to face another direction. His touch was soothing.

She eased her face back, trying to draw deeper breaths so she didn't faint. There was no pain, but her thigh looked like sausage without a casing. Mariskka felt tears on her cheek again, for no good reason. She had seen plenty of patients who looked like bad sausage. None of those patients had been her, though.

"Mbube tell you story. Make laugh."

Mariskka took the bait. It would distract her. She nodded to him.

"Animals see Mbube," he said.

"Animals can see you? All of the angels?" she asked.

"Yes. One dog lift his leg and pee on Mbube. He not like strangers. No dinner for him that night. He missed Mbube but hit new couch."

Mariskka laughed, even though she didn't mean to. It hurt.

"What else?" she asked.

"We hear animals. They talk much. Little ones most." Mbube folded his hand and made the sign for rapid chattering.

Mariskka laughed, not even caring about the pain. "What about cats? Can you hear them too?"

"Cats say only, 'Bring food next time.'"

"Sounds like a cat to me." She tried to turn her head to get a more direct look at him. "Mbube, do you like being an angel?"

Mbube pulled his chin back, as if surprised. "New question for Mbube. Think."

A wind blew her hair from the back of her head into her eyes. She held out her hands over her forehead, trying to keep her eyes out of the blast. Mbube looked alarmed. Squinting, she glanced back. The vulture-angel was gone. In his place, a howling whirlwind spun, growing wider with each revolution.

"Pages turning, Mariskka," he said. "I no strength to stop story."

"What can I do?" Mariskka grabbed his arm as hard as she could. "Mbube, they're all going to die. At least let me help them!"

The Scribe stepped from the whirlwind and held out his hand to her. Mariskka felt nauseated.

"You have no words in this story," the Scribe said. "It is punishment for stealing another's."

The whirlwind swept her away.

When she came to consciousness, she staggered onto her feet and ran.

It was coming.

Chapter Eight

Lazarro jumped out from the darkness, trying to grab the burning woman as she ran past. Gio was watching for him; she landed against him, shoving him away from her door.

"Let her go, Lazarro! I painted her arm with a new thing called Greek fire—it burns without destroying anything. She will not be harmed!"

The woman was too fast for him, running down the steep path, disappearing into the night, shielded by its twists and trees.

He shook off Gio. "You could have killed her!"

"Look at her, Lazarro. It would have been mercy," Gio replied.

"You have no mercy—do not speak the word!" Lazarro said.

Gio was praying her hunger didn't show. She wanted more of this anger from him. She wanted to make him so angry he could think of no prayer to say. Then, as he watched, she would take her sorrow into her hands and crush it until her plain dry fingers snapped and winds scattered the crumbled remains upon the volcano.

He had the words of the Church and of God as his witness. She had nothing but his anger, and this mountain. The rocks here would be her testimony: that not all beautiful things keep their shape, that even red fire can turn cold and sharp. Others would come along, and seeing it of no use, sweep it from the path.

She could be the one to sweep the past clean, leaving no memories behind. She could kill him, in any number of ways. A priest's death was not unusual. They attended the beds of the sick every day, offering Mass and Communion. Or she could wait another year. Someday God would pronounce judgment on him. He would suffer as she did.

"What have you got in there, Gio?" Lazarro was trying to see past her door.

"Nothing that concerns you," Gio replied.

"You concern me, Gio."

"How can you speak such perversion?" Gio said. She raised her arm to strike him and he caught it, forcing it behind her. It forced her nearer to him.

He sniffed at her mouth. "What comes upon you? Why do you hate with such force? I did not wish for this life, but I embrace it for your sake. Why can you not do the same?"

She spit in his face. "When you die, I will rejoice."

"I will never be your husband, Gio, but I will have your secrets. I will put an end to your hatred." He forced her backward toward her door.

She dug her heels in, trying to stop him. "No," she screamed. "No!"

He slammed her against the door, crashing it open, revealing everything to him. She had forgotten to pull the cover back up in the corner.

He let her go, wandering into this forbidden cave. She curled into a ball, hiding her face in shame. Where could she go to hide? She could not leave this room, even if she had somewhere to run. Her life was poured out before her enemy here in the canvases and colours. Nothing was hidden from him.

She forced herself to watch as he took them in, one by one. Once she had been subjected to long, humiliating scrutiny. She would not do this to her life's story. She would stand with it, though her face felt hot and she wanted to vomit.

It was agony to hear his breath.

He was standing near her mortar and pestle. The pestle was heavy stone and as long as her hand. She could smash it on the back of his head, if she got close enough.

"I just wanted to understand what I was selling, Lazarro," she said, standing. She told him the truth. That was what made it so ironic, that he should hear the truth from her before he died, but not the truth he needed.

"I thought if I practiced," she said, "I could perfect them. It is why mine are so preferred among all the church painters."

Her fingers were closing around the pestle. She began to lift her arm just as he dropped his face into his hands. It startled her.

"What have I done to you?"

He lifted his face back up, reaching for one painting, running his fingers over the colours, tracing the river of blue that ran through all the other colours. She had worked at this for years and had not yet made it whole. It was the gentle face of a man, standing in a crowd of peasants who were begging him for bread. His hands were open.

"Don't touch it!" she screamed, dropping the pestle as she pushed him away.

"Is this what God is to you?" he asked. "Is this the face of your Lord?"

"I do not see the face of your God," Gio said, breathing hard. "You forget that He has forsaken me."

"If you did not believe that God sees you, you could not paint. Not these."

"Maybe I paint to forget that no one ever sees me. How long has it been since a villager looked me in the eyes? Do you know what that is like, Lazarro? To walk the streets and see every face turn away? Only the children talk to me, and I suspect some of them get a beating for it later."

"You never lacked faith, Gio. You lack courage."

The words stung her.

"Some things cannot be spoken." She hoped he did not miss the pain in her voice.

"If you had told the truth, you would have been forgiven. I stood there waiting to give you Communion, to cleanse you of your sins. Even when you spat at Dario and his nobles and then fled, I waited. I stood there until the stars came out and rain fell. It was the only time I missed my Matins."

"They were all cowards. As were you," Gio said.

"I traded my life for yours. I am no coward."

"How many years have passed now? Twelve? Have you ever imagined how our lives would be different if I had told the truth that day?"

"You would have a good place in the village, be secure, and be counted as a child of God. I would know peace."

"Perhaps I do lack courage, Lazarro, but you lack imagination."

"Before the winter is out, Gio, I will have you shouting God's name in the streets. I will not live another year of my life seeing you in this darkness."

"I'll do that, Lazarro. Just before I marry a wealthy man and live in a fine house, bearing him glorious blond children and eating dainties by candlelight before we attend our evening Matins."

"That would please me."

Those words, on his lips, cut her worse than any before. He would wish her in another man's arms? He had not the courtesy or courage to lie. Not even now.

She pushed past him, whipping the covers back down over her paintings.

"But why, Gio? Why keep this secret too?"

"I accept what I am. That does not mean I must share it. It is what you are, who you have become, that I cannot accept."

"I will tell you what I am, Gio. I am the reason you are alive. I am the reason you have food and peace."

"You should have let them drown me."

"Maybe."

Gio's hurt flinched, the blood stopping a moment, a pain ripping through her chest. She refused to show it in her face but moved a fist to her chest and pressed down, forcing herself to be slow.

Lazarro's voice became soft, cut by deep breaths.

"I kept you alive for myself, Gio. I thought you would be able to make peace with our destinies, that we could continue in some new way. Please forgive me."

"Oh, I saw how easily you walked into your new life after my betrayal. I cannot trust you."

"Did you ever?" He stood to leave. His face was red. "I feel old, Gio. I will go and sleep."

Gio tried to stop him, rising and blocking the door, holding her hands up to him. She had more to say.

"No, do not try, Gio. You cannot tell yourself the truth. I cannot expect you to speak truth to me."

She would not be made the villain. He needed to know she suffered because she was good. He needed to know there were still secrets to be told. Even if it killed him to hear the truth so late. She did not need a pestle to send him crashing to the floor.

"Test me then," she said.

He stopped, listening.

"The poor have no words, do they, Lazarro? You teach them through paintings, preaching the gospels on the church walls, using colour instead of words. That is why my paints are in such demand. Colour is the only common language of the poor. That is why I give them the best. In these colours they can see the world as even the emperor does."

"You do well to love the poor," Lazarro said. His voice was weary, a priest who has said those same words too many times in response to meaningless gifts.

Gio couldn't breathe. Her face was flushing, her body sweating under her robe. This was too hard. The sting in her heart was coming too hard, too fast.

"I can't," she said.

"For once, tell me the truth. Tell me his name," Lazarro said.

"These paintings are the words I still cannot say. In them you can find the truth. I would not have to say the words that would destroy you. Perhaps I painted for you, in some way, for this night when you would come to my door ..."

Everything she had hidden was pouring out into the beginning of this confession, her shame lingering between them in the hot, dark room. If she could push herself to continue, there was freedom.

"You haven't changed, Gio," Lazarro said, stepping toward the door. "All these paintings? They are one more secret you kept from me." He pushed her out of the way and grabbed the door.

"But there is more to say!" she cried. "Be patient!"

She grabbed his robe, but he kept walking.

He did not stop or slow, even as she stumbled. Gio realized she was holding onto the robes of a man finally dead to her.

She let him go.

He did not look back.

⚜

The troubadour struck a harsh note on his lute, startling Panthea. She pushed Damiano away, stopping his lips from meeting hers.

Damiano's outline rose above her on the walls, the torches making strange shadows. He drew his sword, walking toward the unarmed troubadour.

The troubadour smiled, not standing to defend himself but still playing, watching Panthea.

"I am your servant, mistress Panthea," the troubadour said. "He cannot rid me. But I cannot remain with you for long. You have hardened your heart to my voice, and the voice of the Father. I came to tell you only this: Love can still save you. It is all that can save you."

Damiano began to speak in a language she did not know. The troubadour did, however, and answered with a short, bored reply.

The air around Panthea grew thick, as if she were being crowded in. She couldn't get a clear breath; a veil of this thick air shrouded her on all sides.

A cold hand touched Panthea's shoulder.

Panthea cried out, lurching from her seat. Damiano lowered his sword, his confrontation interrupted.

Armando gave no attention to the other men as he stood before her on the balcony. He had a strange look on his face. In his hand was a necklace she had not seen since she was a child. It looked to her like a noose.

"My years in the desert passed quickly because of you, Panthea. I dreamed the stars were our children, and the moon a lantern you had set out to call us in. You were with me wherever I went. I fought the infidels because that was my job, my duty, but I turned aside every reward, choosing instead to make this house great, giving you a dowry so large that everyone would know."

"Know?" Panthea said.

"That I didn't deserve you. No man could. You have to choose to love me, Panthea. This I cannot win. I cannot make war for you."

"My mother would want me to go to Florence, to marry there," she said. Her words were soft. She had imagined digging her heel into his heart at this moment, relishing the feel of spurning him one last time, but the moment was here, and he softened her rough will. He softened every hard edge she had, and she wanted to be that soft woman. She needed him to teach her how.

"The law says I can do with you as I please."

Panthea looked up from the necklace he was holding. This was what she wanted. She wanted him to grab her and she could rest her face on his chest and just breathe, letting him worry of the stories for the guests who were still waiting, and the strange men in the garden. He was so close to her heart. All he had to do now was take it.

He wasn't saying anything.

"And what would please you?" Panthea said. He just needed to say the words.

"It would please me to give you your freedom," he said.

Her chin was quivering. She wanted to shake him.

"All I will ask is this: for one night, be mine, in name only. Do not make your choice until tomorrow."

He stepped behind her, lifting the necklace to her face before settling it around her neck.

It was a double strand of pearls the size of plump berries, connected by gold loops, running toward a double pendant of looking-glass opals, reflecting the light in new ways at every hour in pinks, blues, golds. The greater opal was on the bottom, the lesser one nestled on top, each connected to the other by a thousand delicate cast strands of gold, no bigger than a hair, weaving a complex pattern from which neither could ever break free without destroying the entire piece.

Her mother had worn it as she died, wearing it with grace and sorrow, resting cold fingers on the cold stones, thinking of her life as the lady of this manor. Death had come for her as it had all the others, but it came too early, and all the gold in the world had not saved her.

Panthea, just a girl, had not known whether to blame this house or this gold for the death, and so she wanted neither. She wanted another house, and new gold, gold that came without memories. She could never be her mother. The woman was too great, too lovely and kind. Panthea had inherited so little from her. She did not want to disgrace her, living a poor second life in this place.

But there was another voice within that did not listen. *Do not be afraid to love,* it said. Sometimes, when Panthea was quiet and still, she heard this voice in her heart and wondered if it was the voice of God or of her mother. She did not truly know either. She did not know what their voices would sound like.

Armando had been to her what her father had not, a strong, shadowing presence in the days of grief, an assurance that she would have a place in the world, a good place. How could she let herself imagine it must be elsewhere, with some man, any man, who could give her more? What more did she need? Why did she allow that thought to take root and grow?

She remembered when it had first entered her body, presenting itself as a delicious distraction, a moment's sin that would be undiscovered. Lust, this craving for what she couldn't have, what she didn't need, felt rich and slick in her mouth. It made her taste salt and roll her tongue across her lips as it slid down, shooting darts of pleasure through her arms and down her legs. It thrilled her, and no one knew. But the pleasure was too brief, and she invited it to enter again. She feasted upon these little secret thoughts, each one making her taste what she shouldn't, each one making her stomach leap with pleasure, and her legs feel light and weak from the thoughts.

Joy did not feel like this. Joy was a steady, quiet presence. It offered no rich, dark thrills. Joy showed on her face and others knew. It had no second life, no secrets she kept close.

But the distractions turned to torment, each demanding more and more of its own, each leaving her weak for another, each burn making her cry when it faded. She became consumed with the pleasures and hungers. She had let one thought in and it became legion. Now she could not bear joy, could not bear to come into the light, for she was a greasy, hidden slave of pleasure. No one would be able to overpower these sins. Nothing of this earth felt as good.

She wished she could go back in time and set that moment right, turn away that unhappy thought, train her mind to see without fear what could yet be if she but stayed true. And she had stayed true—she had not acted on any of these thoughts, not in her physical life. No matter. Her heart was decayed, and her spirit was in shadows so that her body did not want to be true, though it was. Everything had been given over. A thought given time changes everything. She wished now for it to end, but there was no way out. Her thoughts owned her life.

Armando fastened the necklace. "Tonight I am your lord," he whispered in her ear.

She did not respond.

"Let me hold you," he said. "You have never been in my arms. I am your lord, and I have not yet kissed you."

He had his arms around her waist, turning her. She was trying not to move her face up toward him as he leaned down, his hand moving to her cheek.

Panthea held her breath, feeling the hot, smooth touch of his skin and the cold weight around her neck. Perhaps Armando could do it. Perhaps if she forced herself into his arms, forced herself to move her mouth to his, perhaps if she tasted this real man instead dreaming of imagined suitors, he would be enough to save her. She would never tell him of this second life she lived. She would summon the will to try.

As she turned to begin her new life, her eyes widened and she screamed.

Damiano was standing over the troubadour, his sword run through the man.

Armando pushed her down and leaped over the balcony, running at Damiano, drawing his own sword.

Damiano was fast, too fast to be a simple messenger as he claimed. Armando was caught off guard by his speed, and Damiano's blade ripped through his sleeve. Armando did not flinch. Panthea saw blood running along the blade's edge. Damiano lowered the blade and laughed.

Armando seized him by the hair and ran his sword through Damiano's stomach.

Damiano fell, blood on his mouth, serene.

Panthea tried to breathe but could not. She retched, covering her stomach with her hands, expelling nothing. She was paralyzed with horror.

Armando was at her side, putting his arms around her, steadying her, leading her to sit. His touch awakened her and she clawed at him.

"Why did you that?" she screamed. "He lowered his blade!"

Armando tried to pin her arms to her side, but as she spoke, he pushed her back to look at her.

"He killed your troubadour," Armando said. "He might have killed you, too."

"I know why you did it," she said. "Do not feed me imaginations."

"What did you promise him, Panthea?"

"You accuse me? As if this was my fault? I was wrong to have ever softened under your touch."

"You softened under my touch? I didn't notice. All I ever felt were the barbs from your tongue."

"You stood them because you wanted me. And when you thought you might lose me to another, you killed him."

Armando spat in disgust. He sheathed his sword and bowed to her. "I take my leave of you now. Good night, Panthea."

"Good night?" she asked. She did not want to be left alone with a corpse, and certainly not two of them. She had never seen a dead man. She peeked again at them, expecting their bodies to animate or twitch.

"You would prefer good-bye?" Armando said.

Panthea refused to answer.

He started to speak the dreaded word—she saw it on his lips.

"I will not." He shook his head. "You are right to break faith with me. I am a fool."

He looked at the bodies, but not her, and left.

⚜

Gio moved closer to the fire, still unable to feel its warmth. Lazarro had left hours ago; the doves had grown silent, and the light disappeared from under her door.

Lazarro knew what she did and why. She had no more secrets from him. Except the one. That secret was so much a part of her now—it had spurred so many decisions and words—that even to confess it would be useless. She might as well seek forgiveness for her very self. *She* was the lie.

She sat with all her riches before her, the tubs of finely ground pigments from every imaginable source. She was the reason the cathedrals were painted with such drama and force. Her colours were the voice of God to the Lost River.

"If a man has anything against you, as you stand praying ..." She remembered Lazarro approaching her on that hot, humid night. He had read this Scripture at Matins, and it pierced his heart. He had been gone at his studies for only a year, back in the village to see Dario. Everything was still fresh in his heart.

She remembered how his hands shook, how he restrained himself from weeping, as he sought her forgiveness. There was nothing to forgive, really. She knew that. That is what made her so violent, so angry. She was so ashamed of his meekness. He had always been stronger than she.

She had chosen to scourge him as she should be scourged. Every punishment she deserved was poured out on him. She renounced God just to spite him, so that every prayer he offered would be a reminder of her absence.

The shame of what she had done, what she had done to them all, still burned, years later. It gave her hope tonight, hope that what still hurt was still able to be healed. Dead flesh felt nothing. She knew that from her work with the poor. Pain was a sign that life still flowed into the wound. Tonight, being at last abandoned by Lazarro, pushed to the edge of the darkness in her past, broken in the fall, tonight she would open the wound. Tonight she would tell the story. All of it. He would see and understand.

She pulled the black pigment up into her lap, using her brush to scoop a bit of fat into a mortar. Flicking her wrist in tiny, twitching arcs, she mixed the pigment dust into the fat, making a loose pool of black, an irretrievably dark, shimmering mirror. The black pigment was the only one with an odor that caught your attention. Made from bones burned black until they could be crumbled and ground, it had a musty animal smell.

Gio knew she shouldn't start with black, but this was the first colour that came to mind. It would be hard to clean her brush after using this. This pigment was hard to wash clean. The dead were tenacious.

Black snaked its way down the clean parchment, dividing, cutting. Black was the lie. She had not known, when she was a little girl, how her life could be divided like this. This black line was fixed now, and no other pigment could cut through it or diminish its effect.

She painted on, the paper listening as she told the tale, the sorrows and secrets swirling, dancing together. This was her love letter to him, everything they could have been. Next came red, Venetian red, the poison and passion of life. She held them both in her heart.

She sat back and saw it as another might: There had been the brilliant green days of her youth, when she had loved a boy named

Lazarro. Her parents, poor peasants working for Dario, were happy. Dario's wife was a kind woman, making sure they had enough grain and meat for the winter, sending clothes to them when her mother was unable to sew enough for the family's needs.

Every festival season, the family came across this mountain to Dario's town.

There was the blinding yellow of the first meeting with Lazarro, the golden flush of joy that had swept over her at their first kiss. She loved Lazarro, the house servant in Dario's manor, the servant who distinguished himself with wit and loyalty. He was sure that Dario would consent to a marriage.

They fell asleep together in the stable after sharing a kiss and a bowl of wine at the festival. The day had been too warm, and the labours from harvest had worn them down. When Dario caught them the next morning, he was angry.

Dario demanded payment for her ruin; it was his right as master of the manor for which her father worked. Her father had no such sum and she had no way to prove her honour except by her word. A woman's word was meaningless. Her father had to pay the fine at once or face punishment. Dario could pinch his wages, leaving the family to starve in the winter months, or throw him in prison until the debt was paid, which would ensure the death of her family. Either way, Gio's parents would have to sell off her siblings to other masters to raise money for Dario. In one careless night, Gio had destroyed them all. Her parents could not look her in the eye.

Catching her alone in the fields days later, Dario was quick to make a bargain with her. She could cancel her father's debt if she became Dario's mistress. Or chambermaid, whatever her family preferred to call it. Though she was ashamed, Gio ran home and confessed the offer to her father. She hoped he would rise up in anger and fight for her name. He knew she was a good child. He would not endure this insult.

Her father agreed to the offer at once. She was sent to Dario's home, sick with dread and humiliation. She had never been with a man. Now she would be a mistress and never a wife.

She had not even seen Lazarro since they had been discovered. She was sure he had heard the news, but no word had come from him. No help had come from him, no secret messages by moonlight, no promises of escape. Now she would see him daily, and he would know that she spent her nights in Dario's bed. Lazarro must have been content to watch her father pay that fine. He had had a bit of fun with her. A stolen kiss would be nothing to a man. His honour was not in question, and his purse was not touched. Indeed, his reputation might increase, affording him more picks for a wife to bear him children. After all, men who took women for sport made some women delirious with desire.

Her head hurt, the awful thoughts making the blood pound in her temples. She tried to keep her feet steady on the path to Dario's home. They would think her drunk if she stumbled. They might beat her.

No one remembered she was a good child. No one fought for her. The thought struck her with such force she fell to her knees, hitting the loose stones of the path, falling to her knees like Saul on the blinding path.

That was her salvation! She could never prove her good name and be believed, but were not men eager to believe stories of shame?

Men were always so quick to doubt a woman. Words could spoil herself for Dario, and Dario would be forced to cast her away.

When she was freed, she would tell the truth to Lazarro. Perhaps they could still escape. He had meant that kiss, she was sure. He might have been told her father would pay the fine at once. He might be wondering why she had not come to him. Yes, tonight she would earn her escape, find Lazarro, and they would flee together.

A servant like him could find work in another's house, far away. She would have to be careful to take wine and dried meat for the long walk.

She was still making her list for the flight when she arrived at Dario's keep. It was early in the afternoon and the sun was strong. The doors were made of wood carved with images she had never imagined; lions and winged creatures, bulls and serpents with eyes made of emeralds. Iron handles as thick as a ship's rope hung on the door and did not move as a servant swung the door open to her. The heat, the images, and her fear made her sick. She wanted to hide in the bushes that grew along the walls.

Gio held the paintbrush in the air, remembering the night.

She was led to an upper chamber, her heart going so fast that she made little noises as she climbed the stairs, the same little noises rabbits made before her mother wrung their necks.

Gio tried to think of Esther in all her grace and how God had blessed her courage. What one woman could do, another woman could.

When the servants pushed her in and closed the door behind her, Dario licked his lips. He was reclining on the feather bed, picking at his nails.

Gio did not wait to speak. "You don't want me, sir. You have a fine wife."

Dario was high from his wine even at this obscene hour. "I will let you go if you can answer my riddle," he said.

She nodded her agreement. She did not believe him.

"Why am I rich?" he asked.

"Because you are wise," she answered, straining to sound sincere. Dirty, ragged bits of nail fell on the floor around him. Except for the bits he ate.

"You lose," he replied, sounding bored. "I am rich because I am greedy. I never have enough. So your reminding me that I have a fine wife just reminds me I have no fine mistress."

He gave her a long appraising look.

"These will be your chambers for tonight. You can lay your clothes on the washstand, but pick them clean of any lice first. We'll keep you elsewhere after today. Probably in the crypt. I'll have a straw mat sent down to the cellar for you. When I don't want you, try to busy yourself with cleaning. My wife would like that."

"You don't want me, sir," Gio repeated. Her knees were weak. "I'm three months along. I would add to the burden of your purse and offer nothing to your bed. You cannot take me as a mistress tonight unless you have a good lie for your wife to explain me, to explain where you were three months ago. She would send me away at once, wouldn't she? All that trouble for you, sir, and not a bit of fun."

Dario rose from the bed and grabbed her, ripping her bodice open from the bottom. He shoved his hands under her bodice, digging his fat fingers into her flat stomach. She tried to breathe in and hold the breath to give her stomach some shape.

He slapped her. "You could have told me this earlier. You enjoy making fools of men, yes?"

Gio didn't answer.

"Is it Lazarro's?" he asked.

Gio panicked. *I am a fool,* she thought. She had not thought of this question. If she said yes, she would bring terrible grief to Lazarro. He would be rounded up at once and forced to face Dario. Lazarro would be beaten and heavily fined, the fine doubled just for spite, and forced to break himself for the money to repay Dario. His life would be ruined. They could never marry.

"No, it is not his."

As soon as the words were out, she saw her second mistake. This world of men was too fast for her; she could not think of lies as quickly as they thought of accusations. Who would she say the father was? What would Lazarro say? *Oh, God,* she pleaded in her heart, *let me find him first and explain this, too.*

Dario licked his lips and laughed. He slapped her again, his hand drawing slowly away from her face, his fingertips dragging over her skin, making her feel dirty.

"Your father still owes me the money, you know. It doesn't matter who ruined you."

He was losing interest in her, his body slumping, more interested in his wine than her now.

"I will pay it myself," she said.

"Ah, you have surprised me, Gio." He took a long dreg from his bowl. "Everyone thought you were such an innocent, didn't they? Such a devoted daughter of the Church? And you are really nothing but a tart. Poor Lazarro will be heartbroken. The fool actually fancied you. I have done him a favour. I will be merciful to him today and tell him the full story."

It was four years before she saw Lazarro again. When she saw him next, he was a priest, university educated. Dario had paid for a church to be built in the piazza. His wife had grown ill, some long, wasting disease. Priests could do two things well: beseech God and heal. The health of the body and spirit were one, and none but a priest could properly attend to either. Lazarro would attend to the sick with cures approved by the Church and prayers on their behalf to God. What a priest did not heal, God would. God listened to priests and none else; therefore, no doctors were needed. Any help from a medical man was stunted by his inability to talk to God.

Lazarro came to Dario's wife daily; she did not have to travel for prayer or medicine. Dario hoped he had bought a big enough church for God that God would be pleased to cure her. Best of all, he owned the priest. Dario had paid for his education. There was no need to pay for prayers to be said for his wife night and day.

Gio's own parents had died. They had not wanted her at their bedside. She earned her bread now foraging for herbs and minerals. The men working on Dario's church needed pigments and paid great sums for them. Gio first found pigment dealers on the roads home from the piazza; she traded her family's knowledge of simple cures for their knowledge of elaborate pigments.

Lazarro refused to speak with her alone ever again, or offer her Communion until she confessed her sin. One night she drank two extra bowls of wine and went to the steps of the church.

Dario was there with his nobles, collecting debts from the villagers. When the people saw Gio, a ripple of excitement went through the crowd.

"Lazarro!" Gio cried.

The crowd pushed in around her. Dario began to sweat, but he was smiling at his companions.

Lazarro emerged from the church, his eyes adjusting to the dimming light. "You are a stranger to me. Go home."

"Fine words from Judas!" she said. The wine made her dizzy. She could not hold her course, her planned words of pleading and tears. It all came out as fury.

"Whom have I betrayed?" he yelled back. "It is you who kissed me, then gave me over to death."

"Death? What do you know of death? I will tell you of death: of watching your mother and father die, slowly, not having enough to eat, too shamed to tell their lord of their great need. It is trying in vain to heal them of the sores that came upon them, when they lay too long in their beds from exhaustion, of trying to spoon a little fat into their mouths for strength, having them spit it at me and turn away."

"We are all sorry for your parents," Dario called out. "Whoever had you first should have been generous to your family. If that was your first."

The crowd snickered. Women pushed men aside for a better look. Women who broke the rules were always so fascinating.

Gio was too drunk to kill him, but she wanted to. She just spat at him. She hit someone else instead. She could tell by the sudden cursing and movement on his right.

Lazarro spoke. "Sins can be forgiven, Dario, if they are but confessed. Is that why you have come, Gio? Will you confess and be cleansed?"

"It's lies you have fed upon!" Gio yelled. She swayed, trying to focus on what she must say, but he was healthy, and fed. He knew things now. He had been given a better life because of her suffering. "I cannot take it away," she muttered, turning toward her home.

"God takes away the sin of the world," Lazarro called to her. "Confess and be free, daughter. You owe that to us all."

Gio stopped. "Do not speak to me of debts! You who live in a fine church, who eats every meal knowing the next is not far behind, who have no fear of men in the night! You are a pig in priest's robes! You live well because of my sin!"

Lazarro came down the steps and slapped her. The crowd approved with murmurs and claps. His words were too low for anyone else to hear, especially Dario.

"I paid your debt to Dario with my life. I will never earn my freedom. I will never marry, never kiss a wife, never have children. Yes, I have my meals in peace and I sleep in a quiet room. But I was kept alive against my will, forced into a life I did not want to live. When I learned who you were, how you slept with many men, I died inside. I wanted to marry you, Gio. I fell for your deceits, and I will spend the rest of my life paying for it. Are you happy, Gio? No higher price can a man pay for his bride. Did I do well?"

"It was not as it seemed," Gio said, her voice falling. She just wanted to go home, to fall into her bed and weep, alone. The wine wasn't making her brave anymore.

"No, it was not," he agreed.

He repented later for slapping her, when it did no good. She was sober and had no courage to confess her own mistakes.

Gio held the brush in her hands. Tears mixed with the pigments as she made another stroke. Words had failed her too often to be trusted. They were slippery, like wet shards of glass that cut as you handled them, everyone seeing something different in them from their angle. Only this parchment could be trusted, where she affixed the colours and they stayed, a flat, honest surface that gave all the same picture.

She would say it all in this work and give it to him. She forgave him with every colour she had, and the truth began to emerge.

Chapter Nine

Panthea sat, numb, looking at the two bodies lying in blood beneath her in the garden.

Armando had forsaken her. This is what she always claimed she wanted. But it did not bring her pleasure. It brought grief, an awakening of a voice she should have recognized but didn't. She wondered if it was her heart, dead for many years, returning to scream in her ear.

The bodies before her were a vulgarity, a perversion lying among the flowers as the birds sang.

Why did the birds sing? Panthea wondered. Their song terrified her. How could nature be so ruthless? Birds should not sing when there is death.

But then, she thought how she herself had continued after her mother's death, and her father had as well. Everyone thought it was near miraculous. They were like birds too, rising each morning and doing the work set before them.

Panthea's heart had not been in it, though. Her father's heart had not been in it either. Their hearts were left at the bedside, bundled into the bedding her mother rested upon, lowered into the ground as Lazarro blessed the Lord for His mercies. Her father wept then. Death humbled him.

Her father became tender, softened. He lost his will to live as the man he was before. He struggled to make amends. Panthea panicked, seeing her father change, his will become unsteady, just as she needed him. She became what he could not.

Panthea hated him some nights for adding this burden to her— why did he not fight death? How could he accept it, let it break him so that he became a weaker man? She wanted to strike life across the cheek, to humiliate it, to ruin every good thing it offered. She could not bear to hear the birds sing.

She forced herself to climb over the stone wall of the low balcony and walk to the troubadour's body. Closing his eyes, she thought she should cry, but she could not. The troubadour's wide hands were cupped, blood drying on them, the blood on his clothes turning to a rust brown. Death was changing him, too.

She should repent for her words, for her flirtations. It would do no one any good except God. Could her sorrow save anyone now? Sorrow was the most useless of all emotions, she remembered. You could cry a thousand tears and let sorrow destroy you day after day, but God would not come to your rescue—this she remembered from her mother's death.

But anger—that changed the world. This surely had caught God's eye. Two of His children lay dead because of it, because of the sorrow God had not healed in her. God was the bird in the forest who sang when good people died.

"I should say I am sorry for their deaths," she said to the night air. "But I do not know how to ask for mercy, and I would not know how to bear it now. Too much time has passed since I was willing to receive the Lord's comforts. To turn back now would cost everything I am. I do not know how to save myself, or receive mercy, or even bear the tenderness of a good man. I cannot save myself from the woman You have turned me into."

She spat on the ground and did not say amen.

Panthea forced herself to look down again, to look for purses or gold jewelry. There was no sense in the servants stealing them. The poor ruined themselves by losing money and bearing children. Besides, the troubadour wore a beautiful cross of gold, which she bent to steal, though it was stained in blood. A glance at Damiano's face showed it twisted in his death. He did not look changed. She bent farther in to the troubadour, turning so she would not have to look at Damiano.

A cold hand shot out and took her by the ankle, knocking her off balance to her knees. Her stomach clenched down hard as though it had been struck by an anvil.

Damiano's eyes were open.

She tried to jerk her leg free as he began dragging her to him, his grip crushing her ankle. His hands were so cold and prickly. His eyes had a strange green light as his tongue flicked around the edges of his lips.

She tried to kick with her other leg, but he caught that one too and dragged her on her back until she was under him.

"Tomorrow my work begins, for I have come here in service to another. But I have found you, Panthea, and I will not let you go again."

He bent for a bloody kiss.

⚜

Painting was the art of infinite corrections. One impulsive stroke would give her hours of work. She had practiced, over and over, to make something beautiful from her mistakes. Painting was freedom for her heart, the chance to say anything and know that whatever came out could be built upon into beauty. Here, her heart made no permanent mistakes.

Next came the green earth of Verona, and the yellow of Italy's soil. Cumin gave a brighter yellow, but it always made its way to workmen's pies and not the church walls, so it had fallen out of favour with her. There were other pigments she could use: lapis lazuli, which took hours to grind and wearied her wrist, crushing the precious stones into fine dust.

The pigments would be mixed with fat and sit before her, a language of indescribable words. She would find an order for them, and they would say what she could not.

It took so long to mix each colour, time to think, to consider each stroke that would be made. The paper from Amalfi absorbed the fat quickly, leaving the pigment dry to the touch. If not mixed in perfect proportion, however, the pigment would ball up on top of the paper and flake off. The pigments were the temperamental ones, not the artists.

She made the finest pigments for the churches because she alone was a painter among all the herbal women. She alone could offer a sojourner the prize his priest sought, and remedies for his loved ones as well. How they must have fought for a chance to visit her. It was no trouble: She gathered the stones and the herbs on the same walks and traded for them both at the harbour.

She had transformed the ruins of her life into something desired by the holy men who had once scorned her. She had not meant to stay entwined in Lazarro's world. Now every holy man asked directions to her hut from him; every month he had to sit and listen to a strange man praise her work and insult her name. After all, she was a wretch now, an outcast who did not receive Communion. She once hoped this tortured him.

She never revealed the truth to him of her false pregnancy. When no baby came, the village gossiped that justice came in many ways to a sinner. She buried her shame and pride deep in her heart, layering them over and over with lies, until it became a brittle, calcified rock that no one could break open. It had been hard to climb her mountain with these deep burdens.

But here, tonight, she broke open her heart. The paper was silent and did not rebuke her. Violent pigments swirled and cut through each other. Too much was used for each. A little would have made the impression, but her soul was pouring out and wanted more. More words, more piercing truth. So much truth was needed to cut through the past.

After midnight it was almost finished. *What artist can ever say the work is truly finished,* she laughed to herself. *An artist can only say the work has seen the end of one's talents and burned out from confusion. They were both meant to be so much more.*

She sat on her haunches and looked at it, sweat dripping from her eyebrows onto her nose and exhaustion overtaking her. She would bring it to Lazarro tomorrow, leave it at his church. It was her best work, her masterpiece. He would see the language and begin to find her story, the buried story. He might forgive.

She had never painted like this. She had never been able to make something so beautiful from her life. The painting was all her lost words, tears that had not fallen, kisses never shared. The painting said she was broken with grief, and it gave her heart back to him, the only way he could hold it now.

Perhaps now she would travel with his blessing and see the painted churches she had supplied with pigment. Perhaps now she would share her secrets with the other herbalists, and churches would have colours that the world had never seen. Confession could give her the world back again, not just her heart.

Confession for sins could be heard only by a priest if there was to be forgiveness. Gio's stomach burned at the thought. She had not eaten for hours, true, but it was the thought, the courage she would need to face Lazarro to do this—that was what ate at her. Food could wait. Fear was a stronger appetite. She had to find the strength to show Lazarro her sins, and he had to forgive her in the name of God. Was it unfair to ask him to forgive as a man and as a priest? Would he do it? Would he even hear her confession? Now the painting seemed too bold. She wished she had not used so many colours, such thick, harsh, black scrapings. Alone, she was brave in telling the story. She might have even embellished it.

Gio felt sick. She did not trust her work, did not trust Lazarro to understand and accept her, did not trust God to mediate between them. Why had she painted at all? Now this wretched canvas would sit here, accusing her every moment of both past sins and this cowardice.

A wind moved the door, just enough for Gio to see that there was no light outside, no light except the stars. Some ancients taught that angels were stars, burning guardians holding back the darkness, lighting cold nights for the sons of man. She tried to take comfort in them, tried to believe angels were there. She could take the painting, right now. She could force herself to move, to push through her weakening resolve, force herself to walk to the church and be free. She could do it tonight. She could do it right now. All these years, all her lies, they would be over.

Fear would not leave her. It circled around and around, constricting thoughts and breath until Gio was unable to defend herself.

"Please help me," she said, reaching a hand for the door. "I must do this tonight."

Every movement she made only gave fear new access to her flesh, new places to sting in her belly. Gio withdrew her hand.

"I cannot," she cried. No one heard her. The piercings did not stop.

The door did not move. Gio crouched in the fetal position, helpless. A night wind parted the trees beyond her door. She heard the branches sway and the birds sing out. Gio had not heard birds sing in the still of night like this. They sang with full cries, the way they sang on spring mornings. Something was stirring, but they were not afraid.

She sensed something moving into the room. The broken places in her heart began to heal, the sealed words unfurling, melting away in its warmth. Exhausted from the attack, Gio could not move. She lay there like a child.

Arms wrapped around her, lifting her, cradling her tired body. Her fingers felt new life waking them, new colours she would dream, new works she would paint. She dreamed of a strange, gentle giant in the room with her, with eyes of fire and wide sweeping wings that could touch the walls if he stretched them.

He was like the creature the children of the village described when they had fallen too close to the water's edge or came upon an angry animal. They told of being saved by a fierce man with great wings and burning eyes. But these same creatures had been painted by the Greeks and Romans, whose ruins were still here. Everyone thought the children had created the legend from the paintings. Now she wondered why she had not believed the old painters. Lies destroyed art; they did not feed it. The painters who drew these magnificent beasts were telling her what was true. These creatures existed.

She felt a kiss upon her forehead as he lowered her to her mat and sat at the mat's edge throughout the night, his back to her, his attention focused on the door.

She stretched her legs in her sleep, pointing her toes just to feel how loose and gentle her body was now. Tomorrow she would bring her painting to Lazarro. There were still miracles in this world, and there were still fresh dawns. There was so much time, she told herself.

So much time.

Damiano pinned Panthea's wrists above her head. She jerked her head to the side, smelling death as he lowered himself to her.

The iron serpent, his staff, was alive and crawling up the wall of the castle, its eyes reflecting the moonlight in a wave of greens and blacks, a wave that made her feel the ocean beneath her, and

the fear of losing control, the seasickness rising in her stomach. The
serpent was heading toward her father's chambers. She could see the
candles flickering from the window; her father was still consulting
his attorneys and advisers, finalizing the transfer of estate. He would
be at peace tonight at last—this place and its memories resting on
the shoulders of Armando. He would be free to love the memory of
his wife without the burden of carrying on with their former life.

The serpent's head swung in her direction, its mouth opening,
red foam dripping down. It hissed, spraying red in the air.

Damiano took her gently by the chin and returned her attention
to his face. "You were so beautiful to behold when He first dreamed
of you."

"Get away from me!" She tried to kick, but he dug his knees into
her thighs, making her gasp. The struggle was bringing her closer to
the troubadour's lifeless body, his blood making it too slick for her
to move with force.

Spying the cross still on the minstrel's neck, she tried to move a
hand to it. Damiano allowed her just enough give to rest her fingertips on its edge, then he snapped her hand away.

"Will God save you now? Look what you have become. This is
not how He envisioned you. He is ashamed of you! He will have no
part in your rescue. Come with me, Panthea. There is no hope for
you here."

"I will not! I have my father, and I am pledged to Armando. You
cannot undo that!"

"I cannot undo that," he replied. "You speak truth, daughter
of shame. I cannot undo what has been done. But death has come
at last to your world. It is not the good death of the saints, or the

blessed last sleep of old age. This is a death of agony, and blood, and madness. Your world of angels and good deaths will end. Your world will never believe in goodness again. Lies will become as truths, and few will know it. Come with me and live."

"If you can save, save my father. Save Armando. Then I will be yours. I will go with you."

"You mistake me. I do not control death, Panthea. I am in service to another."

"Your prince? Take me to him then."

"No, sadly, though he is great, he too is in bondage to another lord, and his powers retrained too often. We may do our work here, but we cannot control it. We cannot control who dies. This is very much like your life, isn't it? Though you are rich and have much power, nothing you have done has ended as you planned. There is no power on earth that can give us control. It is a beautiful lie."

"So you cannot save me? This is a lie?" Panthea asked.

"I can take you from here before it begins."

He looked up at the snake, watching it test the glass window for a weakness, forcing its head into the wood edges made soft from rain.

She thought of her mother. The agony her mother felt was not the physical death but the separation from her family. That is what broke them all inside and kept shattering any foundation she or her father tried to build after her death. Separation was an unnatural grief. The serpent moved between her and her father.

No, Panthea decided. For her father, she would stay.

"I will not go with you," she said.

He slapped her, sticky cold blood on his palm smearing across her cheek. It made the sting less sharp. It sounded like a wet thud, not a sharp clap.

"What are you staying for, unloved child? A father who does not see you? Or a knight who has fully seen what you are and fled?"

His words stung, making her shoulders hunch down, shielding her heart.

"Do I lie?" he whispered. "You know this is true."

"I can turn from my past," Panthea said. She did not believe it, but she had heard Lazarro say it. "I can redeem myself in their eyes."

"You cannot!" he shouted. "Do you know how much evil you have done? How daily you have crushed hearts under your heel? What is broken would take a thousand years to sweep together and mend. You ruined them. And then you made it known to all at the feast that you wanted more, more than Armando. You wanted me. Let them have one last moment of peace without you harping in their ear, selfish little beast that you are."

She slipped a hand free and grabbed the cross from the minstrel's neck before his hand caught hers again.

He spat on her. "Gold and silver cannot save you. Was not our Lord betrayed for it?"

He glanced at the window and she followed his gaze. The snake was gone; a tiny flap of light shone through a space in the window frame.

"Come with me! Now!" he said.

"No."

"I cannot save you if you stay."

"You said I did not deserve to be saved."

His face softened. "Do you believe that?"

She wouldn't answer. The truth humiliated her.

"If you tell me you believe that, perhaps I will let you go now. Say it. Say you will not accept the Lord's mercy ... that it could never blot out your sins." His fist landed near her head. "Say it! Say you do not deserve mercy! Renounce God's grace forever, and I will let you go!"

"I cannot renounce God," she said.

"You fool, I do not ask you to renounce God. Renounce yourself. You know you do not deserve to be saved. Cling to who you are, what you have done, and I will let you go. I will even save your father." He nodded toward the window.

Panthea licked her lips, trying to prepare herself to say it. He was right, she knew.

"My time here is done. I must move on. Give me your pledge, speak the truth out loud between us, and you will be free."

His touch called up every evil she had done, the foul images and lusts she had entertained, the countless ways she had betrayed the goodness set before her by God. How many chances had Armando given her to love, or even speak kindness, and she had repaid him with wounds. She had torn her house apart with her own hands, and now there was no time to build it again.

She looked straight at him. "I deserve no grace. I have done evil in the sight of the Lord and betrayed every kindness shown me. It is who I am, and I cannot change. I will never receive enough mercy to cover my transgressions. I am damned."

His face came closer, and she smelled rancid death, a dead animal left to rot, away from the light.

"When you awake in a dark wood, and there is no light, I will be there. I will carry you across the burning river."

Chapter Ten

The straw mat crunched as a weight lifted off of it. Gio opened her eyes; the Italian sun was charming its way in again this morning, finding the gaps in her old thatched roof.

She was alone, of course. She always woke up alone. Why, then, did she feel someone's absence this morning? The empty air haunted her, and she tried to remember what she had felt as she drifted to sleep.

Italy was a land of wonders. No one ever spoke of ghosts, though angels were known to walk freely in the streets. Some of the peasants said they had seen them, great men following the children as they harvested, so that snakes shied away and sickles never swung too close. The children, of course, had many more stories. The children said you could hear angels laughing in the streets at night when the adults slept.

Gio had seen the angels her pigments had created in the churches, the sample boards the painters discarded as they tried her pigments, carried about by the monks seeking more of the same colours. These angels were mighty guardians dispersed among the Bible stories along church walls and ceilings. She considered them fanciful embellishments to the story. She had never considered they could enter her story. To believe they were real made a strange chill sweep over her, as if invisible hands had guided artists' brushes, revealing a world she had yet to imagine.

Gio looked around the room. Someone had watched over her during the night, she was sure. If someone had stayed so close in here through the dark hours, why? What other strange creatures might walk the earth? What else was she blind to?

Something sharp scraped down her door, like the slow rattle of a snake. Gio clung to her blanket, not daring to set her feet on the floor. She pressed her hand into her stomach, forcing herself to breathe.

"Who is there?" she called.

"Help me, my sister," someone said. "There is blood!"

She slid her feet to the floor, curling her toes to test it, to see if this was real and not a dream. The dirt and scattered straw bunched up between her toes, prickling her. This was real.

Grabbing a shawl, she set one unsteady leg in front of the other, walking to the door. She saw the door as if a hundred miles away, and her tiny faltering steps did nothing to bring it nearer.

Gio wished for someone to slap her, the way she slapped the new mothers during their deliveries. They panicked, saying they were too weak, or the baby was too big.

She lurched, taking hold of the door like a drowning woman grabbing an oar.

What would flood in when she opened it?

She turned once to look at her masterpiece, the bitter confession that had become beautiful as she poured out her heart. The sun was dancing around it, the pigments bursting from the paper, casting rainbows through the air.

Taking a deep, painful breath, she forced open the door. A man fell upon her, his wide, dead, open eyes flying toward her as she screamed and fell under his weight.

She kicked at the corpse with one leg, wresting herself out from under him, throwing his lifeless arm behind him so she could move.

"Hail Mary, full of grace, blessed art thou among women. Intercede for me now at the hand of the Son!" she cried.

She pushed herself into a corner, repeating the words she had heard at so many bedsides. The body did not move.

The robes of the man were familiar. She told herself not to see that, but she did. She knew those robes.

She wanted to turn him over. *He is dead,* she chanted in her head. *He is dead. He cannot harm me.*

Standing, she grabbed one arm and pulled straight up so that the body lifted on one side, then she jerked it over.

The Old Man landed with a wet thud at her feet. Gio averted her face, covering her mouth as she screamed.

No one deserved this death.

His skin was covered in deep purple blotches, blood pooling just beneath his skin. They still moved along his skin, though he was dead. Great swellings, the size of market oranges, ringed his neck. They were black and split open, with horrid black, stinking fluids running down them onto her floor. The black fluids reached her feet and she gasped, jumping back. She had never seen this. She looked up, around into the air, remembering the world she was blind to. This was not a death of her world; it was a punishment from the next.

The rancid fluid from his mouth and ears and eyes made Gio retch. The smell was strong and sour, like a wet, rotted animal left in a dark place. She stumbled backward, feeling along her wall, trying to find her way to the door, keeping her eyes on the corpse. Her fingers recognized the edge of the door joints and she felt the open air.

Gio turned and ran.

Panthea opened her eyes, alone in the garden. Gasping for air, she sat up, running her hands across her mouth, still tasting rancid blood.

She held the hand at her face out, looking at it. The hand was clean.

The garden was empty. There were no bodies, no blood, no broken or bent blades of grass or leaves. But the birds, she noticed. The birds were not singing. She looked to the edge of the garden, where tall trees separated her world from the next, the land of the common. A robin fell from a tree, twitching as it died, its beak opening and closing.

What had she dreamed? Something awful, something she had stirred up from her shame and secrets. She had been light-headed when the servants brought out the wine at dinner. The room had been warm. She had been provoked by Armando and the stranger, too. Her hand went to her neck; her mother's necklace still rested upon it.

She tried to sit up; she must never drink wine when she was so warm and preoccupied again. She had probably drunk her share and more, staggering into the garden to dream frightful things, just like the filthy peasants the sheriff dragged from the streets and beat.

She looked in all directions to make sure no servant was trying to catch a glimpse of her. But where was Armando? If he had seen her like this, he would have carried her into her chambers. She would upbraid him if the matter arose.

The marriage would happen today. The stranger had no doubt upset the plans for it to occur after last night's feast.

It was too much for her to think of, undressed before Armando, his last conquest. He would be gentle and kind with her. She couldn't bear the thought. When she was undressed before him, alone, with no one to pretend for, no prize to win, no bolts of cloth and weights of gold shielding her, he would know. She wouldn't be able to hide herself forever, not in that chamber. He would not love her.

She had not yet kissed him. Her stomach tightened as she imagined the feel of his lips, of his hands upon the small of her back. Realizing she was already submitting in her imagination, she broke away from the thought, shaking her head. She was not trained in this art, this way other women had of submitting. She did not know how to yield and no man had yet to force her.

Gold caught her eye, something gold hidden in the grass at her side. Reaching for it, parting the grass with her hand, she saw it was a gold crucifix, covered in blood.

Her breath caught in her chest and burned.

"I did not dream."

She looked at the window above her, where her father was meeting with his advisers. The candle was still burning, though it was almost dawn now and the sky was lightening. No voices came from the room.

She clutched the crucifix to her chest.

"I did not dream.

"I did not dream."

She found no strength from the cross, just a sharp, cold accusation piercing her palms.

Shoving her hand into her pocket, letting the cross tumble into her skirts, she stood. Her legs could not find their balance. It felt as if the ground was shifting beneath her.

"My father is up there," she whispered.

Running in the fragile dawn air, Gio leapt across the rocks and hollows of the path. The lights in the village were all burning, the festival over for the night. Those who had drunk would be passed out in doorways, and the somber wives would be sweeping them from their thresholds, muttering about the *tempestoso* nature of men. The church bells broke the predawn silence. Lazarro was beginning Matins.

She felt the vibration of the church bells in her legs. Every peasant she knew relied on the bells to tell time, having not the wits to read an astrolabe. This made the merchants angrier still at the hapless workers. It was one argument Dario did not bluster into, and all were glad. Of course, Dario would grow rich either way. If the peasants told time by church bells, they would still rely on the church for the fundamentals of life, the counting of hours. They would remember the necessity of prayer and tithes. Dario's Church would do well.

If, however, the peasants learned to tell time by mechanical clock or astrolabe, they had less need of the Church. The working hours would rule the day. Prayers would be forgotten. Time would become nothing more than a silent reminder of duties to earthly masters. Church bells reminded the people that God owned each of the hours. All of Europe was debating the matter; Dario was content that he would prosper either way.

Lazarro would be tired by now. He had had little sleep. He rang the bells for Compline prayers just after dark, then watched for the appearance of stars. He would read the Psalms aloud, standing in the doorway of the church, using these readings to count time until he could say Nocturn prayers just after midnight. Then it was sleep, but no food, until Matins. After Matins came Terce, Sext, and finally None, when he could break his fast at lunch. The peasants came to call it noon, having not the tongue for Latin.

Gio heard the bells finish and knew Lazarro was beginning his long day of service without adequate sleep, without adequate food. He would be weak.

Gio stopped. She had put enough distance between the horror she had witnessed and her path here. Clear thought was returning. What right had she to add to Lazarro's burdens? Her heart had changed toward him last night, but had not his been hardened? Would he even receive her in the church? She had thought today would be a day of confession and reconciliation, and instead she was running to tell him that his friend and servant was dead of a gruesome death.

The villagers would want the body burned at once, and it would be Lazarro who must do it.

Worse, the Old Man had died without Last Unction; his time in Purgatory was now extended. She had not even tried to save him. Lazarro would think she had spited him again by letting his friend die. This was a new death, one never before seen. Who would believe her? No, he would hate her for this news and her failing. She thought of the masterpiece. It was ruined. She should have run with it last night, rousing him from sleep, confessing it all and making amends. There had been time. She thought she could wait until the new day, but the new day had its own intentions. Now he would never want it even if she offered it to him.

Her steps slowed. Herbalists who let their patients die, especially blind old men, could be beaten or worse. Some might say she was a witch. That she had poisoned the blind old man. His body looked the art of witchcraft. Gio stopped, surveying the path around her. No one had seen her yet, and the sun was not fully risen. She could get rid of the body, carry on with her plans. No one would know. She glanced back toward her home—it would mean a return to her life of secrets. But these would be new secrets. Perhaps they would not be as heavy to bear. She hesitated.

Whimpering, a large dog, its belly swollen with pups, staggered toward her from the low brush. Gio bent down, offering her hand, coaxing it out from the leaves and branches. As it came closer, she saw huge black swellings on its neck, and a thick black bile seeping from its jowls. It collapsed at her feet.

Gio stood back, running her hand over her mouth. "What is this thing?"

Pressing her fingertips onto her closed eyelids, she tried to awaken herself. This could not be real. At her feet the stones twitched. Blinking, shaking her head, she looked closer. Birds were dying, wings twitching as they lay on the path all around her. The world had been poisoned.

Another movement came from the brush, heavier, like the dragging of feet. It came from higher up, behind her. She grabbed up her skirts and tried to get around the dog on the path, not letting her skirts touch it. They snagged on the brush, and Gio heard them tear as she jerked them free and tried to keep moving, her eye on the path above her.

"Murder!"

A woman's scream rose from the village just below.

"My husband lies dead!"

Gio was not safe. A dead man in her home, someone else dead in the village, all these animals. It had to be witchcraft. She would be blamed. She would be the convenient solution.

She pushed each leg forward, her skirt snagging with every step. She stopped to yank it free with both hands.

From out of the trees, a figure in black swooped down on her, its arms raised, face blackened, forcing her to the ground with a snarl. Gio struck the attacker, pounding with her fists, kicking with her legs, but the figure was heavy. Pain had no effect on it. The attacker caught her hands as they slowed, pinning them at her sides, sitting on her legs. Gio's heart was beating too hard; she feared it would burst if she didn't slow her breathing at once.

Gio tried to see past the burned black oil covering the face. The robe was torn enough for her to view a leg patched with clean cloths.

"It's you," Gio gasped. "The woman of no name."

The Old Woman did not move, just kept her pinned and still.

"Do it then!" Gio yelled.

The woman's face crooked at an odd angle.

"You've come to have your revenge on me. I burned you."

Gio saw the woman's chin tremble, but no tears followed. It was not a good sign. She was dehydrated. This woman needed wine, or ale, or milk. She would die within hours if she did not drink.

"You need to drink," Gio said, making a motion for drinking. Maybe the woman didn't want revenge. She could be driven by nothing more than thirst.

"The man I traded with said it would do no harm," Gio offered. "I suppose I should have tried it first.'

The Old Woman began to rise, releasing Gio's legs and arms, motioning for her to follow. Gio scrambled to all fours and stood. The woman was pointing away from the village, moaning. She pointed to the forest beyond them, grabbing Gio's hand, trying to pull her in that direction.

"Why must we flee?" Gio asked. "What has happened?"

Falling to her knees, the woman clutched Gio's skirts, imploring Gio to do something.

Church bells were ringing. It was not time for the next prayers. Gio looked down into the village, wondering what Lazarro knew. When she turned back to face the woman, a man stood with them. His appearance was too sharp, too bright, so that looking at him pierced her eyes like the noon sun.

Gio fell backward, landing on her rear, toppling the woman with her. The mute woman began to crawl to the man, but Gio grabbed her. The woman shook her off, saying something in a strange voice to this man.

Together, they spoke in a language Gio did not know.

⚜

"I'm trying to save her, Mbube!" Mariskka said. "They have no medicines, no painkillers. They don't even have hand sanitizer. No one knows what a virus is."

"Truth sound crazy, in any age," Mbube said.

"You're not going to let me save anyone, are you?" Mariskka asked. The realization made her stomach sink.

"People don't save," Mbube said. "People fight. You fight death."

He gripped her arms and faced her. "Show people to fight. Do not let darkness win."

"How can I fight? I can't talk. I'm useless," Mariskka said.

"This true."

Mariskka waited for him to smile at his joke. He didn't.

"How do I fight darkness, Mbube? I'm no better than they are."

"When you girl, your mother took us church," Mbube said.

"That's right. Except I didn't know you went too."

"You heard Truth. Your heart knew what was light."

"That next week my mother was diagnosed," Mariskka said. "The glow didn't last long for me. The God you serve let a nine-year-old watch her mother die, Mbube."

"You hate light after that," Mbube said. "You hate God."

"You don't know what it is to grieve," she said.

"Hospice workers pull you from your mother's bed. Make you sleep alone on couch. I hold you all night. Only then Mbube sorrow he cannot die. Mbube hurt so bad with you."

Mariskka reached out to embrace him. He had been there. God had not deserted her. Mariskka wanted to say she was sorry.

Mbube raised his arms, crying out to the sky above. Lightning flew from his fingertips into her nostrils, shooting into every blood vessel, making her flesh glow blue. Mariskka looked down, seeing her body transparent from the lights within, her heart beating, the rivers of vessels sweeping her blood along. She felt the anger from that night as thick clotted scabs over her heart, peeling off and falling away. She screamed from pain, the tearing away of the anger, leaving her tender, raw heart exposed.

Muscles all through her body that had been tensed for years let go, stretching, her palms flexing, her hands being opened fully for the first time since that day. She had not realized she had walked through her life with fists.

The storm receded. The air around her smelled like a roll of new copper pennies.

"You have the Blood now," Mbube said.

"That hurt!" she said.

"Now you strong," Mbube said. "His strength will hold."

Mariskka did what she had wanted to do that night in the hospice when her mother had died. She lunged to Mbube, wrapping her arms around him, burying her face in his stomach. His arms went around her and he comforted her at last. He said the words she had waited thirty years to hear.

"All will be well. You never be alone."

A scream from the village startled Mariskka and she released him, turning to look upon the houses below.

She turned back to ask him what to do.

He was gone.

Chapter Eleven

Panthea entered the house from the kitchen, which would be lit and warm, servants working at any hour. A few were there, cleaning, counting, throwing scraps to the old dog chained to the wall guarding the larder. The dog was panting heavily, lying on its side, its jowls a waxy, grey colour. Its eyes followed her as she walked past.

No one else dared look at her. They would be praying, she knew, that every plate was accounted for, and no foods gone missing except that which the guests ate. Many servants had their own home, where they could find their own meals, though the food was far inferior. Panthea had always told them to work harder, for a great appetite was wonderful seasoning.

But tonight, she wanted them to linger. As she edged past, she studied them. All appeared in fine health, with no unusual worries. They had seen nothing to disturb them, although a servant girl seemed distressed that the dog would not eat his dinner. She stroked his head and coaxed him with a greasy bone, but he closed his eyes when she waved it too near, and did not reopen them.

Panthea reached the back stairs of the kitchen. She preferred these to the main stairs in the manor. Only one person could fit at a time. She could climb to her father's chambers without being stopped or spied upon.

"Do not return to your homes," she said, clearing her throat first so all would listen. "You may each eat the leftovers from the feast, and have a draught of wine or ale."

No one moved, as if their bodies were frozen from shock at her offer. She had no explanation. She only wanted people present and lights burning, and that was no explanation for a servant.

"Return to work, and do not leave!"

Panthea began climbing the stairs.

The dull wax still burned in the sconces. The light was enough for safe passage but did nothing to set her nerves at ease. She had seen strange things and would not feel safe again until she had told the story to her father, who perhaps had one of his own. Armando would rise from her father's side and sweep through the castle, making sure nothing evil lingered. He would suppress a smile, she thought, that a woman could be so skittish.

In an hour, it would be over. She would feel safe again and laugh. This was what she meditated on as she climbed, counting each step, each footfall coming faster, unable to slow as she saw the light under her father's chamber door and knew she was almost there. She didn't care if she amused Armando.

"Father!" she called out, shoving the door with a burst of speed.

Panthea felt the whip of air move past from the door's fast arc, catching the smell of the room, her mind fragmenting as her eyes took in the sight.

The smell was death, a bad death. Her mind told her it was the smell on Damiano's mouth, told her she had not dreamed. Her eyes were the only part of her still moving. Panthea's heart stood still, her breathing stopped. Her eyes darted back and forth around the room. It was cruel that she could not remember how to shut them. She did not want to see this.

Her father and his advisers all lay in the room. Black boils the size of eggs covered their exposed skin. Some of the boils had broken open and oozed a black fluid speckled with bright red clots of blood. She leaned against the wall, panting.

An adviser, a young, earnest man from the village council, rose from the pile, smiling at Panthea. He held out his hand to her. She shook her head no. He laughed and began disrobing, peeling away his robes and belt, standing in his linen undergarments, laughing at her.

Turning, he ran straight for the window, throwing himself out. Panthea heard him land. There were no more sounds below after that.

Panthea was swaying, unable to hold her balance. Her mind couldn't hold her balance as it worked through these sights.

Her father was in the center of them, his eyes still open, his arm reaching for the door. She wanted to run to him, to pull him free from the others, but he had the black marks on his body too and thick dark swellings on his neck. Dried blood crusted around his eyes, nose, and out through his ears. He could not be real, she thought. This was a stuffed doll or clever image, but it could not be

her father, her fine, fit father who took life so lightly. Death would
not have come for him this way. He had made amends with God
years ago. He had built a church. This was a death for the poor, the
forsaken, the damned. Death could not be so bold in her own home.
Armando would not have let it happen. What happened here that
Armando let death take them all and all at once? What could have
overpowered a man like Armando?

She did not see Armando among them.

Panthea forced herself to look upon the bodies, some fallen on
the floor in strange, contorted positions, as if they died from a fit,
some still seated at tables, faces plunged down onto the ledgers spread
before them. She tried to pretend it was not real—of course it was
not—to find the courage to look at each one and mark his features.

She backed away, careful to touch no one and nothing. When
she felt the door frame's edges, she turned to the hall and screamed.

"Armando!"

⚜

Gio flinched, whipping her head away from the light. She opened
her eyes, still looking away, and tried to turn her head to see what
wonders were occurring now. She thought she had seen lightning
strike the path and linger, consuming something between them.

From the light walked a figure in robes. Gio squinted harder to
see it, to see its face. It was the mute woman, and she looked beautiful. Her face was soft, the hardened lines gone from her mouth.
She looked like the saints Gio had created pigments for. Always too
bright to be mortal, always serene.

The mute woman pointed down the path into the town and gave Gio a nudge.

"What?" Gio said.

The woman nudged Gio, gesturing down the path again.

"You tried to force me to flee with you. Now you want me to go into town?" Gio did not understand. She did not want to be swept into this until she understood the danger. "I cannot go there yet," Gio said.

The woman walked in front of Gio, placing a hand over Gio's heart, then placing her ear over that. Gio stood still.

The woman drew back and pointed to her own chest, fluttering her hand fast over her own heart.

The woman understood that Gio was too scared to move. Gio nodded yes.

The woman slapped her.

Pointing again to the town, the woman grabbed Gio by the hand and pulled, then shoved her down the path.

Gio tried to scramble off the path, but the mute woman found a switch, whipping it across Gio's ankles when she veered off the path.

Too many people would calm themselves with violence. Gio knew neither of them belonged in a frightened city.

Below a man was waiting, craning his neck at all angles, looking up in her direction. The sun was rising to her east, but there was not enough light to see him well.

"You there! Are you the one they call Gio?" he called up to her.

Gio did not see anyone else with him. She did not know if this was a sign for good or ill.

"Yes," she called back. She did not take another step. The mute woman held her switch still.

"My wife is giving birth. But it is too early. You must come!" He was motioning to her with one arm, toward a shop she had never crossed the threshold of.

His wife made pastries for the nobles, yellow flaky pastries with cheese and berry fillings, sprinkled with sugar, and set facing the glass window to the street. The sugar glittered against the dark berry colours, making the pastries look like jewels, rows upon rows of gems. She had longed to taste one when she was a child, but her parents could not afford this food. That baker had threatened her with a spoon when he caught her lingering. He said she dirtied the glass. Still, the shop had been magic to her, the best kind for a child, the magic you could eat, that would make your head swirl and your belly full. She had not known many foods that made her happy. Most just dulled the hunger enough so she could sleep.

The baker was below her, impatient with her delay. His arms swung in higher arcs above his head and his tone was thin. "Hurry! Why do you delay? Have you no feeling?" he yelled. "My wife is in pain! I will pay whatever you ask, if that is what slows your steps!"

Gio blew the bitter memory away with one exhale and started down the path, the woman behind her lurching forward, determined to stay close. Gio turned, holding out her hands, trying to stop the woman from following so close, but she did not obey. A strange mute woman wouldn't be any safer in this town today than Gio would.

The man yelled at Gio again.

Gio gave up on the woman and raced ahead, hoping to lose

her. The lumbering mute woman could not move fast; she looked to be in pain from her leg. Gio's legs knew the paths here well. She was down to the man in but a few breaths. A crowd grew outside the baker's house, keening relatives praying for this baby, the first for the baker's young wife.

He rushed her through the glittering pastries, pointing to a dark, narrow staircase in the back. Frightened husbands like him would offer their whole fortunes to save their wife, if they loved her. She would settle for a pastry.

He pushed her hard toward the stairs. She stumbled, her cheek catching the stone edge of the wall. She began climbing, shaking off the humiliation. He must love his wife to be so worried, she thought. He could not mean to hurt her.

A woman's grunting was the first noise she heard. Gio's heart began to calm. This was a world she knew. Reaching the top of the staircase, she entered into a room paneled with wood, the floors swept clean, a salty morning breeze coming through the open window.

Sitting in a chair, a young girl was doubled over, her hands pressed against her stomach. She saw Gio and cried out, "I saw blood! I saw blood!"

"Shh, love. We'll be fine." Gio tried to cut through the woman's panic with calm, steady words. If the woman was going to deliver too early, the baby would die. The womb did not negotiate or respond to women's entreaties. No magic or herb could stand in the way of its will, and no prayer could stop it from conceiving, either. Women lived, and many died, at its mercy.

Gio rested her hands on the woman's arms, whispering little words, trying to get a better look at her stomach. The woman, trembling, lifted her arms, letting Gio run her hands all along her body, feeling for her curves.

"How old are you?" Gio asked.

"I don't know."

"How long have you bled?" Gio asked her.

"It was the year after we married," she replied. "It's been two springs since then."

Gio was right. The woman was still a girl, with a girl's reed-thin body and narrow pelvis. She was pregnant, yes, but Gio did not think she was delivering early.

"When did you know you were with child?" Gio asked.

"It was about four moons ago, at the beginning of summer," she replied. A pain caught her, and she doubled over again, crying out.

Gio laughed, shaking her head. It was so good to be back on familiar ground.

"Daughter, you are not delivering early. You just did not recognize the signs of pregnancy. Have you no mother living with you here?"

The girl shook her head.

"My mother died giving birth to my youngest brother. The baker took me from my father just after that."

Gio stroked her hair. "Has no woman watched over you then?"

The girl shook her head. "My husband does not like me talking to the women who bring us our berries. He says they bring disease."

"You had to learn many things alone, didn't you?" Gio asked.

The girl started to cry.

"Shh," Gio said. "You are further along than you know. The baby will be born, and healthy. If it is a daughter, what shall we name her?"

Gio began moving the girl around the room, trying to walk off the fear and help the baby drop down.

"No, no, my husband wants a boy."

"Of course he does," Gio said. "But he's had his fun and has no more say in the matter."

The girl tried to catch a smile before it began, but Gio saw it.

"If it is a girl," she said, grimacing as a contraction hit, "I'll name her after my mother."

She stumbled, apologizing. The girl's skin was burning under Gio's hands.

"I think I would sit now," the girl said. "The hour grows late."

"What is wrong?" Gio asked.

The girl landed on the bed and began undoing the strings at her bodice. "It is so warm in here! Has he no mercy?" Her tone was that of an old, angry woman.

She ripped off the bodice with a jerk, breaking her bag of waters at the same time. Gio saw the fluid staining the bed, the girl's legs kicking in it.

"What are you feeling? What is this?" Gio asked. This was not how women behaved at a birth, even new mothers. Gio began to feel nervous.

The girl was frowning, fanning herself for air.

"Did he give you something before I arrived?" Gio asked. "Did you take something?"

The girl did not answer but began removing her robes, grunting when a contraction hit. She bit at Gio when she tried to help.

Gio had never lost control like this. She knew what frightened girls did at the first birth, and this was not it.

"What is wrong? What is happening?" Gio asked her.

Naked, the girl began weeping, holding her stomach, groaning as she pushed down, trying to find a position that stopped the pain.

Gio saw purple shadows moving under the girl's skin and thought she was losing her mind. Gio grabbed her, forcing to lie back, bringing a candle stand closer to look at her body. A dark pool began to gather under her neck and arms, settling too along the inner thighs. Like bread rising, dark rings rose and darkened.

The girl screamed, causing Gio to drop the candle. The room dimmed. There was not enough light from a window to help Gio.

This could be a strange new herb brought by a trading ship. Or the work of the Devil. Gio should not be alone now.

"You need Lazarro," Gio said aloud. She prayed the baker had stayed close enough to hear.

The girl started laughing. "Yes, Lazarro! He is so handsome! Isn't that evil of me to say? His voice is like the voice of a god calling down from the Pantheon! What a wicked girl I am. I went to hear Matins this morning before I went to the miller's shop. I ran out of the almond flour yesterday and needed but a small batch to finish today's work. I went early before my husband rose, so he would not discover my foolishness and be angry. But the miller was ill and would not come down! Now I have no flour. Gio, let us deliver my husband a child and he may forget about my error."

The baby was crowning and the girl talked on, feeling nothing. Gio began to panic. She had seen everything in her time, but never this. Why was this woman going mad? What were these shadows and swellings? Was she turning into a new creature—a witch, perhaps, or an animal? If it were a strange fever, the same awful death that took the Old Man, she would die, and Gio feared that most of all. Every woman who dealt in herbs did. A healer with a dead body was proof of one of two things: incompetence, or the curse of the Devil. The healer was beaten to death for the first and burned for the second.

If this girl died, only Lazarro would be safe. Lazarro they would believe if he said it was a fast death. If Gio lost a patient, alone, without last rites, the family would be enraged. If people died without confession and Communion, their hand at rest on their heart, sealing up that wellspring of sin, then they would wander forever in Limbo, condemned with Virgil and so many others. The families would want revenge.

"Lazarro!" Gio screamed. "If anyone can hear me, bring Lazarro here at once!"

The baker was upstairs in a few heavy steps. He looked with horror at his naked wife, laughing as she pushed a child out and black boils burst.

"I'll not have a man, even a priest, see my wife like this!" he said to Gio.

The woman turned her head and saw her husband. He squinted, peering at the dark stains around her neck and body.

"Come closer, lover. You won't be mad. Look what I have given you!"

Gio freed the baby at the last push, dragging the child and cord away from the girl. She worked with terror's speed, washing the baby with the bowl of wine left on a nightstand, severing the cord with a knife left from the evening's dinner on that same stand. She took the woman's shawl from the floor and wrapped the baby in it.

The girl was standing on the bed, still naked, her arms spread out like a bird.

The baker made a loud swallowing sound. "Is this how it's usually done?" he asked Gio.

"Oh, darling husband, I have outwitted you! For I will leave you now and see things you have yet only imagined. You must want to kiss me before I depart." She coughed, staggering on the bed. Grey fluid, speckled with pink flesh, flew from her mouth.

The girl jumped down and ran toward the baker. The baker fled, knocking over the mute woman who was standing behind him in the doorway, tears running down her face. The girl saw her and stopped, transfixed. Sweat poured out of the girl's body, and the room took on a wet, rancid, sweet smell. It was the smell of death.

The mute woman held the girl's hands and led her back to the bed. The girl obeyed without question, becoming as meek as a dove.

"How do you know me?" the girl asked in a child's voice. "Who is this you have brought with you?"

The mute woman did not answer.

"Let us name her after my mother," the girl cried to Gio, "after all the lost mothers! I go to find them."

"We must find Lazarro," Gio said to the mute woman. "She needs Last Unction. Now."

The mute woman shook her head no.

The girl, her eyes swelling closed, took Gio's hands in her own. "You pray for me, sister."

"I cannot," Gio said. "I am but a woman, like you."

"I will die in my sins!"

The Old Woman placed a finger over the girl's lips and spoke.

Gio gathered the baby and handed it to the mute woman. "Can you hold her?"

The mute woman nodded, taking the baby.

Gio ran down the steps, bringing up a leather sieve for cooking and a crock of sweetened goat's milk that had been warming near the fire. It should have been poured over bread for the couple's breakfast.

She layered a piece of bread into the sieve and poured milk into it. Opening the baby's mouth, Gio dripped the warm milk down, and the baby swallowed.

The silent woman shook her head as if she had never seen a baby eat before.

"The baker has fled," Gio said to her. "Take the baby downstairs and wait for Lazarro. When he arrives, send him up here. Do you understand?" Gio asked, pushing her out the door.

The girl was raising her arms. Her body moved off the bed as if it were being pulled up. She screamed in joy, and the body collapsed back onto the bed, the head flopping to one side.

The baker was at the door, a crowd behind him.

"There she is!" he yelled.

She needed Armando.

Panthea cursed herself for going too far last night, in every way, letting that foul stranger get so close. She had teased her share of men and servants, but never had one gotten the better of her. She was shamed.

Armando had seen more of the world; he must have known she

was insincere in those pursuits. That's why he humoured her. But he did not humour her last night. She felt dirty.

She spurred Fidato on to move faster. He did not need it. Fidato surely smelled terror clinging to her bones. What she had seen in that room, she would not acknowledge. Not until Armando was there to carry her.

"It is not as it seems," she whispered to herself.

Ugly thoughts were coming fast. She could not remember how to shut her mind to them.

Armando was the only one who could take her father's place. If he was gone, anyone could rise and take the castle. If they did not want Panthea, which was unthinkable, where would she go? She could not work, and she was too pretty to beg. Some ogre would force himself in, proclaim himself the owner, and she would die of despair from rubbing stinking fat feet and wishing she had been kinder to Armando.

"I will not lose the castle," she said, kicking Fidato too hard.

Panthea took no comfort in the morning light. She was cold. Yesterday morning all she wanted was to keep Armando from being named the successor of her father and joined to her in marriage; now she was riding out to bring him back.

"Madness," she said.

Fidato picked his familiar way through the lanes, where the peasants slept off the festival's wine, the merchants' wives emptied chamber pots into the streets and nursed along breakfast porridges hanging inside above their fires. A few wise, eager ones waved to her. A pleasant exchange could convince her father, Dario, to lower interest rates or give larger loans.

Panthea smiled and acknowledged them, surprised that the fake reaction was so quick. She never had a desire to meddle in her father's complicated dealings; she did not know how books worked and what interest to charge. But the merchants, especially those with good fabrics and perfumes, were worth acknowledging.

Panthea passed the church. The strange woman was huddled in the door of the church, feeding a newborn through a sieve. Panthea slowed Fidato to look closer. Who would give this wretch a child? The woman met Panthea's stare with tears, as if Panthea were the one who was a wretch.

Panthea wanted to hit her.

"You know nothing," she said to her.

Armando was not near the church or in the piazza; Fidato would have smelled Armando's horse, Nero, by now. She turned Fidato toward the sea, keeping him moving.

Damiano had done something awful in her father's chamber, some cruel magic or blood illusion. The troubadour's body was gone, as was Damiano's. These were the first things she needed to tell him. Later she would have time to make other sins right with him. She would have time later.

Panthea passed the lane that led to the baker's and miller's homes, which were close to the butcher Del Grasso. They could sweep their refuse into the sea, and if the great stone ovens set the baker's house on fire, there was water nearby. She recognized the sharp tone to men's voices and the shrill cries of women egging them on. Probably a peasant had stolen a pastry. It was the baker's fault for displaying them so lavishly in the case, where all could see but few could have. She hated that quality in him, that condescending pride. Of course, she had always had enough money to shame him in return, so it was only a fleeting annoyance.

She glanced down that lane as she passed it. A rough-looking boy, too young to have wasted his night in wine, crept into the baker's home.

Panthea slowed Fidato. The boy emerged, carrying something metal flashing in the morning light. He was stealing. Panthea could not see well from her perch, but judging from the flash and swing of the piece, he had stolen jewelry. How could that be? The wife never took it off. What would make a thief so bold as to steal at first light?

The world was going mad, Panthea thought. The boy wiped something wet on his shirt, then wiped his mouth with his sleeve. Panthea understood. The sun was warming fast; she was sweating by now too. The boy's mouth left a dark stain on his shirt, but Panthea spurred Fidato on before she could consider it.

Her mind tried to show her again what she had seen in the upstairs chamber of her father. She would not see it. She had the power to turn this thought away. That was something.

The truth looked for a new way in. What had she loosed? It was all connected to her nightmare, the violent dream of a man Armando had killed, one who rose from the dead in the garden, catching her and kissing her with slick, spoiled lips.

Panthea shook her head with such a sharp twist that Fidato stopped and strained to look back at her. Panthea realized what she was doing; letting those awful thoughts find their way back in. Gritting her teeth, she determined to try harder and keep them out.

Armando was standing at the far edge of the lane, near the water's edge. Panthea got down from Fidato, running to him. Her legs were not moving fast enough.

All the strange sights, dead men, but Panthea wanted to talk of herself first. It mattered more.

He spoke. Panthea pinched her lips together and tried to listen. Armando was wrong about her; she would show him. She could even let him talk first, although nothing he said was important.

"Do you remember the story of the Red Sea?" he asked. His tone was even, without deep feeling. "The Israelites were fleeing the Egyptian warriors, the land of their captivity. God reached down and parted the Red Sea. The Israelites fled along the path and God closed it behind them, drowning the warriors of Egypt. Egypt was no more to trouble them."

Blessed Mary, help me, she thought. She wanted to shut him up about this story. She had her own.

"Do you think the Israelite warriors were disappointed?" he asked. "They were told to run."

"There were women and children among them," Panthea said, using a final tone. His question should wait.

"Greater glory, then, for the men to fight. When a man cannot fight for a woman, when God alone claims that right, this is hard for a man," Armando said. He did not look at her.

"Why do men fight at all, Armando? Solve that mystery before you question God about His," she said. No wonder she had provoked him to silence so often.

"We are made in His image," Armando said.

Panthea was looking at her slipper, pulling away her skirt to one side so she could see it well. There was a spot of blood on it. She looked around to see where she might dip her foot and wash it away. She looked up to see Armando watching her.

He sighed. "I think I will return to the Holy Land and see how I may assist your father's cause there. I am thought of fondest when I am farthest away. And I do not feel this pain."

Panthea had a vague sense this was all directed at her.

"Good-bye, Panthea." He walked toward Nero.

"Armando! You stop!" she yelled.

He stopped and turned. The look on his face embarrassed her. He was expecting something else from her.

She pretended she could not read his expression. "Armando, there may be cause for you to stay...." She could not finish. She wiped her hand over her brow, surprised to be sweating this much so early in the day. "Something has happened to my father."

Armando came closer to her, his expression changing.

"I dwelled on sinful thoughts. My mind is corrupted. I saw a vision in my father's chamber. Come with me. Come and see. I will not give you more trouble."

"What has happened to your father?"

Panthea began to shake. Armando reached out and caught her by the arms.

"No, it was just a vision. I imagined it." She pushed against him, trying to stand on her own. "We should be married, Armando. At once."

"Panthea, what did you see?"

⚜

"What did you do in that room?"

Gio was being pinched and shoved in all directions.

"I did nothing!" Gio cried. "It is some new illness, one I have never seen!"

"One you caused!" he yelled. "Did you think I would pay you more if you saved her at the last minute? Saved her from a new death? I am too wise for you!"

"Drown her!" someone screamed. "It is too long in coming!"

Lazarro appeared in the doorway of the church. "What goes on here, friends?"

The baker grabbed Gio by the arm, dragging her up the steps to Lazarro, shoving her to her knees before him.

"My wife was giving birth, and I could not find you. I called for help, and Gio came running, eager to earn a fee. You know how she haunts these streets in the dark hours, searching for the desperate. She gave something to my wife, or did some magic craft, because my wife went mad and died—all in the matter of minutes!"

"Rosetta is dead?" Lazarro asked. He looked alarmed, Gio thought, but not shocked. He glanced back into the church. "Tell me of this, Gio."

She kept her head bowed, not looking him in the eye. He still saw her as the liar who cursed him.

Gio told him what she had witnessed. She could feel the crowd tensing and pushing nearer, eager to hear details of the death. The certain evil thrilled them.

"She did not receive Last Unction?" Lazarro asked.

"No, there was no one to hear her confession or pray with her," Gio said.

"She is in Limbo now?" the baker asked. He covered his face with his hands.

Gio's heart was seared by the thought. The girl had been so innocent. She would wander among the lost, where there was no colour, until all on earth were dead and Christ returned to the underworld to save them.

"How much will I have to pay for her ascension?" the baker yelled, moving his hands to reveal his agony. He turned to Gio. "You will receive no fee for your work, wretch. You will pay Lazarro for her salvation." He grimaced, talking more to himself now. "It took me two years to make her a proper wife."

Someone kicked Gio in the calf and she cried out.

Lazarro held up a hand. "The miller has died this morning in much the same manner. Gio did not see him or visit his house. Good Christians they were. They did not believe in her medicines. I do not think this is her work."

Silence fell upon the crowd. The people worked the matter to its conclusion in their minds. Gio could see them glancing at each other, chewing their lips.

"My wife saw the miller," the baker said. "This morning. She bought flour before dawn. She thought I wouldn't notice if she slipped out of bed so early."

Gio's mind was spinning, trying to weave this new information together with what she had seen, trying to find the pattern in it.

Lazarro counted the sequence on his fingers. He did not speak loud enough for the crowd to hear, but Gio understood his words. "Rosetta went into the miller's house before dawn. The miller died at first light. Rosetta died an hour or so beyond that."

"Gio," he called. "Tell us more of this death. How did it come upon her with such speed?"

"I do not know, my lord," she answered. She had none of the usual boldness in her voice. The hairs on her arms were still standing, goose bumps pricking her flesh. As long as these people moved as a crowd, anything could happen to her.

"What have you to do with the miller?" Lazarro asked.

"I know nothing of the miller," Gio said.

"Send for the miller's wife," Lazarro called.

A woman at the back of the crowd screamed. All turned her direction and began pulling away, stumbling backward. As they parted, Gio saw a boy with black boils covering his neck, his face pale and waxen. He coughed, and a violent spray of blood splattered the crowd in all directions. The boy was trying to reach the church.

Lazarro pushed through the crowd, catching him as he collapsed. The boy reached into his pocket, pushing a necklace into Lazarro's hand.

"I am sorry, Father," he said.

Lazarro began rushing through the words of Last Unction.

"Bring me the Host and wine!" Lazarro screamed.

No one moved. The boy's head hung to one side; a thin black river stinking of decay ran from his mouth. Lazarro put the boy's hand across his heart, to cover the root of all sin. As he pushed the hand into place, more black fluid poured out.

Gio could not breathe. The air stank. The boy was melting, all his humours and blood pouring out together.

Lazarro released the boy, dead, to the ground and stood facing the crowd, staring at the necklace in his hand. It was stained in blood, speckled with pink flesh.

"That is my wife's." The baker snatched the necklace from Lazarro, wiping it clean on his own shirt, tucking it into a pouch on his belt.

Everyone in the crowd was silent, looking around the piazza, straining for sounds or movements.

"Death is here," a woman whispered.

Gio looked at the upper edge of the piazza, up toward where the fields began and the peasants walked through rows of vineyards back to their homes. The fires to keep the wolves away had burned out during the festival and no one had thought to relight them.

"We must light the fires!" someone called.

A young boy ran to relight them, his older brother not far behind, carrying a knife held out in case wolves had already breached the firelines.

"Father, tell us what to do!" a woman carrying her child called.

"I do not know this evil," Lazarro said. "I do not know if it comes by food or air. We must pray. I must pray."

Gio had never seen him unsteady.

"Damiano." It was Del Grasso speaking.

He stood at the back of the crowd, with coarse, hairy arms crossed over his chest, blood all over his apron and legs.

All seemed troubled to hear his voice—one more strange event.

"It is the one called Damiano who brings death," Del Grasso said. "You did not listen to Del Grasso."

The crowd whispered, some feeling their stomachs, the food from the feast still there. Damiano had been at the feast.

A hunched old man got in Del Grasso's face. "Shut up, you blistered fool! This is God's judgment upon your wickedness, all of you! If you repent, He will spare you!"

The baker grabbed the old man, shoving him to the ground. "What sin did my wife commit?"

Lazarro lunged to restrain the baker.

"Wolf!" a woman screamed, pointing down a lane behind the church. "I saw its eyes!"

Gio was sure it was just a dog, one of the many who watched in hope for Del Grasso to sleep with his door open and a bone unattended.

A young man took control of the crowd, cutting off Lazarro from their sight. "Kill anything you see in the village that does not belong here, whether man or beast."

The younger men liked his words, Gio saw. They were pleased to have cause to fight.

"Search the houses! Eat and drink nothing until we find the cause!" Lazarro pushed the young man aside, commanding the crowd. "If people fall ill, send them to me at once. This death moves fast. May we be saved before it takes another!"

The mass that had huddled together so close now scattered in all directions. Women fled to their homes; men brandished knives and sticks and whatever they could uproot. Eyes wild, arms flexed with weapons at their shoulder, they marched down every path, beating on every shop door, kicking every drunk still sleeping in quiet corners. Some of them stood and tried to wipe the boy's blood from their clothes, before it contaminated the air and gave the evil a chance to spread. A woman saw a bloodstain on her child's face and stopped him, spitting on her sleeve to wipe clean his face. Licking the spot on her sleeve again, she wiped one more time to make sure no trace of the curse remained.

Del Grasso crossed his arms over his chest. "You need my help."

Lazarro squinted at him in the morning light, releasing the baker, who was cursing them all under his breath.

"I see the heart of man," Del Grasso said. "Not all sins are confessed to you." He bowed his head, then turned, walking toward his shop.

Gio should have run then, before anyone thought again to drown her. She did not think they would find wolves, and they would find no poison, at least none from her hands. Fear told her to run. Gio felt it there, roiling in her stomach, but it did not hurt her. Gio was encouraged. Last night had made her stronger.

Looking in the distance, to mark where the others had run, Gio recognized a noble, one of Dario's favourite allies, a man whose name she did not remember. He was riding out of the city with speed. Trying not to breathe the air, he wrapped his robe, with its blood spatter from the unfortunate boy, around his face and mouth as he rode.

Lazarro saw him too. "The angels be with him. With all of us."

Chapter Twelve

Armando kept her from falling off Nero, one hand wrapped against her waist, the other holding the reins.

He was spurring Nero to ride harder, but the climb up the stone streets to the castle was steep with a heavy load. Panthea could not look up. She pressed her face against his shoulder, breathing in his scent, feeling the warm skin of his neck.

He might have taken her away if she had surrendered last night. She would not have sinned or seen. This vision, this thing she had seen in her father's chamber, it was her fault. Everything was her fault.

Armando would know how to fix this.

The mute woman grabbed at her ankle and she kicked her hands off as Armando pulled her tighter. The woman opened her mouth, releasing Panthea's ankle to gesture at her, scraping her fingers against her face, motioning for Panthea to do the same. Red scratches ran down the woman's face from her efforts, and she grabbed Panthea again, nearly taking her off the horse.

Panthea kicked, hard, catching the woman in the chest, knocking her to the ground. Armando spurred Nero, and Panthea craned her neck to watch the woman. She was clutching her chest, trying to get a breath back, and tears were running down her face. She began staggering toward Panthea, determined to catch her.

"Faster, Armando!" Panthea cried.

"There are too many people to ride fast," Armando said, his grip loosening. "Look."

Women were pushing children in behind closed doors, slamming the bolts down behind them. Men were dragging grain or whatever they could grab from broken shop windows into their homes. Peasants, too, carried more than their children on their backs. Panthea saw a boy's dead body lying on the steps of the church. No one was attending to it. A black pool surrounded him. His eyes were open, staring into the sun.

A group of teenage boys in threadbare clothes were the only still bodies in the piazza. One nudged another as Panthea and Armando rode by, making Panthea afraid. They did not look away when they saw the crest on Nero.

The miller's wife was walking straight down the street, her children pulling on her hands and crying. "Sshh! Not now, bambini! We must find your father! Come home! Matins are over, and we must grind the flour!"

Sweat soaked her bodice. Dark stains spread from her armpits and neck to her stomach and skirt. She wiped her face with her sleeve; her hair was matted and wet. It was still morning. No one should be that hot.

The mute woman caught up to Panthea but did not move. She

was transfixed, staring at the miller's wife, her mouth opening for a gasp. The woman reached limply for Panthea but did not touch her leg.

The miller's wife collapsed in the street. "I need water, children. Go and fetch your mama some water."

The children cried and would not leave her. One caught Panthea's eye. "Mistress, we need water, please!"

Armando's grip tightened. "Do not get down," he whispered.

The woman stood and kissed her children, extravagant kisses on their faces. "It is no matter, children! See, God has sent Mama a drink!"

She walked toward the sea, singing a snippet of Latin that Lazarro often sang in church. When she got to the cliff, she did not stop or slow. Her body fell and disappeared as her song lingered above.

Panthea screamed. Armando's grip tightened around her waist as the woman turned, her eyes fierce, lunging for Panthea.

Gio was kneeling before the boy. With a light touch, she closed his eyes, and then brushed locks of dirty hair back from his forehead. She removed a silver coin from her skirt pocket and pressed it into the boy's palm, curling his fingers around it so it would not be lost. It was all she could offer him.

He had no mother. She had seen him on the streets, stealing when he could, begging when he could not. He had been too strong to ever need her medicines, but she tried to help him in her way. She saw to it that her coin purse tipped down as she walked by, so that a stray piece of silver would fall near him, especially in the barren months when vendors huddled over their carts and there were not enough customers to distract them from one pie gone missing.

The boys of the street mocked her, grabbing at her skirts when they were drunk, pretending to die of her hexes, staggering into the lanes clutching their throats. She had given them much cruel amusement.

Still, they had no mothers. Gio could not let them starve. She had filled her stomach with water and chewed on bark so she could sleep on those nights. It was easy to sleep hungry, knowing they were fed. They would have laughed to know of her sufferings, but she brushed their hatred away. They could not be held in account for it.

Lazarro's arms went under the body, lifting the boy up, away from her.

"Where will he be buried?" she asked. She would pay for a proper burial, a fine casket.

Lazarro did not answer her question. He carried the body up the church stairs. Gio caught up to him, opening the doors for him. Lazarro passed through and walked to the altar, the morning sun making the dust in the air visible, a thousand swirling worlds under the mighty cross. None ever touched, Gio saw. They all moved, dancing, falling, blown by small currents she did not feel. They never touched. Gio wondered if one even knew another existed.

Lazarro laid the boy on the steps of the altar. Sweeping a gold cup through the Holy Water basin, Lazarro began washing the boy.

"By the waters of Christ you came into new life. By the waters of Christ now you go to the next. God be praised," he said.

"He is eligible for Communion?" she asked. She had never seen the boy going into the church.

"All are eligible, Gio. Few are obedient."

The space between them widened again. Gio felt it in the air.

"He was obedient?" she asked, straining to move closer.

"He did not renounce God, like you," Lazarro replied. "God blessed the boy in the midst of his suffering, always keeping him fed. You would have done well to know him."

"Lazarro, you do not know the truth," Gio began.

"Is this the hour for you to talk?"

He was right. Her time had been last night. She had told herself there was more time.

"I must go and collect Rosetta and the miller," Lazarro said. "I must order coffins and collect money for Masses. A boy will need to be hired to ring the bells. There is much work to do."

"Father," Gio said, hoping the term would startle him and he would look at her, "you must leave these details to others now. Search the Scriptures and pray. This thing is not of me, not of man. You must seek God's face."

Lazarro was not listening. "They will all be buried as soon as Marzcana and his sons have built the coffins. We will have a noon Mass."

Gio shook her head. "Do not make my mistake, Lazarro."

"Which mistake is this?" he asked.

"You do not know what you will be doing at noon."

"I know this, Gio; you will trouble me no more. You will probably be dead by noon."

⚜

Nero rode up the path to the castle, trees brushing past them on the narrow turns, Armando not slowing as they flew through them, the branches tearing at the hem of Panthea's skirts that billowed out. She was being torn apart with every leap. What would be left of her by nightfall?

Shapes were moving all around the castle. This encouraged Panthea. The servants were working, and quickly. Good. She knew about control. Only the matter of her father, and the horror of the upstairs chamber, was beyond her power. She needed Armando for that, and he had come when she asked.

The servants must be brought inside, Panthea thought, *and all the stores of grain and wine secured. Fires need to be lit around the perimeter.*

Let the village worry about wolves. Panthea would worry about keeping the hungry peasants out. None would enter until this madness was sorted out. Any servant with children would be permitted to leave. She did not want to feed those who could not work. Letting them go would cause hardship for the other servants, who would have to work harder, but Panthea had learned mercy, had she not?

"They're running away," he said.

The dark shapes she saw were servants, but they were not working. The bags they carried were not being brought inside. No, every servant was carrying bags of grain and fruits, straining to get into the forest and steal away. Armando drew his sword from the sheath alongside Nero's saddle. When the servants saw it, the slower ones dropped their bags and ran without them. The young ones readjusted their loads and bore down, running faster, disappearing into the trees,

Armando released Panthea and she swung her leg over Fidato,

jumping to the ground and chasing after the servants. She caught up to an older woman heaving a sack of grain. The woman dropped it at once and held up her hands as if to explain. Panthea slapped her, hard, grabbing the sack, pulling it back toward the castle.

Armando had run Nero into the trees and circled back around. "Secure the castle," he called.

There were servants standing who had not fled. Panthea wondered if they were loyal or just slow. Maybe they were both, she thought. She did not doubt she would be left with the worst of the lot.

Armando rounded them inside, Panthea standing at the door to mark their faces as they went past. She would punish their families if they went missing now.

As the last servant approached, Panthea lifted a torch from the wall and gave it to a servant. "Set fires all along the castle. Set them so close that no man may pass except by the main door, and set two guards at this door. The post must not be abandoned."

Armando grabbed Panthea's hand and led her upstairs.

"No!" Panthea screamed. "You go alone!"

He pulled her up the stairs as servants watched her with surprised faces.

Cold fear pierced at her throat, cutting off her breath. Stabbing through her stomach, it impaled her, shaking her without mercy. She thought she was going to die from fear, but still Armando pulled her up the stairs.

He did not pause at her father's chamber but rammed both doors open. A group of servants huddled over the bodies inside, most especially that of her father.

"Oh," Panthea wept, holding her shaking hands to them, "oh,

mercy upon you!" She tried to focus on their faces, their eyes, so she would not look down at the bodies. "You attend my father!"

Armando thrust his sword into one leaning over her father. The man fell at an angle, exposing Panthea to the full view of her father.

He was half-naked, his clothes torn, pockets in his robe pulled out and split apart. The man had been pulling a locket with a woman's picture painted in it from her father's bare grey chest. The gold chain swung from the thief's dying hand, like an executioner's saw, back and forth, back and forth. Panthea snatched it, surprised at her speed when her mind was numb.

"I cannot take this ..." she said, holding the locket away from herself.

Pain was a wall that fell upon her, blunt and wide, breaking every bone and tender place. It forced the air from her lungs, and she fell to the floor, gasping like a fish.

The remaining servants jumped over her, fleeing. She thought one stepped on her hand, breaking a finger under his heel, but she wasn't sure. She could not hear her own thoughts, as if her mind were calling to her from another, distant place.

Armando's arms went under her, lifting her and carrying her to a couch in the hall. He laid her upon it, brushing her hair back, kissing her upon the forehead. She put her arms around his neck, pulling him to her. She couldn't breathe. His breath felt so warm on her dead, cold skin. If she pulled him close enough, pulled him from the cold distance to her mouth, she would feel life again.

"Kiss me," she whispered.

He pulled against her hands, shaking his head. "Not like this," he whispered.

"I cannot breathe," she said.

He pulled her up, resting her back against his chest, wrapping his arms around her bodice, pulling hard. Her ribs felt his wrist bones digging in, his forearms crushing against her. She felt his breath move through her, his ribs expanding, forcing hers out and in, so that she moved with him, his body mastering hers. She surrendered, and she breathed. She let him move in and through her, the first time she had ever been held by him so completely, ever felt a man sustaining her at her point of weakness. She rested against him, knowing why God had given men their strength.

"What was that?" Armando asked.

"I do not know, as Mary and the angels are my witness. What is happening, Armando? Why do the villagers steal grain? Why do my servants flee? What man would dare kill my father?"

"I do not think it was a man, Panthea."

"It was no animal. There were no teeth marks."

"I do not think it was an animal, Panthea."

"Don't be a fool!" Panthea spat the words. "What else is there but man and beast?"

"Plague," Armando answered.

"You must go," Lazarro said. "They will come for you. I will not allow blood to be spilled in my church."

"I can help," Gio said.

"If you stay, it will only be out of fear for your own life. Go back to your home, Gio. Pack what you can and flee."

"The Old Man lies dead on my threshold, covered in these same marks."

The truth burst out between them, ugly and raw. Like life, truth had a will and timing all its own.

Lazarro stopped, his hand in midair over the boy, performing his final baptism. "What did you do?"

"I did nothing!"

"You loosed something," he said.

"Why must you always believe the worst of me?"

He kept going about his work. "I cannot force you to do the right thing, Gio. It was never your talent."

"It's a wonder you became a priest, standing here for God, telling others to repent. You are the sinner, Lazarro."

"This is not the time, Gio. This hour is not meant for you or me. Whatever debts you owe me, I forgive." He pointed to the door, flicking his hand as if to brush her away.

"Have you smelled the boy?" Gio asked, pausing at the door. "We do not know what this death is."

"It is of the Devil," Lazarro said.

"What do you know of the Devil? You do not even know your God." She swung the doors of the church open, the light blinding her as she stepped out of this house of shadows.

"Gio!" he called.

She paused but did not turn to him.

"Gio, if I find you had any part in this, if you profit in any way from this suffering, I will drown you myself."

"Be at peace, Lazarro," she called. "The truth will find you soon enough. Then you will weep!"

Gio stormed from the church.

Someone was waiting for her. Jerking her down the steps, out of sight from the church, he stuffed a thick, dry rag into her mouth as she tried to fight off his restraints, the wires that dug into her wrists as he tied them together, yanking the wire up and tight, cutting her. Forcing her against the side wall of the church, he began pouring brandy all over her clothes. She smelled the torch burning, the wax and fat making it burn white, and saw the torch lowered to her skirts.

Mariskka's soles ached; there was no such thing as medieval sandals with arch support. Worst was the pain in the balls of her feet, stinging with every step. Her body needed rest. How long had it been since she ate or drank? She couldn't remember.

She daydreamed about white foaming milk skimming a perfectly drawn latte. She didn't need a lot to make her happy. Or maybe a latte with a hot bubble bath … that would be nice. She could fill her Waterford bowl with a pile of chocolates and then pour a scented bubble bath. Then the latte would taste even better, and she could eat chocolate until the bath water turned tepid. Or she could skip the latte and the bubbles. She could just fill the tub with chocolates and get in. She could eat her way through the rest of the day.

Another stone nicking her foot made her wince and stumble out of the daydream.

Mariskka staggered across the lanes, picking her way through spitting crowds and little girls who reached out to pinch her in their disgust. Mariskka was a dirty foreign woman. She was easy to blame for this new illness. She smelled it on them and wanted to cry. It was here. Death was here.

What had they taught her in school? She knew the Black Death killed a lot of people. It had been interesting when it was in a book. A stone caught her in the shoulder, hitting hard. Mariskka grabbed the spot, trying not to look afraid. She could hear someone cursing her.

She had done as much to the foreigners when working in the hospice, always whispering about those maids who spoke no English, and the funny way valuables went missing after a room was cleaned. Even if Mariskka was the one doing the stealing, she was an American. Mariskka felt a lump of guilt in her throat. She would give anything to apologize to those women.

Another stone clipped her hard in the back. Mariskka fell onto her knees but couldn't help it. Sometimes patients did that, she knew, when pain was too much.

"Mbube, I know what they're doing!" she called. She felt a peace that made no sense right now.

Mbube was beside her, walking, taking her by the hand and leading her away from the crowd of angry mothers beginning to draw together as they watched her. The hostile whispers were growing louder. They were angry at the foreigner. They blamed her.

Mbube's breath came in low huffs. His palms on her arms were firm and rough, like the pads of a bear. Mariskka tried to pull away from his touch, and iron claws came out, drilling down into her skin.

"Why you grab Panthea?" he asked. "You scare her."

"Someone needs to save her," Mariskka answered.

"She not want to be saved," Mbube answered.

"It's all over her!" Mariskka said. "Like a fog, or a web. It's wrapping around her."

Mbube frowned. "Your eyes opening fast," he replied.

"I can help her," Mariskka said.

"She not want your help," he replied. "Not for that."

"Mbube, the plague: it's not the real danger, is it?"

Mbube was silent, turning her to look into the lane again.

The mists were taking shape, walking and gaining in colour and form, until one looked right at her. It was Death, one of many creatures stroking children's hair like women choosing fruit at a market, licking the skin of weary old men, who brushed at their cheeks thinking it to be a fly. Death liked the young ones, she could see that. They cried out.

The old ones were silent, staring at the mists without expression, infuriating them. Mariskka had seen this face in the dementia wards. She had thought the old, silent patients didn't have anything to say.

She had not been wrong. Silence was the last great voice.

Silence had said so many things in those rooms, and she had not listened.

If she could go back....

Mbube grabbed her, forcing her to focus on him. "You not see all. People always quick to see darkness first. There is more."

"I can't wait, Mbube. These people need help."

"They think you crazy," he said. "You be spat on, hated."

"I'm a nurse, Mbube. I've been spat on. I've been vomited on. I've been peed on."

"Everyone die, Mariskka. No medicines. It called the days of the

Great Death, the Unimaginable Suffering. You not enough. Your little truth not enough."

"You sent me here to fight the darkness."

"You not know who fight with you. That big truth. That truth you still need."

"This is what I know: Death doesn't want their bodies. He has no use for them. Bodies are not eternal, not in any world. Spirits are. These are what he seeks. That's why the Enemy appears as a disease. There is no one visible. No one to blame but God…. Oh, wow, listen to me. I do sound crazy." She laughed.

He flashed his teeth at her, long yellow canine teeth with needle-sharp points. "I not laugh. Not about you."

Pulling her up off her feet until her face was pressed against his, she saw fine gold hairs all over his face. She looked into his eyes with the gold irises, and caught his scent, the scent of air after a storm.

He lowered his head and kissed her eyelids, once on each side. "Now you see more truth."

He set her down and she opened her eyes.

She did see more; the mists now appeared as angels walking the streets. Some had wings made of scales, like snakeskin, that rippled and moved as the angel walked. Those angels had frightening faces— thick-scaled brows, eyes a tornado green, the colour the sky turned before the earth was ripped open. Some had mottled wings, browns and tans, like the skin of rattlesnakes she had seen crossing the roads on summer afternoons. They had black eyes, so you could not tell when their gaze was fixed completely on you. One might strike or move on, you never knew. Even as a child, she'd known it was foolish, but she always locked her car door when her mother drove her down those county roads where rattlesnakes sunned themselves.

"Seraphim," he said. "They are dangerous if you do not know Him."

One stared at Mariskka, his head flicking in her direction without warning. She went cold and looked away.

Mbube clicked his teeth at the seraphim, who glided past. "Many of them follow Satan. Those hide in darkness. Always best avoid."

Mariskka grunted, trying to hold her breath and not panic. Fear was takings its toll on her stomach first. She wished God had sent back a porta-potty with her. She wasn't much for squatting over holes, and the age of the outhouse had not arrived.

Mbube had probably seen her at her worst, anyway. She tried not to think of the parties in nursing school, where she woke up the next morning with leaves in her hair and the sour taste of cheap booze in her mouth. One fine morning in particular she remembered waking up facedown on the dean's front lawn, wearing only her bra and underwear. Not her best moment. But she had avoided being punished. She had written an apology note and signed her roommate's name to it. The girl was expelled, and Mariskka finished the semester with honors. The dean said he had never gotten a good look at the girl's face anyway.

Mariskka knew why God made angels eternal: We'd all want to kill them if we could, just to blot out their memories.

"How you say it?" Mbube asked her.

She shook her head, not knowing, trying to say something. It might help her recover faster from all these shocks.

He lifted a finger to stop her. "Welcome to my world, Mariskka."

Chapter Thirteen

"I cannot believe a plague is upon us," Panthea said. She did not withdraw from Armando's arms. "Plague occurred in the ancient worlds, when God inflicted punishment on His children, and in the land of the Greeks. Never in Sicily. Plague has been dead for centuries."

"Plague is an immortal," Armando answered.

"Only God is immortal!" she said.

"No, Panthea. Immortals cover the earth."

"That is not true."

"Nero and I saw death many times in our journeys. We saw things that cannot be explained."

Panthea was silent. He had never spoken of his years in the desert before, the years of his pilgrimage, fighting infidels and making a name for the house of Dario Campaigna.

"You talk foolishness. I do not like it," she said.

"It is not such a horrible death, for another man to kill your body. There are other ways to die. There are spirits among us. It is not our mortal bodies they want."

"I cannot believe you talk like this to me," Panthea said. "You who will not light candles for those in Purgatory or pay for their release. You believe in nothing."

"One night as I slept in the desert, I felt the earth tremble all around me, as if a great army approached and halted. I jumped up but could see nothing, though the stars were bright. I believe in many things."

"In what?" Panthea asked.

"That we are not the only ones with secrets."

He stroked her hair and sighed.

"Go on," Panthea said, pushing his hand away from her hair.

"I climbed a mountain once, a very big mountain," he said. "There was snow near the top and the wind blew hard enough to peel my skin off." He dropped his hand back to his side, holding her with less attention.

"The wind saved my life. I was a loud, careless climber. The locals there moved with the silence of mist. They would have heard me that day and killed me on sight. But the wind howled and screamed, and Nero and I climbed higher, until I looked below me and saw a clearing. There were a few shrubs and rocks but nowhere to hide. An old man moved down there, weak and slow. His back was bent at a terrible angle and I knew he could not raise himself up to see me. I was slipping back down, out of sight, when I saw a man, a youth really, with a knife in his hand. The boy pulled back as if to launch the knife at the old man's back. He meant to kill him, to cut the old man down without mercy."

Armando shrugged, as if to justify the decision to himself once again. "It did not seem right, so I instead rushed down upon him, cutting off the boy's head with one blow from my sword. He looked surprised to see me, and I do not think the boy felt pain. The old man heard us, though, and turned with difficulty to see what was above him. He saw me, a foreigner to his home, standing over a local boy, whose head now lay a distance from his body.

"I do not know why I didn't turn Nero and flee. I had acted like a warrior, a man of justice, but I suddenly felt ashamed. He had been only a boy. The old man looked between me and the body and motioned for me to approach. I edged Nero down toward him. There was an old man, with no weapon. No one else. He could not harm me.

"When I reached him, I saw his eyes. Green, greener than the soil of Verona. His face was brown and rough, and he kept his hair hidden under a great turban wrapped around his head. He motioned for me to dismount, and then he embraced me as I stood before him. From his gestures I understood that I had saved his life from a mortal enemy. I was pleased. It was not right to cut down an old man like a dog. The boy had gotten what he earned.

"The man—I guessed from his slow words that his name was Amar—led me to a cave deep within the mountain, a cave with many shadows. I heard voices and saw strange shapes flying through the darkness. As they drew nearer, I realized they were children, rushing to welcome home this man, taking him by the hand to lead him deeper in.

"The deepest part of the cave was unlike any palace I could imagine. Light flooded in from above, revealing a home of a god. There were riches there I cannot describe, even to this day. It overwhelmed me. Most of all I saw fabrics woven with gold, woven gold flowers with stones in the center, beautiful coloured gems that glistened like they were wet. The fabrics made rooms, separating boundaries for the children, I think, and the old man. Some fabrics were draped over the most searing light, creating purple flames along the walls. I tell you, no other fabric has ever been seen like these. It would take our women years to construct one like it, and none of our women even have such skills as this weaver. I wondered, in my daze, if this was the home of the lost Greek gods.

"The old man clapped his hands—so soft was his strike of flesh on flesh, I was sure no one heard it. But these were quiet people. The children ran into the darkness, returning with plates of dark, hard bread and clotted milk. It was offered to me first, and I ate. A goat's hoof would have tasted better.

"The children gave me something else, a green pudding of sorts, chewy. It was made from some kind of plant and when I tasted it, I left this earth. I saw the colours around me in new ways. The voices thundered in my ears, and I saw the old man dancing all around me, laughing.

"As I lay there, the world spinning, my mouth numb, my tongue running over my lips, trying to find feeling, I saw a dark spirit. A figure in black, thin as a winter branch, swaying above me. It had no face. All was shrouded in black, the image of every fear I had ever known. From the shroud came a woman's hand, small but strong and smooth, and it pressed against my mouth, sealing my lips to keep me from yelling. She smelled of a desert rose, of a woman's oils, and I felt her touch against my lips. I thought I would die from the kiss, the taste of a woman's soft palm against my mouth. I breathed into it, feeling my breath move along the surface of her skin. The old man hissed at her, and she rose at once. As she pulled away from me, I thought I saw a glimpse of her hair. Long and black, the kind of black you would see before you dove into deep water, shutting your eyes.

"The old man stretched himself out, taking my sword and setting it at his own side, grinning at me. He ran one hand along its handle, tracing the marks. He fell asleep, his mouth open, ropy strands of saliva running down his chin as he breathed in and out. Such little breaths, I thought. He was an old man, a small one.

"I was too weak to move, my legs feeling heavy, my arms unable to hold my weight as I tried to lift up. But she was there, beyond the veils that trembled when herdsmen above moved across the mountain. That was all there was between us, these veils of gold and purple. All night I lay there, listening for her, remembering the feel of her palm against my lips.

"Did you know, Panthea, that if you tie a tiger's neck to a stake in the ground when he is young, when he is old, he will not strain against it? He will remember when he resisted and the rope burned, twisting into skin. The fiercest among us can be ruined if they are caught young. That was me. She was tightening the rope around my neck.

"A storm came upon us while we slept," Armando continued. "Lightning blasts that shook us. The walls of the cave began to glow blue from the strikes all around us. My host, the man, awoke, saying nothing to me. He went outside, right into the beast, to relieve himself. When he returned, his hair wet and dripping, he sat cross-legged and clapped once. She appeared, lifting the veil between us, carrying a tray of figs and flatbread. Still, I could see nothing of her face or form, nothing but those exquisite hands. My mind was clearing. I saw she must be young, for the hands were so smooth. I did not trust myself in her presence, and I clasped my hands together before my face. I feared I would rise and throw off her veil for the thrill of seeing her face, though my host who owned her would surely kill me for the dishonour. This is the only time I have considered a dishonourable death.

"'Who is the man I killed?' I asked my host.

"Hunched over his breakfast, fig seeds trailing down his stubbled chin caught here and there on coarse grey hairs, he grunted. 'A boy. From the village below.'

"'Why would such a boy kill you?' I asked. 'You are a white-haired father, unarmed.'

"He grunted again, but I think it was a laugh. 'The young ones get excited about my coming death.'

"He was more interested in his breakfast than this tale, which upset me. The old man saw I was not eating, and he grabbed my plate away. He ate like a rodent, working his two good teeth in front with ferocious speed, tearing, smacking, and swallowing. It was vulgar, but who could scold an old man?

"When he finished, he looked at me with disdain. I had not eaten what was set before me.

"'These clothes. My wife makes them. No other man has such a wife. I grow rich by her.'

"'The young boys want to kill you so they, too, can have her and grow rich?' I asked.

"He spat, a thick clump of fig seeds in the sand between us. 'Are you a eunuch?' he wheezed. 'I am old, but still I know what they want. It is not cloth.'

"It offended me, though I would not admit it. I would not suggest a rude motive to my host.

"'I bought her in the open market when she was just a girl. She wore a veil as she climbed onto my donkey for the journey here. No one has seen her unveiled, save me, in fifteen years. Legend tells them she is a daughter of gods. Beautiful.'

"'Why do you keep her veiled? Surely no one enters here and may look upon her.'

"'I do not command she wear a veil,' he replied. 'Do you think if we planted these seeds near the cave, in a spot safe from the wind, we could grow figs? I hate paying market price. A man should grow his own food if he can.'

"'Why does she wear it?' I asked.

"He began picking out the seeds from the wet mush. 'Why do you care? She is my wife. A good wife. Does not complain.' He cupped his palm and counted the seeds. 'Will you stay one more night? I must reward you for your deed, but the journey is long for an old man. I need a full day to go and return. Will you wait?'

"I stood and bowed. 'I did what was right. My God will reward me.'

"He grinned up at me and began the process of raising himself—first to his knees, then pushing one leg up, steadying himself with both hands, and grasping for my help, which I gave. 'Yes, your God,' the old man wheezed. 'He is slow when good things are due, isn't He? A bent old man is faster.'

"'I will stay to please you,' I said. And so he left on his journey.

"I made no noise, landing each footfall with care, going heel to toes in a slow, silent arch. My breaths became more shallow as I walked deeper into the darkness. I did not know what I would do when I saw her.

"I saw her standing in a delicate waterfall that came in from above, the light from the parted rocks making the droplets look like diamonds cascading down her shoulders. She was bathing, her back to me.

"She turned her face at an angle, so I could see only an outline of her features. Seeing me there, she cried out, grabbing for her long black veil and running back into the darkness beyond us.

"'I will take you from here,' I called. 'I can take you away, to a land of sun. You do not have to be veiled.'

"Shadows along the walls betrayed her movement, edging closer to me.

"'Why should I leave?' she asked.

"'You are hidden here,' I said.

"'I have my work,' she said.

"'Let me look upon you,' I said. I heard her footsteps as she ran back into the darkness."

Armando exhaled, wiping his brow. "I never saw or heard her again. The man brought me a bag filled with gold coins of many nations. I left that night."

Armando laughed, as if to end the story. "I never understood her, not until last night, not until I understood you."

Panthea placed her hand in his. She would find a way to love him, to submit against her will, her anger, and ambition. With effort, Panthea tried to soften her features, to look into his eyes as another, weaker woman might. "What is it that I have helped you understand, Armando?"

"Not all women want to be rescued." Armando stood. "I must go into the village. They will not know what to do."

"You're wrong!" Panthea said. "I want to be rescued. But I am too strong. I do not know how to be that weak woman you men look for. Why does that make me less desirable?"

"No man can save you from yourself," Armando replied. "You are not less desirable, Panthea. But your beauty is wasted. You will never allow yourself to be loved. That is why I leave."

"If you leave me at this time, you will never be permitted back into the castle. I will see to it that you suffer griefs unimaginable."

Armando bowed to her. "I must go to the people, Panthea. They will need me. Try to understand that and do not blame me. Do not blame yourself."

Panthea took off her leather slipper and hurled it at his head. "I blame myself for nothing, you pig! You were always a coward, afraid to take what you wanted! Alas, I will see to it that I do not make your mistake! I have no need of you! I will have all that I desire!" Panthea was shaking as she yelled.

Armando bowed once again as he exited. "That has always been my wish for you, Panthea. May God deal graciously with us both."

Armando was gone.

The baker was about to set her skirts on fire with his torch.

Gio snapped her head forward, striking him, splitting open his lips. Cursing, he put a dirty hand to his lips, pulling it back to see the blood. He still held the torch in one hand.

The smell of the alcohol was strong but not enough to overpower the stench of death upon him. He was covered in swollen black lumps, some beginning to split along the edges, a dark fluid oozing out.

Gio moved her feet under her skirts, inching back from him.

"You wretch," the baker said. "You poisoned me as you did my wife." He grinned and began lowering the torch to her skirts. "Shall I hold you while you burn, so we may go to her together?"

"I did nothing!" Gio said.

Her words had no effect on him.

"Have mercy on me!" she begged.

"Mercy is God's job," he said.

He fell forward, dropping the torch away from her. The flames licked around his wrists as he twitched.

Flung deep into his back was a mace, the iron spikes along the ball driven into his body.

Raising her eyes from the horror, Gio saw a knight standing over the body now beginning to burn. She did not know if he intended worse torments for her. She tried to move, to keep edging back and away, as the knight stepped closer, reaching for her.

She turned to run, but he was too fast. His arm caught her at her waist, and he dragged her to his horse, throwing a hand over her mouth to silence her.

"I will do you no harm," he said. When she quit kicking at him, he softened his grip, letting her go.

"You are the one called Armando," she said.

"I am," he replied. "Why would this man want you to die?"

"He thinks these deaths are a poison I conjured."

"Are you a healer then?" Armando asked.

"There are ways to heal beyond what the Church allows. This is why I am condemned." It was another lie, Gio realized. But lies had no consequences when all were dying.

"Can you cure this?" he asked.

She did not like his tone or expression. A knight should not have fear, and this one surely did.

"I have never seen this before," she said.

Armando studied her. She felt as if she were being drank in, tested in ways she did not understand. Sweat began to form along her upper lip, and she looked away.

"Collect all cures that might be of use, and come at once to the village. We will save who we can. Children first," he said.

Gio nodded, and Armando helped her onto his horse. She had never seen a horse in such good health, with such fine muscles and livery. The horse had a life far better than her own.

Armando put his leg in the stirrup, and Gio leaned forward to make room for him. The horse danced, not letting Armando on. A wolf was walking around the flames of the baker's body.

"Wolves have broken the fire lines," Armando said. "They will eat the dead. Or anyone too weak to run."

Gio started to cry. She couldn't help it. All the disasters in the world were flooding down. She wanted a safe place, another day, a day from long ago in her past, before she made so many mistakes that couldn't be fixed by suppertime.

"Take my horse. His name is Nero, and he likes a strong hand. Ride with great speed to collect your cures from home."

Gio did not reply. Her throat was too swollen from tears.

"Are you thinking only of yourself?" he asked. "If you are a good woman, you will do as I commanded at once! Go! Go in the name of the Lord!"

He hit Nero's flank with the flat side of the sword, and the horse shot off, just as the wolf growled across the flames at Armando.

Chapter Fourteen

Panthea was pacing across the floors outside the chamber. She would not go in, but she would not go downstairs and leave the room unguarded. She could not bear another servant stealing anything of her father's.

Everything she had been, everything she had set her hopes on for the future, it was all blowing away like smoke from a fire. No matter how hard she tried to grasp and hold on, these things were blowing away.

Her father was dead.

His advisers were gone.

Armando had abandoned her.

The servants were fleeing for their own lives. Soon those within her castle would rebel. Perhaps they would kill her.

She heard servants below, whispering, and caught the eye of one peering up and around the banister to mark her position.

Panthea's mind worked fast, piecing together what she knew,

what she had overheard as a child. Plagues did exist. She could close off the castle, but then would receive no more supplies. If the plague entered a closed castle carried with the supplies, all would die within days.

She needed more time to make a plan. From the window, she caught scent of fire. She ran to it and peered down below. Men she did not recognize were gathering on the road outside the manor gates, carrying torches and whips.

One saw her. "Mistress of the castle! Send down your father!" he called.

Panthea pulled back, pressing herself, hidden, into the wall. They did not know he was dead. She couldn't tell them. If they knew a woman controlled the manor, they would attack.

Sucking in a hard, cold breath, she leaned back out the window. "Why should I disturb him?" she called back. "You have nothing to offer!"

"Has all your gold stopped up your ears?" he yelled. The men were staring at her with hungry, drawn faces. "Death has come to the village! God's wrath is poured out among us!"

"Alas for you!" Panthea yelled back. Her servants were coming up the stairs, most looking terrified at the calls from the men on the lawn below.

"What is it you want here?" Panthea called.

"Gold, that we may make an offering to the Church, and stop this plague!"

"You are nothing but mercenaries! You have no care for the Church! Be gone!"

Panthea was counting those who stood behind her. She had

several strong men and all the women, though those did her no good. Only the reed-thin drunkards were below in the kitchen, plus the grumpy, burly cook.

She would not show fear. It did not matter that Armando had left her. She would hold on to this castle, onto her name and her wealth, all without him. When this was over, there were certainties: the people would need money, and Armando would need a patron. She would see to it that he suffered. His children would hear her name and weep. She promised this to herself and held her post at the window.

"We will have what we came for," he called. Men were testing the walls, seeing if any would give. "But to prove faith, we will offer a bargain: if you will not give gold to our precious Lord, then send a man out that he may be scourged for your sins, and thus cleanse your house!"

This upset the servants, who all began whispering and clutching each other, looking at Panthea in alarm.

"Don't be fools," she said to them. She looked down and her eyes met the cook's as he stepped out, wiping his hands on his stomach. He made no effort to hide his hatred for her, his desire to see her neck broken.

Panthea spoke to the men standing closest to her. "Throw the cook out to them," she said in a soft voice.

The youngest, the one with great muscles from turning the roasting spits, answered right away. "Good mistress, we cannot do this! It is not right in the eyes of the Lord!"

"Then you can go outside and get scourged," she replied.

He pursed his lips. "It's a fine plan, mistress. We'll send the cook."

The men moved as one down the stairs and took the man by the arms, forcing him along the passage that would lead to a gate. The cook sneered at Panthea as he was pulled off. He could not overpower the men holding him, but she could see he had no thought of dying. She felt sorry for the men outside. He could be violent if they were not quick.

Panthea snatched a young boy by the neck of his garment. His mother cried out, trying to pull him away from her. Panthea's slap across her face echoed in the quiet chambers.

"Do you want all of us to die?" Panthea asked her. The mother stood without moving, a red splotch across her cheek.

"I have a plan," Panthea said, trying to bring her servants together as one mind on this. "You must trust me. All of you." She knelt down. "What is your name, love?" she asked the boy.

"Franco," he replied.

"Franco," she said, stroking his worn shirt. It was so thin she could see the tint of his flesh through it. "That is a very nice name. Franco, do you like games?"

The bodies were coming too fast. Mariskka was watching from the shadows, hiding in an arch of the church. Scholars had discounted eyewitness accounts from the medieval writers. Scholars said the writers exaggerated the claims that victims could die in a matter of minutes, or hours. Witnesses, the scholars said, could not be trusted. They did not know what we know today, scholars said. They didn't understand what the plague was, or how it was spread.

Mariskka looked at the bodies coming down the lanes. Modern scholars did not see, or taste, or feel any of this. Time and distance gave scholars unnatural comfort. True history was terrifying.

Lazarro was moving among them, his robes dragging through blood and fluids, the stain creeping higher up his calves. He had recruited help from some rough-looking boys who had no mothers to hold them back. These boys restrained the screaming victims as Lazarro lanced their boils, pouring wine and vinegar on them, anointing the people with oil and praying. Lazarro was begging the victims to confess, but the victims were writhing and moaning, the sea of the dying growing wider all around him.

He could get no intelligent answer out of them. They screamed for water and wailed in hallucinations.

Lazarro fell to his knees and lifted his arms to heaven. "Who failed, Lord? Have I failed as priest? Have they failed in confession and repentance? Only reveal Your will, and it will be done!" he shouted.

Victims cried out, reaching trembling fingers to Lazarro, grasping his wet robes, catching him by the ankles.

"Why has this happened to me?" a girl asked him. Her voice was light and carried above the wailings of the older ones. Lazarro turned to find her and knelt at her side. Her face was bright red, with sweat running down her temples. She was coughing and swallowing back fluid, trying to force a smile for Lazarro.

"Father," she said, holding out a shaking hand, "Father, why has this happened to me? Did I sin? Are you angry with me?"

Lazarro shook his head. "Am I in the place of God, daughter, that I could answer you this?"

"Yes," she answered. "You taught us that. You are the voice of God to us. Why do you not answer me? Am I to have no comfort?"

Lazarro was holding her hand, trying to steady her, but he himself began shaking. He dropped her hand and stood. "He who loves his life will lose it!" he called to them all. "Surrender to God's judgment while mercy may be found!"

Lazarro is quick to see the darkness, Mariskka thought. *He thinks giving the answer, any answer, is his job.* She had to stop him from making her mistake.

⚜

Gio's legs were burning. She had made the climb up the path to her hidden home many times but had never moved with such speed. Her breath made her ribs burn too, and she pressed a hand against one side to keep moving. *Only a little farther,* she thought. She had left Nero below. He was too fine an animal for this rough path.

She ran through a list of herbs in her mind. What did she have? What would be useful? Henbane would ease their pain. And ginger root for the vomiting, but her root had withered a good bit and she had not yet found a trader with fresh. Sage and yarrow, arnica perhaps. She needed cool herbs to counteract the heat of this illness. Cool medicines would balance the heated humours. Gio debated whether to mix these with wine or water. The wine would dampen the smell of death, she decided. She would use wine.

The Old Man's body was still lying in her doorway. Gio stopped, staring at it. She would have to cross over it to get inside. This was bad luck. The Old Man had not received Communion and the Last

Offices before his death. He was in Limbo now, or a wanderer, coming to her across darkness to drag her away with him. The wanderers were often angry. She had heard the stories as a girl.

A noise in the undergrowth surrounding her house snapped her to attention.

Keeping her mouth closed so her breath would be quiet, keeping her hands at her side and her feet in their same place, Gio listened to see if the other creature breathed too. She panicked; it could be a Valkyrie, a corpse-eater. She had heard tell of these strange women from the traders who came from northern lands, but she had doubted the tales. She had doubted much, until today.

No other sound came. Gio closed her eyes and strained to listen harder, to listen with every pore, every bit of flesh and bone. If evil was close, she would feel it. Evil would make itself known somehow.

Nothing. Whatever was hidden would not reveal itself. Gio glanced to her door. She needed to get inside.

Marking where the Old Man's body was and where she stood, she turned her eyes up to the side and inched forward with her arms extended. She should touch the door frame on the left before her feet reached the body lying more to the right side.

Her hand hit wood and she looked down, keeping her eyes off the body as she jumped past it into the cool, comforting darkness. Inside, the faint perfumes of her home, the soft grit of the dirt under her feet, these made her feel better. She knew these things. They were unchanged.

The Old Man's head was faceup on the threshold. Sitting on her rear and using her legs to force the door closed, she grunted as she pushed his thick, wet head back out. She could not look at him or even think on him. His disease sickened her, made her skin feel slick and nasty, made her keep tasting her lips to be sure she was not polluted with it too.

Having closed the door, Gio curled into a ball and shivered. What had he done to deserve this? What sin could be so great? Gio had dwelled on her own sins for so long she had not considered that others might do worse.

She did not want to heal them. She wanted to run. And she could; many were fleeing. One more would not be missed. She did not live on much here; she could live on less elsewhere. There would be new lies. New lies about her past, new stories to drop in small bits, knowing the village women collected them and, in secret, pieced them together, adding their own embellishments, creating a story terrible and almost true. Gio could even claim she had never been able to have children. That was true. And that her husband had died young. That was true in its way. Lazarro had died—to her.

Gio began putting her herbs into her bag, considering all these possibilities. She would need these medicines no matter which path she chose. She had suffered to pluck and steal these cures and salves, bought from dark men who traveled in lands beyond the Church's reach, who would not take Lazarro's bread and wine.

Perhaps she would offer a few remedies to those with heavy purses. She could use the money for her journey. Reaching to the upper shelf that sat back in the shadows, Gio's hand closed on the jar containing the dried mushrooms. Her wrist brushed against the cool marble bowl. Her pigments. These had been her greatest treasure, the only conjuring the Church allowed. She had birthed brilliant worlds out of the earth all around her. But she could not take them if she left. Every painter knew her skill and her instinct for colour; her lies would not hold up in a new land. They would know who she was. Her heart sank and she turned, facing the canvas that whispered to her.

The colours were too deep, the black too harsh. There was none of the blank canvas left, no spot of hesitation or apology. What had swept upon her that night? How could this be her story?

In the painting, a broken woman knelt at the feet of Christ, surrounded by an angry crowd carrying stones. The stones were pitted and sharp, some chiseled to a point by deliberate hand and some stumbled over on a bad path. The faces were hungry, like a dog panting as he surveys a dinner that he must steal. Their fingers strained as they held onto their stones. No crowd gave mercy.

Gio knew these stones all too well, used much pigment to make their punishing edges clear. The stones would pierce. The woman would not rise again.

But for Jesus: Jesus would not permit them to have her. He held out an arm above her. In the painting, she had shown His path behind Him, winding, disappearing over the horizon.

While they had been gathering stones, Jesus had been coming to save her.

Gio blushed at the thought and looked down. She should not have painted a gentle Christ. This is not what the Church taught. Not for women like her.

"Mistress Gio! Come at once! My mother is dying!"

Gio heard hysteria in a child's voice, and she rushed out to meet him, avoiding the body again.

A boy was in the path, no colour in his face. He was shaking, and his eyes darting around as he waited for her to reach him.

"Come!" he called.

"Where is she?" Gio asked. "What are her symptoms?"

"Do not be angry with me," he said, and before she could ask more, a sharp pain split across the back of her head. Gio fell to the ground.

Lazarro was trying to give the Last Offices to those who were still able to speak and respond. Others just moaned, a sharp fever stinging them, coughs rattling their bones. Children were coming, children who were not sick, walking around the steps of the church. The youngest of them held hands with the older ones. Some looked unwell, but Mariskka did not try to stop them. The children were searching for something. Mariskka watched their faces and understood. The children were looking for their parents. Some children found them, dead or dying, and collapsed with a wail of grief and trembling chins.

One band of three children, clasping hands, wandered among the victims but could not find their parents. Mariskka saw that the youngest of the children, a girl with a simple shift and a blue ribbon in her hair, had the black boils beginning to rise under her neck. She was still trying to suck her thumb, though her two older brothers were tugging at her to keep up. The boys looked, and looked again, and then looked around in all directions.

Mariskka ran across the street to the baker's house. It was

unlocked, the shop empty. She grabbed a few rounds of bread and ran them back to the children. Motioning for them to sit, she broke the bread and handed it to each, gesturing for them to eat. She stroked the girl's head as the oldest boy stared at her. He could not have been more than ten. Mariskka had seen children coming into her hospice, in her former life, and was used to their reactions when surrounded by death. Most cried. Their eyes turned red, and then fat tears rolled out one by one, as their voices grew high and strained. An adult always laid an arm across their shoulders or gathered the child into an embrace. The child would grieve from a safe distance. The adult would let them see death, watch it at its work, viewing it from a distance like a patron watching a famous artisan at his worktable.

Mariskka saw it in the oldest child's eyes. He knew. His parents were not dead, but they were gone. Mariskka guessed they had fled when they saw the spots forming on the girl's throat. She took a big breath to say something, then let it go. The oldest boy wouldn't understand. And what could Mariskka say even if she had the gift of words? No one had stood with her, either, when death came for her mother. Death had gone about his work while she lay whimpering, helpless, watching.

The boy's hand reached out, resting on Mariskka's arm. She looked up at his face, surprised that she had wandered in her mind, surprised that hot tears of her own were rolling down her cheeks. The boy looked at her with a somber expression. She lifted his hand and placed it, palm to palm, against her own, then one by one entwined her fingers with his. She closed her eyes and did something she had not done since that day. She prayed.

"God, help us."

It was all she could think of.

There was more shouting from the village. The boy's arm went around his little sister, and he helped her lean against his shoulder. Her face was flushing, and she resettled herself in his lap, her tiny body nestling down like a bird in its nest.

Her throat burning from the tears, Mariskka went to see the source of the shouting. Lazarro looked up, not stopping his work. He had found a needle and was lancing a dark abscess on a man's inner thigh. The man groaned, his face turned away. Lazarro covered his mouth and nose with his sleeve to keep from breathing the rotted smell.

Angry screams were growing louder. Mariskka hurried. The stone lanes were confusing, all shooting out at crazy angles from the church steps in the center of the village. Echoes carried only a moment in the sky above her. Mariskka listened again and chose a lane.

Armando had a skinny man by the neck, slapping at his sides with the flat end of his sword. The man was twisting and screaming as his companions watched from a distance. Coins and jewelry were falling from the man's pockets onto the street.

Armando released the man, screaming a threat to the others. All fled, though not with shame. They would return once Armando was gone.

"Do you come to loot?" he yelled at her.

Mariskka showed him her empty hands, shaking her head. In the sunlight she saw a red indentation on her wrist, the usual spot her watch rested. The watch she had stolen from a dead patient. Her guilt made her sick. Her memories punished her. Mariskka tried to remember she had been forgiven.

"Come!" Armando commanded her. Tucking her wrist into her robe, Mariskka hurried to him.

"Go into the houses. If anyone be ill, close the door upon them, upon all who are inside. None is to leave that house."

Mariskka shook her head no.

"Do you want to die?" he yelled at her.

She shook her head no again.

"Neither do I," he said. "Do this at once. I will send others to help."

Mariskka nodded.

"In every lane, look for women who will help you. Care for whom you can, but do not forget you must save the living."

He was gone before she even caught the last of his words. She furrowed her brow, looking at the smooth stones under her feet, the dirt and food scraps that collected in the gaps between each.

Armando treated her with respect, though she was not capable of earning it, not as a woman who lived in this age. A broken, mute woman.

Armando was a man who would do well in any generation, she thought. *God bless the Armandos of this age,* Mariskka thought, *and of every age.*

Mariskka looked around at the houses. Those who could flee, already had. Heavy furniture and lumpy sacks were scattered in the lanes ahead; within a few hundred yards their possessions had become too heavy, and the wealthy had to flee without them. These things were worth a fortune, she thought. Medieval furniture? Medieval silver bowls and woven tapestries and bed stands carved with dragons' wings? If only there were a way to get these back to her world, she thought.

So much was going to be wasted.

Mariskka pulled up her coarse brown robe and crept down the lane, stopping and listening every few yards.

A wood door, plain and cracked, was ajar, windows rising above it. Mariskka guessed the house had three narrow stories. No one appeared in the windows, no sounds of movement came from the house, save one soft moan. Mariskka's stomach tightened and she licked her lips, breathing out as she pursed them.

She had walked into many rooms with dimmed lights. Dimmed lights meant someone was close to death. (And the irony, she thought, was that labor and delivery rooms were so bright that babies had to squint, shielding their eyes from the pain. *Let the dying have strong light,* she thought. *Babies should be brought into a softer world.*)

Picking her way across an uneven wood floor, she let her eyes adjust to the darkness. A moan just to her left guided her deeper in, and she saw the stairway, no wider than her own hips really, going at a sharp angle up to the next floor. It offered only the stone wall along its side for support, and she braced herself with her left hand as she felt with her foot, searching for a safe landing with every step. *God bless the guy who came up with modern building codes,* she thought.

One more step and Mariskka saw her. At first she thought someone had dropped a sack in their hurry to flee. The family had fled this house, that was clear, but this sack moved and Mariskka hurried those last few steps to it.

An elderly woman was lying, spread across three steps, hanging upside down.

Mariskka cradled the woman's head and tried to lift her without injuring her, moving her head back above her body, smoothing out her legs and arms. Mariskka took long, gentle strokes across the woman's thin, slipping skin, hoping her touch would communicate her intentions.

The old woman's eyes were watering, an ugly tumor along one eyelid pressing against her cornea. It was not a swelling of plague. Mariskka looked her over. She was not ill, but she was very old, too old to survive alone. Too frail to flee unless someone carried her. From the empty house, Mariskka knew someone had decided to carry a piece of furniture instead.

"They left you, didn't they?" Mariskka asked.

The woman turned her head, not understanding.

Mariskka pointed to the door. The old woman followed Mariskka's finger with her eyes, and nodded.

How can I get this woman down these awful steps? Mariskka thought. *She needs food and water. She needs to get away. She doesn't deserve to die just because she cannot fight death.* The old woman might be helpless before her own death, she might even think she should welcome it, but death had no absolute right to the weak. The weak belonged to Christ.

Mariskka tried to focus again on taking the woman's pulse. She felt a wet, hot breath on the back of her neck, and the woman's eyes opened wide in terror.

A tall, heavy man of no more than twenty years stood over her, dark hair covering his arms in a dirty thatch. Underneath his open linen shirt, stained with sweat and the soil of the village, she saw them: black rising swellings, looking like black shiny eggs popping up, straining against his skin.

"I bring you good news, ladies," he said.

If he knew she was mute, and alone with this elderly woman, they would both die. No creature could be more defenseless than a woman without her voice. Mariskka wiggled her eyebrows as if she didn't care what he said or why he was there.

"I offer you a way of escape from this new death," he said. "For today it has come to your house." He coughed, holding his hand against his sides to brace himself from the pain.

Mariskka felt the tiny blood drops splatter on her face.

"You tell me where the treasures of this house are kept, and I will let you escape with your lives."

Mariskka looked at the old woman, whose pupils were dilated to an extreme. The woman was going into shock. She would be dead within minutes.

The man shifted his weight on his feet. Mariskka wondered how he found the strength to even stand—most victims could not rise from their beds when the symptoms began.

Mariskka's stomach constricted around something hard and cold. He was greedy. Greed had forced him from his bed, forced him to steal. Mariskka saw herself in him. She could not hate him.

Reaching out her hands, Mariskka felt his forehead with the back of her hand. His fever was well over 100 degrees, perhaps 105 or 106. He would be dead within hours, and he was not free. She saw a dark spirit hovering behind him, ready.

He laughed at her, pushing her hand away, but she brought them together, running her hands over his cheeks, stroking away a spot of blood with her thumb. He turned his head to avoid her eyes, his body stiff with anger, but he did not take a step back. She stroked his arms until she could feel him beginning to calm, then peered into his shirt at the black welts. Every one was almost transparent, a sign that the abscesses were about to burst. His time was short. Though he had been strong, he would die like the weakest among them. Greed had probably lengthened his life, she thought, unwilling to let him go so soon, wanting to twist the knife again and again.

Anger flushing through her cheeks, she felt it setting her lips. No one would die like this in her arms. No one would die without a chance to live.

She bent down, drawing on the dirt floor, the only symbol they shared across seven centuries.

Straightening, she again took his face, stroking her fingers against his forehead to whisk away the sweat, waiting for him to look in her eyes.

When he did, she pointed to the floor.

"Are you mad?" he said.

He pushed her away with one sweep of one hand, knocking her several steps off. She came at him again, but he jabbed his palms into her face.

"Look at them!" he screamed.

Mariskka took his hands into her own. Each hand was the size of a plate. Studying them, she could see nothing.

"They are unclean. I am unclean," he said.

She knelt down, smearing away the image of the cross, scooping the dirt of the cross into her palms. She poured the dirt over his hands, scrubbing hard until dirt covered his skin.

"I can't even see my hands now," he said, as if he were trying to joke.

She looked up, breathing hard, then lifted these hands to her mouth, kissing them and laying them against her own cheek.

He did not pull them away. "I can't tell my hands from this dirt," he said. He was starting to say words in tight little bursts. The plague had gotten to his brain. "I am covered in it."

He looked at her and she knew. He understood. He was covered in the cross.

He slid to his knees, crying out for God's forgiveness, then slumped over. He was gone.

Mariskka checked the old woman's pulse and, finding none, closed her eyes.

Her own heartbeat was becoming steady and firm. She understood more big truth.

A woman's shriek from just beyond the door made Mariskka lurch and say a curse word that would have made Crazy Betty from the hospice blush.

"Don't hold anything I say against me, okay?" Mariskka hoped that counted as a prayer, even though she wasn't folding her hands.

Mariskka knew God didn't have a reputation of answering the general sort of questions. She asked anyway. "What's out there?"

Chapter Fifteen

Gio woke up, her face pressed into the cold dirt, her arm tucked under her body, pinning her hand at a bad angle. It was burning with pain.

She used her good hand to force herself up, rubbing the throbbing hand, trying to blink, or scowl, or move her face enough somehow to clear her vision and make sense of this. Everywhere around her were wide columns, set into the dirt, rising to wooden beams above. She could hear noises from above but could make no sense of them.

Her bags were there. She grabbed one, pulling it close and opening it. Everything was there, even some items she did not remember packing. Some items she would never use, like the bat teeth she had bought from a desperate boy. She knew his type too well, always wandering, searching for odd elements that a healing woman or alchemist might use. She had no need of them; there was no magic in teeth of any kind, only decay. But she had paid well and he had been a faithful merchant, always bringing to her first the treasures he found in sleeping villages and stark countrysides.

She stood, trying to see behind the dozens of columns. Mist moved along the far walls, and her steps echoed.

"Greetings?" she said.

Nothing.

In one corner was a straw mattress and table, one of its legs propped up by a collection of old, broken plates. It did not look steady and she feared for the beer mug stationed upon it. Who would live this way?

Whoever slept there was gone. She felt the bed, and it was cold.

A rattle of chains and a dull scrape made her twist around in time to see a brilliant light shining down a shaft.

A woman emerged in the light above her, with a gown of blue silk that radiated its own light. Gio knelt in confusion. She had never been admitted to a high court of men, much less been approached by one so radiant. Gio wondered if she had ever seen this woman in the square. She had never been allowed so close to a noble, not since her youth.

"You are the one they call Gio?" the woman asked.

"Yes, madam, so it please you," she said. The words didn't sound like her own. She sounded like a marionette, a puppet she had seen in a funny market show. She tried to think of which puppet it had been. *Ah, yes,* Gio thought. That was the line from the foolish servant just before getting a beating.

Well done, Gio, she thought. *You cannot speak but invite a beating.*

The woman descended the steps, her feet peeking from beneath the full blue robes. She had little feet in little slippers. These were not feet like Gio's.

"Rise!" the woman commanded.

Gio did.

The woman's face was beautiful, a young Sicilian with deep black hair that fell around her shoulders, her golden skin making her green eyes flash. Gio had imagined that these women, these women who lived other lives, would be so much more beautiful than herself.

I was right, Gio thought.

"I have heard from my servants that you are a learned healer," the woman said. It sounded like a challenge.

"I offer herbs to those who need them," Gio replied. "What treatments I know of."

"You know of this plague?" the woman asked.

"I have seen it," Gio replied. "I know nothing of it."

The woman considered the answer.

"Have you anyone you love?" the woman asked.

Gio swallowed and glanced down. "Only God," she said. She could feel her cheeks growing hot from the embarrassment. It was a stupid way to reply.

"Is that all?" the woman snapped.

"Is that not enough?" Gio replied.

"I can think of one person you love," the woman said.

Gio bit the inside of her cheek. Who was this? What did she know of Gio or Lazarro? The smell of roasting lamb and stale beer from up above reminded Gio of something. She knew this smell, this combination of everything that should be pleasant but made her queasy.

"Do you know whom I speak of?" the woman asked.

"No," Gio lied.

"Everyone loves themselves," the woman answered. "Even people like you." She said "people" as if there were a question.

Gio exhaled. The women knew nothing of her.

"Can you treat this plague?" the woman asked.

"I don't know. I have not tried. It kills the victims so fast. I do not think there is hope."

"Oh, but there is!" The woman smiled and crooned as if talking to a pet. "Hope is the pearl beyond price, the one thing a man would give his entire inheritance for. Hope is the only treasure in the world now. And it is scarce. Men will kill for it."

"I do not understand," Gio said. She swallowed again. A memory pressed its hands against her neck, waiting for her to remember and scream before it tightened its hold.

"You don't understand what? Treasure?" the woman asked. "You've probably never been rich enough to hold two coins at the same time."

"What do you want of me?" Gio asked. Whatever it was, she would agree at once and then flee. This plague had brought companions to help it spread. Greed was the first.

Greed.

The word brought to mind other words, words that had stained her life. *"Reminding me I have a fine wife only reminds me that I have no fine mistress."*

"You are Dario's daughter, Panthea," Gio said. "This is his castle."

At the mention of Dario's name, the woman flinched, looking away. "You know nothing of my father. If he needed healing, he would never go to a woman like you."

"I know more than you think," Gio said. She did not care that her voice trembled, or that Panthea could hear the terror she felt.

"Your life depends on it," Panthea said, pulling her skirts to walk back up the stairs. She did not turn back to look at Gio as she talked. "When the cellar door opens, a fool will be thrown to you. Try to cure him if you can."

"What if I cannot?" Gio asked.

"If you love your life, you will find a way to cure it. I shall have no consequences if you fail. Every one of them will pay me first, whether they get a cure or not. The rest of the castle is well quarantined from this area, so we will be safe. I think you can get through a good dozen before it takes you, too."

A smaller figure was forced into the light at the top of the stairs.

"Do not send me back out there!" a boy's voice cried. "I got this Gio for you. Let me be done, mistress!"

"Find the nobles. Find anyone with a heavy purse. Proclaim that in the house of Dario, in the cellar on the north end, there is a renowned healer. She can cure this plague. But she is greedy and wants much money. Tell them I have negotiated. Their fee need not be so great. But they must come at once."

"No, please," he cried. "It is horrid! And the smells—I might die from those alone!"

"For every paying customer you send me, I will set aside a fat gold coin for you. Think of your mother. She needs this money, doesn't she? Did she raise a son who would spit in her face like this? Have you no love for her?"

There was more conversation, but Gio did not hear it.

The door was closing, taking with it the light.

❧

The man's eyes were white with fear, his arms and legs thrashing against the men who were forcing him into a house. The men fighting him were well fed and muscular, not like the men who spent their days haggling over prices, fighting only against stingy customers. Armando had moved quickly, calling knights and good men from many estates.

The men forced the terrified man into the house, slamming the door shut on him, nailing it closed.

Mariskka looked up and down the lane. Many doors were nailed shut.

But this was not the cause of the screaming she had heard, those awful shrieks. These men were already moving on to another house, yelling for plague victims to identify themselves. Plague houses would be nailed shut, with all inside.

"Do not bring the plague into the streets!" the men yelled, "or we will kill you before it does!"

"The plague may yet show you mercy," called another. "We will not! Do not test us!"

Whatever shrieks had come from that end of the lane, those people were beyond her saving now. Mariskka ran down the rougher lane, stubbing her toes on the uneven stones until she bled, the jagged cuts collecting dirt and leaves and other rubbish. Mariskka wanted two things right then more than she had ever wanted anything in her life, more than money, more than that cursed watch or the cursed manuscript.

"Tennis shoes and hand sanitizer," she said. "I took you two for granted." She sighed, trying to keep moving without her toes collecting further filth. "I would give anything for you now."

The small shrines plastered against the walls of every home obscured her vision, so she had to squint to be sure she saw it right. A woman was leaning out of an upper window, dangling a baby into the street below, shrieking.

Stumbling to the spot under the window, Mariskka extended her arms.

The woman was covered in death welts, her face so red it hurt to look upon it, a tongue protruding out from swollen, cracked lips. She was dying of dehydration, Mariskka thought. It might kill her before the plague. What virus or bacterium could drain all a person's fluids so fast? Nothing like it had ever been seen in her own age.

"Don't touch that child!" a man screamed at her. "It comes from a plague house!" The man was watching from his doorway. He was armed with a dagger that had a broken blade, covered in rust. He made no effort to hide it from her, laying it flat against his belly as he yelled.

Mariskka had once imagined a mother's love would be soft. She had lost her mother too young to remember it well. She had daydreamed about mothers, the kind who cradled their children in the night and rubbed their arms when they were hurting. But this woman's eyes were fierce, her face brutal.

Mariskka looked back at the man in the doorway, then lunged for the baby. The woman wailed, pulling the baby into the window with her.

The beating began with a kick to her calves, sending her to the ground. Mariskka was stunned, not able to connect the force she felt with what she saw. She saw men moving all around her, like a pack, but could not process their faces. She thought maybe one kick broke her rib, but she couldn't decide which kick, or which rib either. Maybe every kick had broken a rib. Mariskka tried to think back to nursing school. How many ribs did she have?

The mother was back, in the window, leaning against the frame to keep herself upright. Mariskka saw her scanning the street in every direction. No one would save her child. Mariskka's spirit eyes saw too.

Dark mists were collecting under her window, jaws snapping at the baby in jest. They pretended to devour it. Why were the angels harder to see? Mariskka wondered. Why did you have to look hard for the good in this world?

Del Grasso was moving up the lane, keeping his bulky frame close to the bricks along his side. The men were busy beating Mariskka. They did not see him.

Mariskka gave her body to them, willing them to strike harder, to drive their boots deeper. She began to taste the most exquisite wine flowing in her mouth. It could have been blood, but she was not considering it. She was welcoming death. The baby would be saved.

Del Grasso extended his arms to the mother, but she shook her head no. She saw the men beat Mariskka, their boots stomping her. She would not drop her baby down into that.

One man stepped back from Mariskka, twisting his lips in satisfaction, as if he had had a good meal.

He's going to stop beating me, Mariskka thought. *They'll all stop. But the baby isn't safe yet.*

She was on her back, staring at their faces, being jerked like a rag doll with every blow. She whipped around to her stomach and lunged for the man who had stopped, biting him hard on his calf. He screamed as he tried to kick her off, sending all the men into a new round of blows and curses.

Del Grasso kicked down the door. It cracked in with one sharp split.

Mariskka counted eighteen more blows. *I should be dead by now,* she thought. *I didn't know I was this hard to kill. It must be the estrogen.*

Del Grasso emerged with the wailing baby.

"Leave off," one man said to the others. "She's as good as dead anyway."

They saw Del Grasso, their eyes moving together.

Mariskka struggled to reach up and bite another one but could not raise her head. She saw the healing angel, the one with the wings of a vulture, moving toward her. Mariskka let her head flop back down and waited for him.

Del Grasso held the baby to his shoulder with one hand. With his other, he held out a cleaving knife, well oiled and sharp, turning it so that it winked at them all.

"Are you mad?" they said to him. "It was in a plague house!"

Del Grasso tightened his grip on the child and took a step back, glancing in either direction behind him. "There are no marks on this babe," he called.

"It might yet be sick!" they screamed at him. "Leave it to die!"

They began taking steps toward him, small steps, Mariskka saw, no man wanting to put his foot farther out than another's.

"I have butchered animals twice your size," Del Grasso replied. "My blade can split thicker necks than yours."

The dark spirits were leaving the men, moving toward Del Grasso, with their dripping grey jowls and snapping teeth, spindly hooked fingers on fibrous arms. They were going to torment him with fear.

Mariskka moaned. It was the best she could do to warn him.

Del Grasso caught Mariskka's gaze, and recognition passed between them. Del Grasso understood death as she did. He had seen enough of it. Death was not eternal; Death was the only true mortal God ever created. *It is no wonder we stare in horror at it,* she thought.

Del Grasso knew judgment too. That was not a hard sign to miss. It was in his face. She understood their mistake. Big dogs were thought to be mean dogs; big men were thought to be cruel men. Del Grasso lifted his chin, a silent acknowledgment, and disappeared down a lane, carrying the baby.

Mariskka was alone again, alone except for the terrified faces staring down from window ledges, some who were trapped, and those who hid from death. Curtains moved back into place as she looked in any direction. The living wished to shut out the foul odors, knowing that foul odors caused plague. Though she was bleeding, none offered help. None could see her being tended to by the angel.

Others were receiving visitors, men and women carrying all manner of bags and satchels. Mariskka knew their type too well; they were the medieval version of multilevel marketers. Medieval fright was as good as modern greed to get people to buy, and buy these people would. Their down lines would be dead by morning, she thought. Not that they would listen, though. Not in any age.

A young man staggered into the lane, laughing, holding his sides and bending at the waist, unable to contain his hysteria.

Mariskka watched the movement of his head to decide if he was drunk or crazy. *Or just young,* she thought. That could be every bit as disorienting.

She could not get a clear glimpse of him long enough to decide; a woman stumbled out into the street, just as hysterical, wiping the back of her mouth with her hand. They disappeared into a home, and Mariskka stood, feeling strength coming back, the angel moving on to another home, slipping in between the cracks of a door nailed shut. She followed to see what could have made them laugh, wiping her face clean with the edge of her sleeve and trying not to notice the blood stains. Mariskka edged the door open, craning her neck to see inside without having to take one more step closer in.

Young men and women were sitting, roosting really, all over someone's home. There were kegs of beer and flasks of wine, some flasks lying on their side, dripping red wine onto the floor. There were noises of passion, and the sound, from way in the back, of a youth being sick from too much alcohol. These had chosen to gorge on sin before they died.

Mariskka grew cold. A night wind had found her lane and was sweeping past, grazing her shoulders with its brittle teeth. She shivered and thought of refuge, a chance to rest her battered bones. She closed the door on the youths, saying a prayer.

Night was coming. Night was coming for them all.

Panthea went over the ledger again. The inkwell was dry, and she did not know where her father kept the extra ink. Digging the quill into the glass sides of the jar, willing it to find some retained ink, she tried to keep writing.

The flame of her candle was the only present comfort. It was a good light that did not tremble like her hands. Panthea set the quill down to shake her hands out and force herself to think.

The ledger showed thirty servants remained with her. She did not know how many had fled. It had never occurred to her to ask her father how many they kept in total. After all, servants were for serving, and as long as she was comfortable, it was no matter if they were one or a hundred.

She had seen the larder and wondered how to estimate her provisions against her needs. She would need more, very soon. The feast had used much of what they had. The problem she could not resolve was this: Whichever servant she sent out on this errand would of course have to return and bring the goods inside. Contact would be made in this way with the plagued village. If Panthea sent her smartest servant, he might know well how to escape the sickness, but if he was damned by God and caught the plague (and how could she know this in advance?) then her loss would be twofold. She would lose her smartest servant and expose her estate to this evil. She could send a fool, but she assumed these were already plagued by another sort of judgment.

She could not resolve the issue.

"I can do nothing tonight," she said to herself. "I should content myself with today's business."

It was something her father had often said. Panthea could understand him more now. Great plans never ended in the same form they began. It did not matter if small things went awry. Panthea was crafting something the world had never seen before, an estate controlled by a woman, a woman who commanded all of Italy. She could do that. She should not be bothered if it didn't move as she planned. There were no plans for this.

A shadow moved on the wall. Panthea jerked her head to catch it, to find its source. She was raw from surprise, every unfolding moment of the last three days sickening her, sweeping her off balance. Panthea felt she had no place to put her feet. Perhaps that was why she was pacing so often today, unable to rest. Anywhere she put her feet seemed wrong, felt dangerous. Nothing was solid anymore. She kept feeling the world being jerked out from beneath her.

A wind outside made the wooden beams above creak. Panthea heard the doors outside pop as they settled into the hinges. Nothing was firm, Panthea's fear reminded her. Not even this castle.

"Panthea!"

Someone called to her from outside the castle.

She knew the voice.

Pushing open the glass window, set into the wall on stubborn, dry hinges, she leaned out to look on him.

Armando stood in the meadow outside her window, holding Fidato's reins. Panthea's heart softened. Seeing him there, healthy, strong, ready to ride, soothed her nerves. All was not lost if Fidato was well.

"What are you doing with my horse?" Panthea yelled down to Armando.

"Panthea, this death spreads too fast. I cannot contain it within the village. You must flee!"

His tone of concern offended her. He should be crazed with fear and anxiety about her. Such simple concern was an affront.

"Flee? So you can come in behind me and claim this castle?" she called.

"Don't be a fool! I care nothing for your castle, or your wealth. If you do not leave tonight, I cannot guarantee your survival! Please go!"

Fidato was losing interest in their conversation. He began nosing around the greens at his feet, investigating the area to see what might be edible.

"What have you been doing in the village?" Panthea asked. She watched Fidato. He shouldn't eat the wild onions. They troubled his stomach.

"There is no time!" Armando called. He was getting agitated. It pleased Panthea. He needed to show more emotion.

"Answer my question first," Panthea called down. "What have you been doing in the village?"

Armando did not look at her as he said something she couldn't hear. Then he answered. "I have called for men who can assist me," Armando called. "We are sealing up houses where victims are known to be. We are battling against *bellechino*, young men who steal, using their own illness as a weapon. Wolves have been seen in the city. The smell of the bodies is calling them. Villagers are frightened. If one survives this death, one must still face violence from men and nature."

"Thank you," Panthea said. "Your report is as I expected. I, too, smell death, but to me, it smells like money."

Armando looked ready to strangle her. It gave her butterflies in her stomach. She had not toyed with him in days. She missed him so much.

"Even now, as I stand here," he called, "people are dying, and not always of plague. What is your answer?"

"This is the reason I could never love you, Armando," Panthea replied. "You see danger and you act. A real man would see danger and think."

"I am a fool to speak to you again," he said, turning. "God be with you, Panthea."

"I don't need God at the moment," Panthea replied. "I have a cure. It is available to you, to all the villagers, for a reasonable fee. I didn't even need a man to think of this plan for me."

He stopped.

"The medicine woman is here, Armando. For a fee, she will heal those afflicted. She can even offer medicines to ward off the death, should someone come to her in time."

"This woman," Armando said, "what is her name? Is it Gio?"

She didn't know how to read his expression. It looked like grief.

"Yes, I think that is her name."

Villagers were coming up the path into sight. They were carrying purses.

"Go fight your battle, Armando," she said. "I have business to conduct. If you know of a knight who needs sponsorship, send him to me, won't you? I can pay well."

"Medicine is needed in the village, Panthea."

"No, those medicines are needed by the villagers. A difference you have missed. All are welcome to come and buy. I withhold nothing."

"Think beyond today, Panthea! For once in your life, think without greed for more. If plague victims come here, you will die the same death."

He had underestimated her again.

"They are allowed in the root cellar, not the castle. They enter and exit by a door that is well away from all living quarters."

Armando let go of Fidato's reigns. He bowed to her, a cold, short bow as if they were done. He should be praising her for her wits, she thought. Someday he would count this money and laugh.

It is odd, she thought, *that Armando would see this crisis and show fear, when I see it too but feel power. More the pity, that he will not praise me.*

Unbelievable, Mariskka thought. The sun was setting late in the day, its horizon lavish red, just as in her own age. So many things were the same here. A sparrow looked the same as in her own century. Birds sang the same songs. The sun was still clean and warm on her skin, and baking bread made her stomach growl. Her mother's generation had seemed like aliens to her, yet these people, centuries past, were as close to herself as any she could imagine. Their faces were no different, whether they comforted a crying child or went about their business.

And the church bells—that constant low ringing she felt vibrating through her tired legs—was a nicer sound than the shrill alarms and constant beeps she was raised with. In her world, beeps and alarms were like little electronic bites, sharp punctures against the fragile skin of the harassed. Bells were a melancholy nod to each passing hour, and when they rang for the dead, everyone paused in respect, searching their hearts. Machines had marked all Mariskka's hours and kept the watches of the night.

Mariskka thought of how many nights she had spent at her nurse's station watching the bank of monitors, each blinking screen representing a patient. She wished she could go back to those nights and unplug all the screens, all the machines. She would watch patients instead, looking into their faces for signs of discomfort, stroking their arms when the IV line hurt and they looked helplessly at it.

How many times had they suffered alone in those sterile rooms? Only the alarm of a machine could bring Mariskka to their side. She regretted that.

Three days had passed. Her body felt numb all over, the bruises already turning yellow at the edges. It hurt to bend over or move quickly; her ribs were hurt, but not broken. She was still able to take deep breaths and thanked God for that. She had been healed beyond her expectations, but she still hurt. Life hurt.

Her first year as a nurse, she had kept vigils at bedsides. She had excused herself to the other, older nurses, saying she needed a soda, leaving that control room of monitors and screens. Mariskka had spent those secret moments at the bedside of her patients, especially the older women, women dying alone. She held their hands as they thanked God for little mercies. She understood these better now.

Life hurt. Death was a relief to some of her patients, a conclusion they were ready for. It was as if those patients read only the end of a book, flipping through the other pages with little interest. They did not want to live.

Mariskka had been changed, little by little, one by one, by those sorts of patients in her first years. One patient would open the window and chain-smoke all night, waiting for her breathing treatment in the morning. Another patient with coronary disease had beer and onion rings sneaked in by the lift team, those young college guys who roamed the halls at night, helping nurses lift and rotate bed-ridden patients. Sweet guys, usually, who just needed to earn extra money. They picked up plenty of business as bootleggers. Medicaid paid for you to get well, but that's not what these patients wanted. Mariskka realized patients came to hospitals for treatments, not heal-ing. Treatments made them more comfortable. People loved being comfortable.

Mariskka had learned something more about those patients: They didn't want to miss a new episode of their favorite *CSI* series, or that hospital drama with the sexy doctors and sexy patients and sexy nurses. TV seasons kept patients alive. They tried to hold out until the end of the season. Every summer there was a rise in deaths. Patients didn't always have the strength to wait for the new season.

After her fifth year, she transferred to a hospice. Here the under-standing was implicit between patient and nurse. They were dying and she would let them. No one spoke about healing and she didn't feel frustrated with them anymore.

Church bells felt like kicks against her back, making her return, with fear, to the sights before her. The sun turned cold on her skin, making her shiver, unable to feel its warmth. Night was already in the air. Everyone could sense it coming like a storm, brewing just behind the horizon. The sun could not hold it back.

Mariskka didn't remember being this exhausted at work, but she had practically been a kid the last time she pulled back-to-back shifts with no sleep. She squeezed her eyes shut a few times to get her tears going, to moisten her dry eyes and clear her vision. The short walk to the church had loosened her stiff muscles. Strong-looking boys were bringing pails of water into the square in front of the church. Lazarro was talking to them. They returned, walking back down the same path, keeping close together.

Mariskka glanced at the torches surrounding the square. They would hold one more night.

She turned her face back just in time to catch a slick blob of spit on her cheek. A man was cursing as she wiped the spit off with her sleeve. He was pointing to a child, a child with a burning red face, moaning, little bubbles forming on his lips. Mariskka pushed the father aside and went to the child, taking his wrist to feel his pulse. The father frowned and cursed her again. Mariskka pulled down on the boy's under-eye skin, checking the colour, and then pulled up on his eyelids, checking his pupils.

The father yelled at Lazarro, who turned to watch her, shaking his head.

"She does no harm," Lazarro said. "Let her work. We do not know where she comes from; perhaps she was trained in the Arab arts of healing."

He went back to lancing boils. He used the same needle for each patient, wiping it on his sleeve between each lancing. Mariskka was going mad watching him.

Witness the birth of universal health care, she said to herself. She had to make herself laugh, otherwise she would be forced to strangle him.

If she could speak, what could she say to him? He didn't know there were germs and viruses. He would have insisted this was the hand of God, a judgment on sin. He would have refused her explanations because he had contented himself with his own. Knowledge was useless in the age of faith. At least when men thought faith meant the world held no more mysteries.

"God help us," Mariskka prayed, though no one heard. "They think they know You, and maybe they do. But they don't know *all* of You."

Her prayer made her laugh. *All those years,* she thought. *All those years spent battling in school, science fighting faith, as if they were enemies who could not be in the same room. Science is faith, Mariskka thought. Science is God beckoning us into further and deeper mysteries. God wants to be known, whether it is under a microscope or above our heads in the stars. God wants us to tear down the walls and root up the earth until we've found Him everywhere He can be found. We should be exhausting ourselves in the search for God, in our drug trials and labs, in our nurseries and hospices. God is too wild, too powerful, to ever be fully explained in our world of maps and measures.*

Yet she knew Lazarro could not see any of this.

Oh, God, she thought, *how You must be suffering today. None of these people should have to die.* She wondered if prayers could horrify God, people moaning for deliverance when answers were all around them as they died.

An idea wedged itself in, in between her prayers and worries. Mariskka jumped and ran across the street, irritated it had not occurred to her before. A baker had foods and seasonings.

Inside his shop, she pulled out woven baskets, tossing supplies on the floor, jerking open leather satchels to see what they contained. Useless. Along the wall, dark glass bottles gave her hope. She yanked the cork free on each until her nose recoiled at the smell of one. Perfect. Lazarro had run out of his own.

Running back across the street, she was careful to cradle the bottle close into her abdomen so she wouldn't lose a drop. She stopped at the edge of the makeshift hospital, ripping off a section of her robe and dousing it in the vinegar.

Looking to find one victim more alive than the rest, she picked her way to the woman's side and pressed the vinegar against the hot swellings. A few had already begun to crack. The woman moaned, staring at Mariskka in confusion. Mariskka clucked her teeth at the woman to be quiet. Mariskka coated each wound in the strong fermented vinegar, moving on, down rows of the dead and dying, searching for someone who might be saved. She finished her walk of the rows with more than half the bottle still left.

Mariskka wanted to cry. She wanted to sink to her knees and let this awful stinging apple that was lodged in her throat out. She had one thing that could help. It could not cure, but it could help. And there was no one left who could use it. Death was winning.

Mariskka saw a young girl, with wide eyes and smooth hair, staring at the victims, her chin trembling. Mariskka stood and walked to her. The girl saw her coming but did not move. Her little chin just bobbed, and the corners of her mouth turned down.

Mariskka clucked at her, taking her little hand and pressing it to her own chest. *Feel my heart,* Mariskka thought. She placed her other hand over the girl's heaving chest, willing her to slow her rapid breathing. Every time the girl turned to look at the dying, Mariskka clucked at her to get her attention, to help her breathe, to calm her heart.

This is the fight, Mariskka said to her in her mind. *Do not give in.*

Dark spirits were circling the edges of the square, some swooping in and taking a bite as someone lay in pain, causing the victim to cry out. The spirits watched Mariskka with this girl. She saw their faces. They wanted this girl more than the others.

Mariskka hugged the girl to her side and spat in their direction. She saw a flash of iron teeth as a freezing wind knocked her off balance, but they did not come closer. She had a feeling she knew them. How many times had they walked the halls of her hospice? How many times had they followed her into a room?

They had been bold back then, when she read machines instead of faces.

Her arms were still around the girl, who had stopped shaking. Mariskka could feel the girl leaning into her embrace, allowing Mariskka's warmth to revive her, allowing Mariskka's steady heart to slow her own down. Mariskka bent her head and kissed the girl on top of her hair. When Mariskka looked up, the spirits had moved on to find a new victim.

The girl pushed against Mariskka and ran. Mariskka picked up the edge of her robe, trying to follow the girl through the rows of the dead and dying, which extended now in all directions. A cart was at the edge of the lane, and men were accepting gold from Lazarro. They were here for the bodies. Mariskka yelled at them, and they turned in her direction.

They were picking up anyone who did not move, throwing them into the cart. Mariskka wanted to check vitals. Not everyone who was still was dead.

She lost sight of the girl.

Chapter Sixteen

Gio loved that light. Every time they cracked the door open, the light illuminated the steps all the way down to her. She wanted to catch it, to reach up her arms and pull it in. Gio stayed at the bottom of the steps. Any closer, and they would have kicked her back down.

She had taken light for granted.

Her candle still had tallow left to burn. It could last for hours, but it was not light. It was not the sun. People moaned in the darkness all around her. It did not frighten her anymore. The healthy were dying just like the ones who stumbled down here already ill. Panthea had sentenced them all to death, taking their money and sending them to see her here. She had probably assumed they would leave once they got their medicine. Panthea did not understand how fast the plague could kill. Some fell dead before they reached the stairs to return.

Gio had no marks upon her. Yet. She marveled at that.

She was trying to piece together what herbs she had, trying to make sense of what could ease suffering. When the people had first come down here to her, they had not waited for her help. They had ransacked her herbs, drinking or mashing or burning whatever they thought looked potent, some stuffing it in their pockets, thinking they would escape, even as the black bubbles began to appear.

She was not used to seeing all her work scattered, poured out at her feet. She tried to line them up, to make order from them. Perhaps if there was order, there would be understanding. She checked the pockets of the dead to retrieve a few herbs.

The fools above had forgotten her mortar and pestle. Some of the harder stones and herbs were useless. What did they think she could do with nutmeg in its shell? She tried to bite it. Useless to her.

She made some sense out of the dried herbs. Florals and peppers went together. Mustards were laid to one side. Gio tore her robe in uneven strips along the bottom. It was filthy, spotted with blood and cow dung from the festival streets. Gathering the chamomile and lemon balm in one hand, she twisted a strip of robe around it, tying it off. She did this until her floral herbs were gone, then she laid the mustard between strips of her robe and tied those into bundles with the mustard hidden inside. She did the same with the peppercorns, but then she smashed those underfoot. The smell was strong even down here, where she was overpowered by mould and damp earth.

Gio picked a dying torch up off its bracket and felt her way along the walls, keeping her eyes down. There they were.

She plucked the mushrooms up and stuffed them down her bosom, careful to get every one she could find, no matter how dead it looked. Any power left in it was power she needed.

These she brought back to the other herbs and laid them out

with her other medicines, in groups of three. *God bless my work,* she thought. *Having one thing you must do—now that is salvation when the world falls apart.*

She cocked her head at a sound. She listened, trying to tell which angle it came from. She moved in that direction, keeping her feet quiet, listening, not even bothering with a light.

Lazarro.

She had to see him. She had to warn him. This plague was stirring violence in meek hearts. It was not safe for him, a gentle man of the cloth, to be out among them. He had to return to his church and pray. She looked at her piles and bundles of wilted herbs and mushrooms. In the firelight of her home, surrounded by her paintings and amulets, their magic was real enough to cure some. But here, alone in the darkness with the dying, Gio felt ashamed that she had asked so much of these little greens. What use were they for the real diseases of men?

She pressed her ear to the cold stone, but it made his voice no clearer. *Oh, God,* she prayed, *do not let him leave!*

She ran to the top of the stairs and pounded. "Do not send him down!" she shouted. "I will sell nothing to him!"

"Get away from the door if you don't want a broken back," someone replied.

"He is a man of God," she said. "You'll bring a curse on yourself for this. Send him away!"

She heard the stutter and grind of wood on wood, the dry wood door being forced open in little pushes. Gio stepped back and moved down several steps, knowing it was better to keep her distance when this door opened.

The light was too strong for Gio. She shielded her eyes and turned her face away, dizzy from the intense blast of sunlight.

"Gio."

His voice was manna.

"Lazarro?" she answered.

She could hear him sit down on the steps. The guard above him closed the door only enough to let him listen in without giving them room to escape.

"I heard you were here," he said. "Selling your herbs."

"You cannot believe I would do this. I have given away my medicines for years. I would—"

"Hush," Lazarro silenced her. "I have come for these medicines, Gio, not talk of the past."

Gio's eyes were comfortable again in the half-light. She looked at him, her hands open and raised, as if she were trying to explain his answer to herself.

"What is this?" she asked.

"Give me everything you have. I have made my terms with Panthea," he said, flicking his fingers at her, motioning for her to move down, out of his way. He wanted to go down into the darkness at their feet.

"No!" Gio moved to the center of her step. "The sick and dead are there. You are not safe. And I will not let you buy. You do not believe in that kind of healing, Lazarro. You should not be doing this. You should be praying!"

"Get out of my way," he said.

"No! You cannot have them! It is a sin for you!" she said.

"Then I will take them."

Lazarro grabbed her by the shoulder and pushed her aside, making her scream and push back, trying to catch him by the collar as he ran down the steps.

She could hear the guard above laughing.

At the bottom of the steps was darkness. On the corner columns were the torches, but they were not equal to this void. Some below must have recognized his voice. They were calling out in strangled sounds for water, or prayer.

"Lazarro?" She could not see him. "Lazarro, what are you doing? Come back up here!"

Her hands were shaking as she forced her legs to move into the darkness below. Wherever she strained to see him, he was not. The cellar had swallowed him alive.

Taking a torch off its bracket, she was careful to tip it first so a little tallow would empty out of the well around the wick. Being burned by hot fat was a burn more painful than any other.

She moved back up to the steps, holding the light in front of her, trying to stare around it. She saw his shoes at the bottom of the stairs; his body was lying at an angle into the darkness.

"Lazarro! What is happening?"

She ran down to him, thinking he had been hurt as he grabbed for the herbs. The dying were not always weak.

Lazarro was sweating in great beads all along his forehead and upper lips. His eyes looked weak, retiring into black sockets, his handsome face puddling under them, swollen from tears and work. She had not really looked at him when he came in; the light had blinded her.

"Have you anything to drink?" he asked.

"Only some bad wine they offered me," she replied.

"No wine could be bad at this moment," he said.

She fetched the green glass bottle and poured a little into a leather cup for him.

"You did not come to buy herbs from me, did you?" she said.

He licked his lips and raised his hands to his neck, watching her as he loosened his robes, pulling them down to reveal his chest.

Gio couldn't hold her head up; the dizziness made her start to fall forward.

Lazarro caught her, pushing her back.

"No," she said. "No. No. Why would you come to me for this?"

"My prayers do not work. I have failed them all," he said. "And now I must die too."

Gio pressed her fingertips on the ruthless black blisters claiming his chest. Most of them were clustered near his armpits.

"Lazarro," she whispered. His name was the only word she could bear. "Lazarro."

He picked up her hand and pushed it away. "You mustn't touch me, Gio. I am damned."

"No, Lazarro. This is not God's work."

"God sent plague on His people when they displeased Him." His voice was the voice of an old man with white hair.

"I cannot argue with what you say. But this is not God's work," she pleaded.

He smiled. She knew that look from so many years ago. He was indulging her.

"No, Lazarro, I have seen God's work. I have seen sunrises from the volcano's edge, sunrises no one in the village was awake to see. No one saw it, Lazarro. But still He ringed the sky through with brilliant colours. I have seen His work in the village, too. I have seen babies open their mouths and wail, thrashing in the wonder of a new world. I have seen puppies born to the thinnest of mothers, doomed to die, but then our villagers drop scraps for the dog and croon to it as it feeds in great, frantic rushes. I have seen the puppies pressed up against her for warmth and milk, and her considering the villagers with wonder and suspicion. It is all strange, this is all beyond our understanding, but this disease, it is not God's work. God's work is to get as close as we will let Him, and He feeds us. That is all God's work."

Lazarro closed his eyes and took a long breath. "I did not come for Mass, though you give it well." He laid a hand on her leg and smiled.

"Why did you come? There is no peace between us."

"I came to ask forgiveness. I pledged myself to you once. When I heard you had betrayed me, I was filled with anger and fear. I could do nothing to rescue you from your sins. That is what I told myself. You were lost, beyond my help as a man. It was my excuse."

"Lazarro, there are things I did not tell you. I wanted to, but I was afraid."

"I should have been a man you could tell those things to. I was pledged to you. I gave you my word. It was wrong of me to run. All these years, I hated you for scorning the Church. Didn't you understand that? If you had only come into the Church, I could have heard your secrets and given absolution. I could have given you everything as a priest that I could not as a man."

She lifted his hand and pressed it to her lips. "Forgive me," she said, and added a soft word. "Father."

His eyes filled with tears. "*Ostebde nobis, Domine, misericordiam tuam.*"

Gio nodded. *Yes, Lord, show us mercy.*

"*Et salutare tuum da nobis,*" she said to him. *Grant us your salvation.*

"*Domine, exaudi orationem meam,*" he finished.

"He will," Gio said. "He will. The Lord will hear our prayers."

Lazarro looked broken.

Gio said it again, louder, trying to force the words into his heart. "The Lord will hear our prayers!"

The cellar door opened. "You've had enough time, Lazarro! Come up."

Gio wanted to run up there, taking the steps twelve at a time, beating this fool about the head until he begged for mercy. Lazarro caught her by the arm and shook his head, motioning for her to stay.

"I am coming," he called up. "She had not so many cures as you promised, Panthea."

"She has enough for the village." It was Panthea's voice. Gio was surprised she would come near the cellar. She must have felt safe if Lazarro was there, as if God would not let a priest die.

Lazarro stood, a grimace passing over his face, keeping a hand pressing on his back as he bent. He took the bundles she pointed to. "I am coming, Panthea."

"And you will sign the papers," she called. "If you want out with my medicines."

"I will," he answered.

Panthea did not sound afraid, Gio thought. Panthea did not

know that Lazarro had the swellings, the tokens of this death, growing beneath his robes. Lazarro had brought death to her, and she did
not know.

He was walking to the bottom of the stairs, where Gio sat out of
view. Turning his back to the light, he reached a hand for her.

"What have you done, Lazarro? What are these papers?"

"These papers opened the door to you. They bought me peace,
to see you before I die. They bought medicines to try in the village.
All Panthea asked for was wealth, the wealth that dying men had
entrusted to me for safekeeping. It doesn't matter, Gio. Most have
no heirs alive now."

Gio gathered all the herbs bundled together, pushing them to him.
She was pushing him away as she did it, afraid she might grab him and
not be able to let go.

She wanted to press her face into his chest and remember those
days once more. How she longed to return, just to taste for one moment
those days, to shake off everything she knew now. The sack around
his belt was full to overflowing. She began to wrap her arms around his
waist, raising her face to kiss him on the cheek before he left.

He put a hand between them and held her off. "You must not,
Gio."

Her throat burned. She tried to swallow the pain back down, but
she couldn't. "If I had known that day, if I had known what would
come …" she said. She could not look at him. "It was the last kiss."

He lifted her face to see him. "No. It was our first, Gio, not our
last. If God has mercy, I will see you again."

"I wasted my years, didn't I? There is so much unsaid. Our story
is unfinished."

"When you finish a painting, do you say you are done?" he asked.

She frowned. Why did he stop her from confessing her regrets, and talk instead of painting?

"Yes, I say I am done."

"But do you mean it?" he asked.

She thought about the question for a moment. "No," she replied. "Nothing seems finished. There is always something more it waits for."

"I go to that place you wait for. God will finish all things for us: our unwritten words, our paintings, our half-lived lives."

She wasn't sure if she believed him, but he needed to hear those words. It hurt to talk. Her eyes were burning as badly as her throat. She dug her fingernails into her palms to be able to say those words.

"He will begin a new story," he said, and left.

The deepest blue sky soothed Panthea. The world was unchanged after all. Night was a relief to her, a predictable event that did not fail. Panthea ran her hand over the papers spread out on her father's table in the study. The room had been cleaned and put into order by one of the servants. She did not know which one.

The papers were thick and uneven. In days past, the paper from Amalfi had not been perfected. These deeds had been written long ago, some perhaps before the time of her father. All had a new seal, the seal her father had created for Lazarro and the church.

Panthea pushed her fingernail under one, cracking the wax, peeling it off the paper. It tore the paper, lifting sections of it away as Panthea picked at the seal. She looked round the room, hoping to find something better than her nails for this work. There was a stack of papers to get through before sunrise.

Her candle blew to one side and Panthea checked the window. It would be a cool night ahead. A wolf bayed in the darkness, his call making her cold. She was not the monster Lazarro and Armando must think her to be. She felt terror and fear, like them. She was not blind to suffering. A wolf in the village meant blood was in the streets. A prayer came to her lips for those people still out there. If they had no one as wise as herself to protect them, they would not last the night.

But Panthea did not say the words of the prayer. She turned back to look upon the papers from Lazarro. He had traded all these papers for the cures to save the village. As the priest, he had witnessed the wills, taking many of them in the name of the Church. He would see to it that estates were settled fairly. He had collected papers and deeds from almost every family in the village. The plague moved too fast for the lawyers to keep up with it. Most just turned their property over to Lazarro. If they died, they trusted him to do what was right with their property and their heirs.

In exchange for these deeds, Panthea had let Lazarro take everything Gio had. No one below had need of them.

She had what was of true worth, what would outlast this plague. If God did not answer Lazarro's prayers, herbs were worthless anyway. The people would die. Only one thing would survive this plague, only one thing she would cling to.

Wealth.

She set back to work ripping free the seals.

God was silent. God did not act. He could have stopped her if this was wrong. It wasn't wrong. It was shrewd.

She owned it all now. Every home in the village could be hers by morning, every business, every pasture. They were dying out there. Panthea tore away another seal and swept the scrapings onto the floor. She would begin again now, affixing to each the seal of the house of Dario.

It would be a long, profitable night.

Chapter Seventeen

Mariskka woke and wiped her mouth. She had drifted off without meaning to. Strange, she thought, that her body still had its own rhythms and desires. She did not want to sleep, or eat. She did not even want to think. All that mattered to her was the work.

Mariskka stretched. Everything hurt and was hard to move; she was stiff with exhaustion. Her back felt like it was made of hot twisting needles. Her eyes were dry and painful. She couldn't remember if she had taken her contacts out before she had slept that last night, before the Scribe swept her away. Chances were, they were glued against her corneas now. Even if she tried taking them out for some relief, it would only cause more alarm among these people.

The morning looked different. She could see dim white outlines moving alongside her. They looked like the white misty phantoms she had seen in badly done late-night ghost movies, except that these looked more real the longer she stared. They were made of something like breath against a window on a winter morning. She liked it, liked the way they changed shape, their edges evaporating and returning as another part of the spirit. Mariskka suspected these were another class of angels. Sometimes she heard footsteps but never saw a form. The steps were marked not by the sound of a shoe, but by the shifting of gravel crunching together, as though someone extremely heavy walked over the stones. Mariskka knew the sound of shoes; padding the hospice halls at midnight had sharpened her skill. She knew a doctor from a janitor, a young lift-team kid from a bereaved husband. These steps were a man's. A man of impressive size, and she guessed he wore soft shoes.

She couldn't see the man, but some of the dying could. They would turn and look at her with their eyebrows raised, as if to ask if she saw him too. Mariskka could only smile and nod. He was real to them. That was enough.

Mariskka's body was falling apart, breaking under the strain. Her bones were grinding against each other in their sockets, her eyes burned, her lips were cracked, and her tongue was thick and dry. She was aware of all this, but she didn't feel it, not in her heart. In her heart she was weightless and free.

Mariskka had never been much in favor of joy; not after she had known grief. But now she felt joy, the real stuff, not the cheap holiday plastic imitation, and was surprised to find it was fierce, defiant, and sweet. It kept her on her feet when her bones were in agony. It kept her serving the dying, wiping brows, hushing men who were humiliated, losing control of their bodies before her, lying there with nothing to do except die. She felt the joy pushing her to nod briefly at pain and keep moving. She would comfort and nurse and pray right until the moment death claimed them. She would not forfeit even one minute of life to it.

Joy was stronger than fear. It pushed her on. Everyone knew fear, sinners and saints alike. Not everyone knew joy.

A boy, no more than seventeen, she guessed, but probably already married, was trying to motion for help. She didn't see the priest anywhere, so she knelt at the young man's side. He pointed to the church. He wants to make confession, she realized. He wants the Last Unction. He knows his time is short.

She pressed her hands together as if praying and then laid them on his chest, nodding. Lazarro would never be back in time. The boy would be dead in minutes.

He turned his face away from her.

Mariskka saw the bitter spirits moving between the rows, coming right for this boy, iron fingernails scraping the air in anticipation. *This isn't right,* Mariskka thought. *They can't come for a believer. Death can have the body only after he's gone.*

She couldn't speak his language. His face was still turned away from her, facing the spirits. He couldn't see them.

Mariskka panicked. She craned her head in every direction, looking for someone who could help her, someone who could pray with him. He was dying with something awful inside, something that called the bitter ones to him. He was not a believer. There was no Blood.

No one was near to help.

Mariskka grabbed the boy's face, jerking his neck, making it pop, wanting him to focus on her and not see what was moving in. "Help me!" she screamed. "Someone help me!"

The boy flinched and tried to pull away from the awful sounds of Mariskka's voice. She knew what she sounded like. She had done a rotation in the state wards. She sounded like a woman born with no tongue, a woman whose mind was pocked and ruined on the CT scans.

The spirits were leaning over the boy, running leather tongues over their iron teeth. Something grey dripped down onto the boy's face and rolled into his eyes.

She watched as his pupils grew wide and he turned his face upward, seeing the spirits for the first time. He opened his mouth to scream and the spirits shrieked, rushing down toward the opening.

Lightning knocked her off balance. Mariskka fell forward onto the boy, cutting her palms against the stones beneath him as she tried to catch herself. She pushed up, seeing more strikes across the sky, hearing the terrible, rushing growl bursting above her from that first blow of lightning.

The spirits hovered just over his mouth, a steaming hiss coming from the blackness beyond them.

"Oh, God," she prayed. "If he does not know You, show Yourself. Give him another chance."

I am not willing that any should perish.

Mariskka heard the words and turned her head to see who had spoken them.

Do not look upon Me, Mariskka.

She felt a gentle hand push her face to look forward.

The boy was standing beside his own body, looking at the corpse. He stared next at Mariskka, shaking his head.

"*Thank you,*" he said to her. "*You fought for me. You fought.*"

The boy then extended a hand to someone standing behind Mariskka.

"*I am sorry,*" he said. "*Receive me now.*"

The boy's body released a breath and the spirits plunged in after it, but the life was gone. The shrieks made Mariskka's ears bleed. She pressed her hands against them. The back of her hands, exposed so close to the words, burned.

When she removed her hands, there was a fuzzy bubbling in her ears. Mariskka swallowed to make her ears pop. It didn't help. This strange bubbling was all she could hear, although she looked around and saw people talking or crying, moving and reaching for her.

She was deaf.

The spirits had retreated again to the outer edges of the patients. One grinned at her, snapping its teeth. She couldn't hear it. The spirits moved in a line, swaying like seaweed in dirty shallow water. The grinning one covered its ears. One covered its eyes. One covered its mouth.

Mariskka got it. She spat back, "You got it backward. 'See no evil, hear no evil, speak no evil.' The eyes come first." She had spoken out loud. Somehow they would know her language. They would understand.

The second spirit held up one finger and spoke back. "No, the eyes come next."

Gio was numb, even hours later. She could not guess how much time had passed since she had said good-bye to Lazarro. Her heart had stopped in that moment, like a church bell caught in its arc. She did not know how to measure time in this new way, when her heart was stopped.

Lazarro would probably be dead by now. He'd had only hours when he left her. Gio thought these hours had passed. She wondered if even a whole day had come and gone. She couldn't be sure. The cellar gave so little light, and the servants were not regular in bringing food or fresh torches. There were no more sounds from the darkness around her.

Gio did not know herself. She kept looking for some familiar sign or feeling, something to remind her how to step back into her old skin, how to remember who she was. Nothing came to her.

A light pierced her eyes, making them water and sting. Gio brought her hands to her face, turning away.

Strong hands came around her body, cradling her like a child and lifting her up. She recognized his strong, blood-soaked smell as he carried her up the stairs and into the morning light.

The morning sun made the stones glitter along the window. Panthea raised her head, smiling. She had fallen asleep at her work. It had been good for her. She felt stronger. Every sunrise that passed would give her relief.

She pulled aside the curtain at the window and looked down. A breeze was stirring the roses below. She was surprised how many blooms still opened, even this late in the fall. Her garden was not ready for winter. Some years it seemed to take the garden by surprise, making the blooms drop overnight, and some years, like this one, her garden gave the coming days no thought. The roses drank the dew and opened to the sun.

Panthea felt a stirring in her belly. Yes, she was hungry. This was a good sign, she thought. And she was thirsty. It was time to live. There was time to live. *This is what my garden is telling me*, she thought. *Eat, drink, and grow strong.*

She dropped the curtain back into place and turned, inhaling for a sigh.

"Good morning," Damiano said.

He sat in her father's chair, his dark hair combed into place, his beard groomed. The serpent cane rested under his palm, the emerald eyes dead and still. Damiano wore wedding garments of dark green velvet with gold embroidery.

"Did you think today would not come?" he asked. Panthea stood still. Her eyes darted to the door behind him, and into the hall. She listened for a noise, any noise.

"They have all fled, my darling," he said. "Undo your gown."

She was lost, that feeling when she played a song in her head and forgot the next verse. She was lost between notes, falling, grasping for a hold to begin again.

"What?" she asked. "Undo my what?"

Damiano rose and walked behind her, his cold hands touching her collarbones as he slipped his fingers under the neck of her robe. "They are all gone, Panthea. They fled in the night. Look upon yourself."

His breath crawled over her skin. She bent her head and looked down. Her gown was stained with black, wet fluids, her body growing thick, dark bubbles.

"No," she said. "No, I was careful."

"In time, no one will remember," he said. "They will think of these days and talk of numbers, of masses, of death as a general accident that befell all. But how perfect, how precise, was the war."

"Is it over then?" Panthea asked. "The plague?"

"The time of the angels is over. Never again will men believe in unseen goodness. The Age of Fear has begun."

"You are finished here then?" She wanted his breath off her neck. She could feel it moistening her hair, making it stick against her skin. Panthea wanted to reach a hand up and sweep those slick wet hairs off her neck.

"I was finished long ago," Damiano replied. "But I am not done."

She waited. He would say more. She knew he would.

His hands tightened on her neck, as if displeased she did not reply.

"I forget how you love to tease," he said in her ear.

She jerked her elbow back, into his ribs with all her strength, and lunged toward the door. Grabbing it with both hands, she flung it open and ran to the stairs, taking them two at a time, lifting her robe so she would not fall in the flight. On the bottom step she released the gown and looked to the entrance leading to the main gate. The plague was out there; she could see newly dead bodies steaming in the morning light. Her servants had tried to flee but had not made it to the gates.

She felt the breath on her neck, his hands going around her waist, pulling her back up the stairs.

"No!" she screamed.

Damiano laughed and put an arm under her knees, twisting her
so she was cradled in his arms. "I like that," he said.

"Let me go!" she cried.

He moved up the stairs with her. She could not feel his feet
landing on the steps or a heart beating beneath his robe.

"My bride," he said, looking at the bruised swellings still growing, not splitting open yet. "Come away with me."

Chapter Eighteen

Mariskka brought a cool rag to the girl for her fever. She shook her little head, giving it back, motioning for someone else to have it.

"Do not stop fighting!" Mariskka said.

The girl stroked her dying mother's face and shook her head. Her mother could not open her eyes or move. The girl did not leave her mother's side, though Mariskka saw the swellings on the girl's neck, the fever making her sweat.

She is fighting, Mariskka thought. *She is fighting for one last moment of kindness to pass between them, one more sign of love.*

"*Love is stronger than death.*" Mariskka remembered that Bible verse from a sermon so long ago in that other world. Odd those words would follow her here when nothing else could. "*Love is stronger than death.*"

Mariskka wiped the back of her hand across her forehead to clear it of the sweat and grime and flecks of blood that kept finding their way into her hair and onto her face. She examined the back of her hand, then looked up.

Mariskka's own mother stood before her. *"Love is stronger than death,"* her mother said.

Mariskka nodded in agreement. She was not shocked to see her mother. It all felt right, this field of the dying, and an apparition she could name. *It all felt right,* Mariskka thought, *to die this way, so far from home.*

"I am dying, aren't I?" she said to her mother.

From the corner of her eye, she saw Lazarro stumbling toward her, his arms outstretched, lips moving. She could not hear him.

Her eyes began to fail her, making the world break apart in pixels of grey and black. She was losing her vision. *It's a shame,* she thought. *I wanted to see my mother.*

The world went black.

"I have no more cures," Gio told Del Grasso. "You have wasted your strength on me."

He took the cup of fresh water from her. It looked like a thimble in his hands. He did not speak.

"How is it no one stopped you from entering the castle?" she asked. "And does Lazarro live?"

"Of Lazarro, I do not know. Death came for everyone above in the castle," he said.

He opened his bag and took a piece of dried beef, tearing it with his teeth into a smaller strip, handing it to her. She refused the dried meat. She did not think she could swallow it. He ate what he had offered her, then began to walk back toward the village.

"You do not flee?" she asked.

He did not reply.

"You are not afraid of death?" she asked.

She wished she had spent more time in the company of this man. His eyes spoke languages she did not know. She could not read what was in them.

He looked down at his hands, marked with scars from knives that slipped, razors that slashed across his skin every day. "No," he answered.

She looked back at the manor.

Del Grasso watched her. He answered her before she asked. "She is dying. I heard her voice," he told her. He began walking away, back toward the village.

"You were not loved by any of them," she called after him. It sounded like an argument.

He did not stop.

"You shouldn't do these things," she said. "You were not loved."

She looked up at the windows circling around the castle. She did not know which room to find. She could be in there for hours. If Lazarro was still alive, if he had returned to care for the victims in the village, he would certainly be dead when she finished here. She would have to give up that last moment with him if she did this.

Love is stronger than death. The thought rang through her mind.

Lazarro would want this.

Gio pressed her hands against the stones of the manor.

The stones were warm. They still felt the sun.

No guards were posted at the front of the gate, and she guessed no guards would be posted at the door.

She didn't know Panthea. She had known only Panthea's father, and that for a brief day. Nothing good had come from her bravery that day. Their manor had overshadowed the village all her life, sitting there like a big stone fist.

The heat from her hand spread, hurting her. There was no justice in this sacrifice.

If she had only truly known Lazarro's heart back then, her whole life would have been different. She would not even be here at this moment.

To that one brief thought, God replied, *If you had known My heart, your life would have been different. Trust Me with today.*

Panthea had seen fish caught in a tidepool before, in her young years. They darted from side to side while Panthea and her friends straddled the pool and laughed. The shadows made the fish flee, but there was only a wall no matter where they swam. Only a wave could save them and waves were predictable. No waves were due. Not for hours.

Panthea and her friends would lose interest soon enough and return to the water's edge, looking for shells and pinching crabs. Sometimes bits of ships would wash up, ships that had been lost at sea, somewhere between those terrible sisters, Charybdis and Scylla. Panthea would find polished wood or leather shoes, or sometimes even a ring. She loved those treasures. They were all hers. No one had given them to her. They did not smell of the village or her manor. They smelled of a new world. A cruel, beautiful world.

Panthea now breathed in small gasps, like those fish in shallow water. She did not waste her energy in trying to flee. She did not want to entertain him.

Damiano was at her side, stroking her hair as she lay on the bed, her chamber ready for her wedding night.

She had never kissed Armando.

Kissing Armando would have changed everything. But she had never been able to trust love. Panthea trusted herself. She did not trust Armando's love, her father's love, or Lazarro's loving God. She had trusted in love once. Those years ended in desolation. Her father had not saved her mother from dying, instead she died without saying good-bye to either of them, slipping away in disappointment. God remained unmoved. Trusting in love was a woman's mistake. Panthea vowed to never repeat it.

"It won't be long now," Damiano said. "Though some have lasted for three days, even four if they have much strength, you are doing very well. Death is working through your body with great speed."

"Just end it," Panthea whispered back. Her neck hurt too much to move it. She could only look up at the ceiling as she talked or strain to see him out of the corner of her eye.

"I have no power here," he said, pushing his face closer in so she could see him. She could see in his mouth rows and rows of teeth lining its roof, waiting to descend. They were ugly and sharp, like the spines of a fish. He craned his neck until he was nose-to-nose with her. She tried to hold her breath so she wouldn't smell him.

"The only power I ever needed, you gave me, darling. Though I waited through time and age for you, I never imagined the splendor He would give you on earth."

He stroked her face. "I will be sorry to see this gone. You really were quite beautiful."

Panthea heard heavy steps coming up the stairs and the cracking of the hinges as the chamber door was opened. Damiano spat in that direction.

Panthea tried to move, but the plague had weakened every muscle. She could only shift her back a finger's width and try to look.

Damiano's hand went to her neck. She could not even whisper.

Gio leaned over her. "You do not have to die this way," Gio said. "There is forgiveness for you."

Damiano leaned over Gio's shoulder.

Panthea tried to nod. The swellings on her neck made any touch, even from her own skin, agony. She felt her eyes stinging, but no tears came.

"You need wine," Gio said. Her face disappeared.

Damiano receded, moving back above them both, hanging there along the ceiling.

Gio's face came into her vision again, and Panthea felt Gio lift her head and pour a little wine into her mouth. Panthea tried to swallow. She felt some go down her throat, and some pour down her chin and neck. Both felt exquisite. Had she ever tasted wine like this? Had she ever truly known thirst?

Damiano was studying Gio. Panthea did not want another one to die for her.

Panthea opened her eyes as wide as she could, trying to signal her.

Great God, Panthea said, knowing no words were coming from her mouth. She could only hear herself speaking in her head. *I am lost. But she is not, is she? She came back. Only You would send her here. Open her eyes. Open her eyes and she will flee!*

Gio's face changed as Panthea's words were spent. Panthea watched as Gio's mouth opened, her eyes watering.

"Angels," she whispered. "Panthea, why are there so many angels?"

Gio's face changed again. Panthea could tell she felt something along her back, and Gio turned, in a slow, deliberate arc to look up at Damiano.

Gio did not scream as Panthea expected. Instead, Panthea felt Gio's skin turn cold and stiff, her fingers digging into Panthea, holding onto her.

"It's a Valkyrie," Gio said. "Why is it here? Something is already dead, or it could not come."

Gio looked down into Panthea's eyes. "What have you done, Panthea? Is there something dead in this room?"

Panthea nodded yes.

"Can you tell me what it is?" Gio asked. The angels were not moving. Everything in the room, even the dust floating in the air, froze.

It is me, Panthea whispered. She could feel blood in the back of her throat, the effort destroying the last bit of smooth flesh in her mouth.

"I don't have any herbs for this," Gio said. "I don't have any herbs. Panthea, I don't have any herbs! What do I do? I don't know what to do!"

Panthea narrowed her eyes, trying to get Gio's attention. She tried to lift a hand to cover Gio's for comfort. Gio's herbs were not needed.

Get out, Panthea thought. *God, if You have any mercy, get her out.*

Gio moved her shaking hands and placed them over Panthea's heart. "I don't know the words. I'm a woman. I was never taught."

Do not let her stay! Panthea screamed in her mind. *This punishment is mine.*

"Panthea," Gio said, sounding like a child reciting a poem she has no understanding of, "God is not willing you should perish. All is forgiven, Panthea. All is forgiven. You can go home. You have only to choose."

The words fell like arrows against stone. Those last words, Panthea thought, those came from Gio, not God. God could not mean that.

Panthea closed her eyes, and Damiano descended closer to the bed, like a spider letting out a line of webbing.

"Panthea, your heart is like flint. Stop it! Take this mercy offered! You are only a woman, after all! We are only women! We must take mercy however it is offered!"

At this, Panthea sat up with a snarl, not knowing where the power came from, except that it was somewhere deep beneath her stomach, something she had felt stabbing her all her days. She was only a woman. And that had not been enough. Not for her.

She threw Gio on the ground with a sharp whip of her arms.

Nothing God gave me was ever enough, Panthea said in her heart.

She fell back on the bed as Damiano spun down, hanging inches from her face, his cold skin making her frightened. This was not what she wanted. But she would not accept pitiful, cheap mercy. Not when it was offered by a medicine woman who had never known power. Not when it was offered by a God who asked for nothing in return.

"Stop this!" Gio screamed.

A flash of lightning splintered outside the window, making Panthea wince from the piercing blue light. Dark shapes began to pour in from between the stones, all gathering to Panthea's bed like purse strings being cinched tight around her.

Gio crawled on hands and knees to a corner of the room, shrinking her body into the space.

Damiano spread out his hands as if addressing a crowd. "My bride has spread a wedding feast, and we have all been invited!"

Panthea's mouth was forced open, and the dark shapes rushed in, taking her last breath, the last beat of her heart. Her eyes rolled up to look at Damiano as she died.

"Truly I tell you, my darling," he said, "tonight you will be with me in hell."

Chapter Nineteen

Gio was aware of an itch. Her scalp itched. It had been itching for an hour perhaps. She didn't really know. It bothered her, but only from a distance, as if she had not quite returned to her body but regarded it. To scratch it would mean she was back.

Gio wasn't sure she was ready to be back.

Panthea lay on the bed, her eyes open and jaw bent to one side. She had been dead for hours.

Gio felt the burning itch on her scalp. It demanded attention.

She closed her eyes and rested her head against the wall. From outside the window, she heard the wind rustling the leaves of the trees. It carried the scent of a fir tree into the room. Gio liked firs. They were always green, in constant agreement with the world and each other. The firs of Sicily did not change, even when the volcano and the waters raged.

She reached up and scratched her scalp, immediately wishing she hadn't. She was back now. She had to move.

Her legs were stiff, and she was cautious as she rose, putting her weight on them. Lifting one leg, setting it down, lifting the other … this is what she focused on. The door seemed a long way off. A noise struck her as odd—a choking sniffling. Her cheeks felt wet, and Gio realized she was crying. *Odd,* she thought, *that my body would express emotion when I feel nothing. Nothing except the buzz of my leg muscles stirring awake and the air on my cheeks.*

She kept doing that, lifting one leg and setting it down, then lifting the other, until she was out of the manor, standing in the late afternoon sunlight. She should be shooing the last of the *fiume perse* away, back to their own homes, and making sure the Old Man had not eaten so much that there would be no dinner for her.

But the *fiume perse* had grown too wide, spilling its banks and swallowing the whole world. All were lost. And the Old Man was dead. What would she do now, with no one to heal?

She blessed her legs, her thick, full, strong legs, that were carrying her down the path, and then away, up into the difficult way. Her legs were taking her home, and she reached out to hold back the branches, keeping them from brushing or scratching her face. The wood and leaves felt so good in her hands. God had used a rare alchemy to make a tree. Man, he made from dust. Man was born to be trampled underfoot. But a tree: born to stretch and rise to the heavens, sinking its roots deep into the earth, drawing from it water and life. Trees were His language. He had sent trees as witnesses. Yet when He grew angry, He sent storms and lightning that swept clean all He had written with His heavy hand and began the page again.

How many of His stories have we missed? Gio thought, *running past these trees, never pausing to consider what they might tell of Him?*

Why did God need so many languages, so many words, to describe Himself? Everywhere she looked there were different trees, or flowers, dense crinkled moss, and the footprints of animals, who made His words their refuge.

I have only now begun to listen, she thought.

Gio felt the stillness of the world around her as she picked her way up, stepping over bare roots and smooth rocks, the sunlight coming in greater patches now.

Gio heard grunting and curses, and the dull echoes of blows. She moved quickly, jumping over the roots and rocks, ascending and running into the clearing ahead. Her home was just beyond her and she saw them, a mass of young men circling around Del Grasso, hitting and kicking, darting in and upon him. Del Grasso looked calm and steady. He was not giving them anything, not pleading or jerking away in fear. Gio knew this expression he wore on his face too well. It was the same steady look a big animal had as it was led into Del Grasso's butchering room. He was not afraid to die, but neither would he forgive and go in peace. His face was a smooth, unmoving accusation.

More men were streaming out of her house, their arms full.

One emerged, holding her painting of the adulteress standing before Jesus. He said something to the men hurting Del Grasso, and they laughed. Del Grasso looked and saw what was in the man's hand. He lunged through the men, grasping for the painting. The youths shouted, carrying her treasures off. They ran in the direction of the next town.

These boys would be richer than they had ever dared imagine by nightfall. Most would be dead by morning.

Gio ran to Del Grasso, who was on all fours, panting. Her hands were so small and insignificant on his big arms as she helped him to sit and wiped his brow. She would have to run for help. There was no way she could get him down the path into the village.

"How badly were you beaten?" she asked, keeping her voice soft and gentle, the way she spoke to children in pain.

Del Grasso smiled, then his mouth dropped back into a grimace. "They are weak and foolish. They did not hurt me with their fists."

Gio exhaled and pressed her face against his shoulder. His skin felt so good. She had been cold and alone for hours. He was warm.

He shifted his weight and looked at her. "It is over for us."

"The plague?"

"No, I do not mean that."

"What? What else is there?" Gio asked.

"Secrets. All has come into the light. We have seen all men for who they are."

"Do not give in, Del Grasso. Do not die. We must rebuild." Gio felt stupid saying that. There was nothing to rebuild. The houses all stood.

"No! You will not!" He grimaced again.

They must have landed a strong blow to his abdomen, she thought. He was in pain.

"You must never rebuild," he said. "You must begin something new."

"Why?" Gio asked, tears wrenching through her abdomen so hard she thought she was going to be sick. "Why did it happen? Why to us?"

"Make me one promise. With your life," he said. She could see him fading.

"Anything," she answered.

"Never ask that again," he said. "Only ask how. How, then, will you live?"

Gio saw a red, wet mark spreading across his belly. She ripped open his shirt and saw an ugly, ripped flap of skin, blood pouring out. They had stabbed him.

"That life is over, Gio. No time for why. Only how. Ask how."

He grabbed his belly, hunching over it with a deep exhale. He would die without making a sound, she realized.

Lifting his head to her face, she pressed her lips against his. He couldn't hold his weight up. His body pressed down on her, and she struggled to keep him sitting up.

"Del Grasso, I was wrong about you. We all were."

She pressed her lips against his forehead, cradling his head as his body slid down onto the ground.

He was dead.

She saw her painting in the dirt, the door to her home torn off its cheap hinges. Crocks lay overturned near its entrance. Ashes from the fire and from the burning bones were tracked out and back. Inside she could see nothing. *Truly nothing,* she thought. It was all destroyed, all her paintings gazed at by unclean men who cared nothing for them and tossed them at their feet. All her secrets were broken open and left in the dirt, covered in ash.

The fire had a red heart. She could see it burning under the destruction.

Del Grasso was slumped over in the sparse grass. His face was covered in dirt, the dust attracted to his sweaty forehead. There was another boy lying inside her home. She assumed he was dead. The Old Man's body had been dragged off. She could see his feet under some scrub brush not far away.

Movement in the brush did not surprise her. She knew the wolves favoured her house. People who were very weak as they left Gio sometimes didn't make it home. The wolves patiently waited.

Gio looked around, wondering where to begin. If there had been time, she would have gone into the village to see if any man was able to assist her, in God's name. But the wolves were already near, and she could not leave the bodies alone. The Church taught that the bodies must be given a sacred Christian burial, under the earth, or the souls would be punished.

Gio had to work fast. She had little strength to cut a trench for one man, no less two. The robber she would let rot. But the sun would fall in a few hours, and then the wolves would come, not caring if she beat them with sticks.

Gio needed fire.

She forced herself to look at her home, and the paintings made vulgar by rough hands that had tossed them out into the dirt. If she did this, there would be no going back. She exhaled, and prepared to burn them all.

She picked her way inside her home and found a hand trowel. It worked well for harvesting onions and breaking up hard clumps of earth that stood in her way when she needed a root. She glanced back outside at the bodies and back at the trowel. It would be a long night. She would have to build the fire high. It had to hold.

She tossed the trowel out of the door and moved to the shelves that once held her herbs. The herbs were gone, most of them in Panthea's cellar. Gio tore at the shelves, and they popped away from the plaster, their thin nails not strong.

She tossed the wood outside.

In the corner were more paintings, the stories of her lonely nights and the things she had witnessed on the mountain. These paintings were what she thought she had learned from her life, the words she had thought God had once spoken over her. On her worst nights, these were all that had kept her alive.

She tossed them in groups of two and three onto the fire, unwilling to study them any longer. The past was gone. It was not important that she leave a record of it. All that mattered now was tomorrow. Everyone in Sicily had a past. She did not know of many who would have a tomorrow. She would keep only the blank papers, the ones that had not yet been written. Those she would save for another—another woman, perhaps, who would take up the story after Gio died.

Gio continued through her home, tossing out blankets and her thick wool robe, her chair and the straw from her mattress. When she finished and came out to stand in the afternoon sun, there was more outside her house than in it. If there was any chance the stones would burn, she would have used them, too.

Gio stooped over, picking up the refuse and placing it around her. Over and over she bent, lifting and carrying and putting the debris down in place, until she had a wide circle with both of the bodies in its center.

Near the body of the robber was her original fire, the one that had kept food warm for the Old Man and bones drying for the painters, and stones heated for her water in the winter. That fire still burned, but only just a little. Gio picked at the upper branches and rocks the robbers had placed over it, one last indignity before they fled. It should have gone out, but it hadn't ... not fully. Gio didn't know if that might ever count as a miracle. There was no one to witness it except her, and miracles were not performed for women like her. She thought of her last painting, buried in the pile. Jesus had forgiven the sinful woman. He had stopped justice from demanding her life. Was that not a miracle, at least to her? Maybe God was the miracle. To lost women, His gentle disposition was nothing less.

Gio found her leather glove and reached into the red fire, pulling out a branch, touching it to the top of the pile, waiting for it to catch. The fire did not catch. Gio heard another noise from the brush beyond her home. This had to catch. Again, she pressed it to the debris of the circle. This time a little smoke rose, but she could not see where a flame was started. She was starting to panic. She didn't have patience or faith at this moment. The plague had left her stripped and exhausted, too weak to bear a small setback.

She crouched down, still holding the branch to the debris, and then got down onto her knees, stretching out, still pressing the branch into the circle. Gio was lying down then, the branch near her face. Its heat and glow made her face burn.

With a soft exhale, Gio blew into the fire. Its red embers grew white, and she repeated this. She breathed into the debris that had been her life, willing it to burn with the touch of her breath. It was an intimate good-bye.

✤

Beautiful.

It was a word she once coveted, hoping someone would use it when describing her. A small word, really. It fell short in describing what angels looked like. Mariskka watched them walking in the streets, leading children from empty houses, carrying old women who gazed up at them like infants. Peace wrapped around her when one came near. Life was infinitely more dangerous, and more beautiful, than she had ever imagined.

They are not of this world, she thought.

Mbube stood beside her. "Yes, yes. They are."

"I never knew," Mariskka said.

"You never look," Mbube replied. "Not with your heart. Look now. See."

Mariskka could see again, but she saw nothing the same way. The streets were illuminated, though it was dark, late into the night. She could see thousands of them in every direction. Only when she squinted did she see the dark spirits. There were few of them now, and they did not like the light. They tried snapping their teeth at Mariskka. A man of light walking by saw this and tweaked the spirit on the nose, making Mariskka laugh. The dark thing spread its wings until it rose above them all. But it did not scare her. Not when she was surrounded by these men of light.

"There are so many of them," Mariskka murmured.

"Yes," Mbube said. "Much goodness in this world."

Mbube picked her up in his arms. He felt good, like a big pillow that Mariskka could curl onto and be safe. She was glad it was her time to die.

"Thank you, Mbube," she said. "Thank you for what I became here. Thank you for fighting for me. I'm ready."

"No die, not today," Mbube said. He was carrying her inside the church, not away into the night like the others.

Mariskka tried to push against him and sit up. "What do you mean? I don't want to go back now!"

"You go back. Not my idea," Mbube said.

"I don't want that life anymore. I don't want the money, or the fame, or even that stupid shower! I have belonged in only one place my whole life, and it was here. I was a real nurse here."

"You save no one," Mbube said.

"I was not brought here to save anyone except myself," she said, surprising herself. It was true, though. "I was brought here to fight."

"Did you?" Mbube asked. "Did you save self?"

"No. God did." Mariskka motioned to the people, some lost, some in pain and dying, some darting between houses and looting.

"When I reached out to heal them, healing came to me, too. I had to open my arms before I could open my heart."

"You talk much," he said.

"I understand now, Mbube. I couldn't accept grace because I refused to show it to anyone else," Mariskka said. "I'm ready to die."

"You not ready," Mbube said. They were inside the church now, the air feeling cold and dry, the candles at the altar brilliant in the darkness. Mbube laid her on the steps of the altar and took her hands in his.

"I don't want to go back, Mbube. I've seen too much here to be happy again in that other life. Just let me go."

Mbube let go of her hands and began to back away.

"There is no one for me there, nothing! I can't go back to nursing—I'm a celebrity. I can't go on as an author—I don't know how to write. I can barely fill out a check."

"God does not want you there for what you do, Mariskka. He want you there for what you are."

"Why? Why, Mbube? Why does it have to be me?"

"You do not have the language for those answers. I cannot give them."

"Why? What's going to happen, Mbube?"

The candles on the altar rose up, their light blinding her as Mbube became part of the darkness. The hard, cold stone steps under her back softened, becoming like down feathers. She saw the stones of the altar growing higher and then arcing back down, burying her in softness and light.

Gio was drowning in tears. The waters rose up from within, and she struggled for breath. Her breaths were shallow and cold. Her body shook, and she could not get warm.

She sat on the ground. Her hair was matting from the sweat running down her forehead and neck. She thought of running her fingers through the mats, to loosen and free them, but she had no energy.

She was sluggish and tired. The world looked so cold and distant. The green trees did not give her joy; the warm stones under her feet left her listless. This world was someone else's home. She did not know it.

The heaviness grew in her throat, making her head dip down unless she forced it up for breath. She had no appetite, no will to force food past the thick knot that slept there.

Gio had been sitting on the ground like this for two days, having lost it all: the people of the village she could not cure; the two men who helped her come home to the Church and herself ... Lazarro and Del Grasso; her pigments, her words, even her body. Her only victory had been burying Del Grasso and the Old Man. She had no feeling left in her limbs; every inch of her was pierced beyond mending, bled out by tears and grief. She was dizzy when she stood and tried to walk. She could not convince her legs to move as they once had. She could not make anything work. She did not think she belonged to this world. It did not seem to recognize her.

Gio had made it down the path to the village but couldn't force herself to move any closer. She sat on its outer edge, where she could see and be seen. She did not feel as alone, but she did not want to return there either. Lazarro would be dead by now, thrown in the back of the hay wagons that came through the streets at night, collecting the dead, carrying them away to a mass grave. She had forced herself to turn away from the sight.

He would be glad to know they all got a Christian burial, even if sometimes there was only a woman available who knew the right words.

This scandal would be forgotten, she knew. Women had stood at the bedside of the dying, saying the words only the holy men of God were authorized to use. They had been priests, willing to die to speak God's words to the weak and the lost.

When the women contracted the plague and died, as they knew they would, most had been content. They died quiet deaths. These women had seen a glimpse of the true Christ, here on earth. The Church that had denied them so much, kept them ignorant and poor, this same Church broke itself at the right moment, sacrificing custom and appearance, and embraced its women.

They had stayed, and prayed, and loved. They had fought.

If she lived on, she promised herself, she would tell this to the world: *Do not trust in yourself to gain your freedom from sin. Better to wait than regret.*

Gio thought of Del Grasso's words to her. If she asked "why?" she might never come down off this path. She might never return to the living. She should only ask "how." That was his dying wish.

"How, then, will I live?" she asked out loud. The only reply was a soft grinding noise in the village.

Gio saw a man wheeling an empty, stained cart along a lane. She admired him. He knew what to do. A chore, even a little chore, was a soothing comfort. To watch your limbs know what to do, to be taught by your body how to live again—that would be a comfort.

Gio wished she had a chore.

If she had words, she thought, she would dare to pray, even to pray alone, without a priest to make it pleasing to God. She would pray for a chore.

A hand rested on her head, stroking her hair. Gio looked up and saw Armando. He stroked her hair, but Gio did not think it was a chore. He was not trying to return to the living, as she was. He had seen death before, she knew. He had seen its face in a distant land. But still, he had returned to the village, to this life.

Armando knelt beside her in the dirt, brushing the hair away from her face. "Are you hungry?"

Gio shook her head no.

"Are you alone?" he asked.

"Yes," Gio said, whispering the word. She didn't want to hear it. That word was too big for her today. She would speak someday, but it was not today. Words needed time to come home, and hers were buried deep in the earth. They would need time to push through the soil and find her again.

He lifted her up, one arm around her waist, the other steadying her from sinking back into the dirt. "Night is coming," he said.

Chapter Twenty

Armando wrapped his arms around her waist, pulling her back to lean in to him. It was his nightly ritual. He loved running his hands through her long, soft hair after she brushed it. Inhaling the perfume that scented it—a present he had given her after their marriage—he pressed his face into her neck.

Gio let him love her and never pushed him away. She wondered if other women had this love. It was a revelation to her. All it required was a soft spirit.

Armando moved his hands from her hair and rested them on her belly. Gio laughed. The baby seemed to know his father's touch, because she always felt it kick at his flat, wide palms. She marveled at God's creative mercy, that a man such as Armando took such pleasure in her. He loved watching her become a woman of grace and mercy, the wife of Armando, the woman who turned no one away from her door hungry.

"I should check on the others," Gio said. "The candles burn low. Some still fear the night."

"The children are sleeping," Armando replied. "They had both Nero and Fidato out today, looking for apples and racing down the quiet lanes."

Gio sighed. "They need to be picking more from the crops, not playing. Winter will come soon."

"Ah, let them alone. Too long have these streets been without the sound of children's laughter. It is good to see them happy again. They lost much. Let me worry that we will be ready for winter."

"And the other villagers," Gio said. "They will need food. They look to you as their baron."

"Yes, all will be cared for, Gio. The house of Dario will not fail them again."

"We should change the name of this manor," Gio said.

With a satisfied groan, she pushed away the plate of pastries he had brought her. She ate far too many these days.

A wind came through her window, but it did not smell of the dead anymore.

This wind smelled of coming rain, and earth that would grow crops again for hungry mouths whose cries had shocked the survivors of the plague into labouring long hours in the fields.

Life would continue. It would not be stopped, not by the death of one, or of thousands. Not by the death of dreams or love. Life pushed past death and did not stop. Life would continue, and children would be hungry.

While their parents fretted and kept candles burning through the night for comfort, all the children in the house of Armando, the orphans, foundlings, and heirs, slept well and safe, resting in the arms of immortals.

❧

Amber-Marie groaned as the phone went to voice mail again. Mariskka was so typical of overnight-success authors: She thought everyone was her fan just because they promoted her books.

Fans didn't mind being kept waiting.

Amber-Marie did. Time was money.

Thankfully, at one overpriced dinner she had slipped her hand into Mariskka's bag and stolen her keys. Excusing herself for a phone call, Amber-Marie had handed the keys and a fifty-dollar bill to the waiter. He knew the drill. Before they finished dessert, Mariskka had her keys back and Amber-Marie had a secret, second set.

Not that Amber-Marie was the villain. She was protecting Mariskka from herself. New money, new fame, and new expectations had done many authors in. Her publisher had spent a fortune on Mariskka, totaling an amount that rivaled a smaller country's gross national product. Mariskka was a walking investment account. If she did well, her publishing team would have a nice retirement. Those same executives had hired Amber-Marie's independent public relations firm to guide Mariskka through this first year, keeping her safe and sane until she delivered book two. Amber-Marie didn't mind. It was good money, and Mariskka didn't know enough yet to be a real pain.

"Wait here, Jim," Amber-Marie said to the driver.

She took the elevator to Mariskka's floor.

She fished out her author keychain and moved the keys around until she found Mariskka's.

Mariskka's apartment smelled like a Girl Scout campout, filled with smoke and something toasting in the kitchen.

Smoke.

"Smoke!" Amber-Marie gasped. She ran from the foyer into the main room, which was separated by two massive marble columns.

Mariskka was lying facedown on the floor. Something smoldered red in the fireplace. Amber-Marie looked again. It was a manuscript, burning.

She'd save Mariskka later. Grabbing a fireplace poker, she tried to fish out what fragments she could. The poker was useless. She stuck her hand into the fire's edge and pulled them out, burning her fingertips and getting black soot all over her clothes.

"No!" Mariskka yelled, grabbing Amber-Marie from behind. "Let it burn!"

Amber-Marie fell back on top of Mariskka and pushed free. "What are you doing, Mariskka? Tell me that's not your new book!"

"New book?" Mariskka asked. "That's why He sent me back!"

Amber-Marie reached out to pat Mariskka on the shoulder with one hand. With her other, she slowly pulled out her cell phone. This was spectacular.

"Why don't you rest here a moment?" Amber-Marie said. "Let me fix you some hot chocolate, and we'll talk."

Mariskka looked up at her with unabashed adoration. "I'd love hot chocolate. They didn't have it back then."

Amber-Marie's mind worked especially hard when she was up to no good. She took the stairs in leaps and ran into Mariskka's bedroom.

"Gotcha," she whispered, grabbing all the pill containers she could find, even Mariskka's vitamins. Running back downstairs, she sprinkled pills all around Mariskka, then handed an empty container to her. Mariskka held it without question.

Amber-Marie held her cell phone up, snapping pictures. "Back in a jiffy with your hot chocolate," she told her.

"Stop!" Mariskka said.

Amber-Marie froze.

"I have to tell you something, Amber-Marie. A confession."

This isn't wrong, Amber-Marie told herself. *This is good business. Profit margins in the publishing business are getting smaller and smaller.*

Amber-Marie pressed "record" on her phone and waited.

"I didn't write my first book," Mariskka began. "I stole it from a dead patient. And her watch. I stole her Rolex watch. I should have been ministering to her, but I wanted her watch. I am very sorry for that now."

"Forget the watch. A patient at the hospice made your first novel up?" Amber-Marie asked.

"No. It wasn't a novel. It was more like a biography, I guess. An angel appeared to my patient Bridget on the night she died, because there was no Blood on her. There was no Blood, and she wasn't safe. So he showed her the past. She saw a woman named Rose, and it was her ancestor. Then she let Him save her, and then she died. But I was different. I lived the story. But I didn't know anyone. And I didn't die."

If Amber-Marie had had any pity at all, she would have turned her cell phone off and called 911.

She didn't.

Mariskka shoved a thick stack of odd, rough papers to Amber-Marie. Amber-Marie had never seen paper like this.

"It's from Amalfi, 1347," Mariskka said. "Take it, Amber-Marie. I shouldn't keep it. I'm not a writer!"

Amber-Marie took the papers without looking at them. "Everyone feels that way when they turn in a new manuscript, Mariskka. It's just nerves."

"No, it's the truth! Read what the Scribe wrote down. It explains everything," Mariskka said.

"Why don't you get cleaned up, Mariskka? I'll alert the studio we're running behind."

"I must look terrible," Mariskka said, putting her hands on her cheeks. "I haven't bathed in ages."

When Mariskka had climbed the stairs, groaning as if she were in pain with each step, Amber-Marie exhaled to keep the butterflies in her stomach from going wild. This was just too good.

She entered *67 and then a longer number.

"City desk, please," she said, and waited.

"Hi, I'd like to call in a tip," she said. "A huge story is about to break. What is it? Well, send a reporter and a photographer to the address I'm about to give you. A hint? Okay, imagine this headline: 'Best-Selling Author Goes Insane While Alone in Apartment, Finishing Sequel.'"

She hung up and gathered as many fragments of the papers as possible. They would be worth a chunk on eBay.

She hoisted the papers into her oversized black leather satchel. She was walking to the door when she felt something moving in the bag. She heard a scratching noise from inside, like a rat working on a piece of wood.

Amber-Marie swallowed hard and set the bag on the floor. With her foot, she pulled it open.

There was nothing. Just the papers. They did stink, though, of smoke and something else she couldn't name.

She opened the door and walked to the empty elevator, pressing the button. It opened at once and she stepped in. Amber-Marie glanced down at the bag. She could swear she heard something with her, panting. It didn't sound like a dog. More like a cat, she thought, the way the big lions sound on *Animal Planet*.

"Welcome to the story," someone whispered to her.

Epilogue

The Black Death annihilated Sicily—and all of Europe. Eyewitness accounts often described a stranger arriving in town just before the Black Death was unleashed among them. Estimates of the death toll ranged from one-third to one-half of all Europe, approximately twenty-five million people.

Scientists today still do not know what the Black Death was. Some believe it was a bubonic disease carried by rats. Others insist it was an Ebola-type virus. Scientists don't know what it was, but more important, they don't know *where* it is. It could still be in existence somewhere, perhaps buried deep in the plague burial pits, waiting to return, waiting for us to make one mistake. A contractor, perhaps, digging a new line, or a flood, or even an earthquake.

Historians know this: The Black Death moved the realm of science and medicine out of the authority of the Church, launching the Renaissance. Some would see this as a great victory for science and a defeat of the Church. Never again would the Church have such

control over intellectual research and discovery. Science would go on
with or without God's blessing.

To many Christians, intellectuals themselves, this was not a
rebellion against God. It was, rather, the direct hand of God. Science
is the search for God. When a scientist enters a lab tomorrow morning, looking for a cure for AIDS or Alzheimer's, she is searching for
God. God's will is to see suffering ended, the lost found, and the
broken made whole. Scientists have faith this can be done. They are
radical optimists about the human condition.

Some scholars would say the Black Death's real victim was God.
The Church's medicines, spiritual and physical, and all the prayers in
the world had not stopped the plague.

But neither did the plague stop faith. The Church lived on, mul-
tiplied now, in one way the plague had not considered. Church is no
longer the four walls and painted windows; the Church lives in us,
and we are the Church to each other. Women, who had previously
been allowed no voice in the Church, were allowed to pray with
the lost and the sick. Women were sent out with God's message of
forgiveness and hope. The pope authorized women to speak the holy
words of priests to a dying world.

I have always wondered why God remained silent in the worst
disaster of human history. In Scripture, great disasters are well
explained. The plagues of Egypt were brought on by Pharaoh's hardened heart. The exile of the Jews was caused by disobedience to the
covenant. But the Black Death? Why?

Why did God not speak? I often asked myself.

But at last, in finishing this book, I understood. God had never
been silent.

In the time of the Black Death, the Church doors were thrown wide open, and the faithful were pushed out into the world. Women, who had no voice in the Church, were now encouraged to speak for God, and their message was one of deliverance, hope, and redemption. The Church was willing to die to itself, to suffer the pain of change and reconsiderations, that the suffering would not die alone. The Church fought darkness, and women took the front lines.

God is our refuge and strength,
an ever-present help in trouble.
Therefore we will not fear, though the earth give way
and the mountains fall into the heart of the sea,
though its waters roar and foam
and the mountains quake with their surging.
There is a river whose streams make glad the city of God,
the holy place where the Most High dwells.
God is within her, she will not fall;
God will help her at break of day.
Nations are in uproar, kingdoms fall;
he lifts his voice, the earth melts.
The Lord Almighty is with us;
the God of Jacob is our fortress.
—Psalm 46:1–7

... a little more ...

When a delightful concert comes to an end,

the orchestra might offer an encore.

When a fine meal comes to an end,

it's always nice to savor a bit of dessert.

When a great story comes to an end,

we think you may want to linger.

And so, we offer ...

AfterWords—just a little something more after you

have finished a David C. Cook novel.

We invite you to stay awhile in the story.

Thanks for reading!

Turn the page for ...

- **Q & A with Ginger Garrett**
- **Discussion Questions**
- **How to Survive the Black Death**
- **Careers That Pay Well During the Black Death**
- **The Medieval Herbalist's Medical Kit**
- **Bibliography/Suggested Reading**
- **About the Author**

Q & A with Ginger Garrett

1. Where did you get Mbube's name and how do you pronounce it?

Mbube is a Zulu word for *lion*, and it is also a form of African song, sung most often by men. Mbube is pronounced "Em-boo-beh." I like to think of him as Bob Marley meets the Hulk. I don't know why, but all the guardian angels in my stories appear in my mind as Africans. Africa was the continent that sheltered Jesus Christ as a young child when King Herod was hunting for Jesus to kill Him. God reminds us in the Bible that "out of Egypt I called my Son." Africa gave shelter to a young Christ, to God, and I believe there is an evil out there that has never forgiven Africa for that. If Africa protected the young Jesus, it's easy to imagine angels as supernatural Africans who protect us, too.

2. You're saying you believe in the Devil?

I believe there is an active, intelligent evil in this world, an evil that is at work to destroy everything God considers beautiful. This evil has several names in Scripture: the Enemy, the Evil One, Satan, Lucifer. Those names have become so perverted in our culture that I hate to even reference them. The Devil to us is a mascot for canned ham. It's a masterful piece of public relations, don't you think? The Devil as a mascot for ham, angels as sweet cherubs that offer no protection, and Jesus as a wise teacher in cool sandals but not really capable of outrageous miracles. Everything in that scenario is so innocuous; it makes the hairs on the back of my neck stand straight up. There is a shocking truth hiding beneath that thin frosting. Someone is hoping we don't scrape through it.

3. How did you choose the subject matter for each book in the Scribe series?

I picked the three most important moments in medieval history that changed women's lives forever:

- Anne Boleyn gave us the right to read, including, but not limited to, the right to read the Bible. (And thus, book one, *In the Shadow of Lions.*)
- The women who survived the Black Death, though their names are lost to us, created a culture of survivors who launched the great Renaissance of science and art. We, too, must answer the question they faced: Amid so much suffering and pain, how then shall we live? (And thus, book two, *In the Arms of Immortals.*)
- For the final book in the series, I will be telling the tale of the witch hunts in medieval Europe. Women with strong wills, strong minds, or women who no longer had families were targeted for death. "Christians" both instigated the murders

front perilous questions: What, and who, defines a
woman? Are women more prone to sin and moral
weakness? Do women have an equal place in God's
kingdom? (And thus, book three, *In the Eyes of
Eternity*.)

I think book three will be, by far, the most difficult book to write
in the series. But it is my belief that we are indeed "surrounded by a
great cloud of witnesses." These women of our past are waiting for us
to make courageous, dangerous decisions … or suffer again as they
did.

*4. Did you exaggerate the symptoms of the plague? It seems that people
died very quickly. Were you just in a hurry to finish the book?*

Eyewitness accounts claim victims could die within a matter of minutes. Many stories were of a plague victim walking down the street,
and if someone went out to meet them, the healthy person died
within minutes of contact. Some historians and scientists refuse to
believe these claims, for the claims do not fit our modern beliefs of
the plague.

We also assume past generations were not as smart as we are.
(This applies to the Bible as well. Although the books that compose
the Bible were written by eyewitnesses, we refuse to believe what they
tell us because it doesn't fit our modern beliefs.)

One question I try to ask myself as I research is, "What if it is
all true? What if those eyewitnesses were right, and some died within
minutes?" We would be able to immediately rule out all the plagues

we know, which take much, much longer to kill. We would be left with no explanation … and we are of an age that cannot bear to live without explanation.

Which was, for me, the greatest problem of the Black Death and this novel: the question of *why*? Why did God allow a plague to sweep in and decimate the world? We often hear the estimate that the Black Death killed up to half of Europe. That's true, but we should also say that the plague wiped out a huge number of people all over the world, including Africa, the Middle East, the Far East, and even remote frozen islands. Why would God allow that? Was He mad? After all, every plague mentioned in the Bible was associated with a divine punishment for bad behavior. God had set a precedent of sending plague as punishment.

When the plague struck, everyone asked, "Why?" They immediately began pointing fingers. The Jews, in particular, were blamed. Thank God, the wise Pope spoke out against this belief and ordered that Jews be left unharmed. (But he was unable to stop many mass murders.) I can only begin to explain this violence when I remember the AIDS epidemic at its beginning. The hate and violent speech directed at gays stunned me. Those claiming to be Christians said they "knew" as a biblical certainty that God had sent AIDS to punish gay people. (Children were dying, too, but this was conveniently ignored. Was God mad at them or did His divine wrath just have a scattershot pattern?)

So much damage is done by Christians when we attempt to answer the question of *why*. No answer suffices, no words can heal that wound. It is a sacred suffering.

Perhaps if God gave us answers, we would find comfort in them instead of Him. How many senseless words are spoken at bedsides and funerals? "It was God's will." "This was God's plan." "Everything happens for a reason." We find comfort in them and we shouldn't. There may be a truth in those statements, but none of them is the whole Truth. We have to find comfort in the mystery of God, and there are no human words that can reach into that place and illuminate it.

We were not created with minds that allow us to comprehend the ultimate answer, yet God left us with the capacity to question. That's the mystery in itself, I guess.

5. You say the Black Death was the death of the angels. How did you see this reflected in art from the period?

In the art that was created after the Black Death, Christ became more "human." Crucifixes began to show a suffering Christ, a God in pain who was naked and bleeding. Christ was still portrayed as divine and "untouchable" in many paintings, with gold and illuminating light, but we now needed to emotionally connect with His suffering. Art also began to show Death walking among the living, walking with priests, menacing unsuspecting women from dark shadowy corners. A fascination with demons crept onto our canvases, while angels went from strong, sizable defenders to chubby babies who could barely hold their heads up, much less carry a sword.

Art from this period has profoundly impacted our spiritual lives today. We still picture angels as sweet, innocuous beings, while we imagine demons as powerful creatures to be feared. We are out of balance.

6. How long does it take to write a novel?

I don't know. I've never written one. I have, however, written a lot of sentences. I write one sentence, and then do this over and over, day after day, until I find I have filled up hundreds of pages. Then I begin deleting sentences, one by one, over and over, day after day, until I find I have deleted dozens of pages. Then I send it to my editor and bury myself face first in a plate of chocolates.

If I begin thinking about writing an entire novel, I'll choke from stress. Novels are big undertakings. But sentences? I can write those.

𝔇iscussion 𝔔uestions

1. The plague was merciless. Suffering was extreme. Everyone was in anguish. Why do you think a merciful God would allow this suffering? How can we call God merciful when thousands, or millions, are brutalized?

2. How can we learn to live without answers? Does this make us fools or faithful? Explain your answer.

3. What are we to do with the anguish we feel when we (or those we love) are victimized without reason and there is no justice to be had on earth?

4. Only Lazarro, as priest, was allowed to hear confession and give last rites (Last Unction). As the plague progressed, the pope allowed all women to assume this role too. Priests could not attend to all the dying, so women were allowed to comfort others in the name of Christ. This was the first time women were allowed to speak in God's name to a dying world. Why was this moment important in women's history? Do you see any ripple effects of this decision down through the ages and in society today? If so, name a few.

5. What does it mean to be healed? Is it only physical, or is there more to it? Do you believe there can be total healing on earth? Why or why not?

6. In his final scene, Del Grasso tells Gio to never ask the question "Why?" Instead, ask the question "How?" In your life, have you ever been tangled up in the question of why? If so, tell the story. In what way(s) have you let go of the whys and started exploring the hows? "How, then, shall you live?" (Bonus points for anyone who can find the Scripture verse that inspired this line!)

7. The Black Death was called "the death of the angels." It was the time when the Age of Fear began. Which rules your life: faith or fear? Why? Why is it easier to respond to a crisis out of fear, rather than out of faith?

8. If you could change the ending to *In the Arms of Immortals,* which two people would be alive and married to each other at the end of the story? Why would you choose this ending?

9. If you could go back in time and witness any event in history, what would it be and why?

10. If you could talk to your guardian angel, what questions would you want to ask?

How to Survive the Black Death

From my research,

I have collected the following helpful household hints:

Breathe only good air.

Inhale deeply the fumes of urine and excrement, preferably straight from a sewer.

Practice moderation in food and drink.

Avoid lovemaking.

Eat no fruit.

Eat only fruit and vegetables.

Think happy thoughts.

Avoid stress.

Build a circle of fire and stay within its center.

Whip yourself until you bleed (if you punish yourself first, perhaps God won't have to).

Pray, especially to Saint Sebastian.

Elevate your bed.

Bleed a pint of blood out.

Balance your humours.

Analyze your urine by smell to select a proper remedy.

Check your pulse—avoid a racing heart.

Send someone else to run your errands.

If none of these methods appeals to you,
do what many people in the plague did:
abandon all caution, reason, and morals.
Eat, drink, and be merry ...
for there is no escaping the Black Death.

Careers That Pay Well During the Black Death

- Trench digger
- Body hauler
- Body inspector (often elderly women, these inspectors were in charge of looking at corpses and determining what had killed them)
- Guard (to keep the enforced quarantine and prevent looting)
- Quack physician
- Quack spiritual adviser
- Quack supernaturalist (to help you chat with the deceased, in case the dead forgot to tell you where the will is)
- Lawyer (any surprise there? Estates must be settled, deeds must be transferred, etc.)
- Thief and looter
- Messenger and personal assistant (the rich could afford to send servants out into the plagued masses, and thereby reduce their own exposure)
- Celebrity chef (because herbs and spices are powerful medicine, the rich and famous must hire the best chef in town, who knows how to season food both for taste and health)

The Medieval Herbalist's Medical Kit

As a medieval medical professional there are a few items you must keep about your person. I've listed those below.

Where noted, you will find a few medieval remedies that are still regarded as beneficial. Note, however: these are medieval medicines and not for modern use. If you try a remedy against my wishes and die a gruesome death, you'll have no one to blame but yourself.

Now, for those who love to reenact medieval life, if you want a medieval career in medicine, you have some choices to make. You may prefer surgery to the healing arts, but you should know that surgeons were regarded as crude tradesmen who cut and sliced, rather than practicing the more sophisticated form of medicine: healing. Also, specialists were seen as rather dull-minded. A truly great healer could treat any condition. If you specialized in one area of disease or the body, it was because you lacked the talent to treat anything else.

Medieval medicine relied on the certain truth that the human body was controlled by humours and crafted out of the elements. As such, we are all composed of earth, fire, water, and wind. (Authors are all wind.) These elements translate roughly in the humours that control us:

> Sanguine: associated with the element Wind and the
> bodily fluid of blood. These people are, accordingly,

flighty and free, blown easily in new directions. Sanguine humours are both wet and hot. If a patient is too sanguine, treat with dry, cold herbs.

Choleric: associated with the element of Fire and the bodily fluid of yellow bile. These patients are fiery, sometimes sour and caustic, but always interesting. If an excess of bile is suspected, treat your patient with herbs to induce a cooler, wetter body environment.

Melancholic: associated with the element of Earth and the bodily fluid of black bile. Although black bile had never been seen, and doesn't actually exist, they needed a fluid to associate with Earth. Black bile tends to shift around the body, much like Hippocrates believed a woman's uterus tended to do. When the uterus got lodged in our brain, we suffered from "menstrual derangement."

When black bile accumulates around the brain, a patient will have muddled thinking. Black bile around the heart brings depression. Melancholics are given to morbid reflections, excessive sensitivities, and composing poetry. Melancholic patients need herbs to introduce more warmth and moisture. Again, black bile has never been discovered in the body. However, scientists needed a rational explanation for the existence of poets.

Phlegmatic: Associated with the bodily fluid of phlegm and the element of Water. Phlegm, as you might expect, is wet and cold. A patient suffering from an excess of phlegm needs dry heat supplied through your cures. Since phlegm has a reputation for being, well, nasty, the medievalists tried to associate a few positive traits with it. Such as, phlegm is always there when you need it. (So phlegmatics make loyal friends.) However, the appearance of phlegm (or a phlegmatic) is well known to put a damper on a party, so phlegmatics are shy. Phlegm rarely changes throughout your life. Phlegmatics may have a hard time with change and prefer a predictable routine. This can make them dependable companions, however.

Basic Ingredients to Keep on Hand

- Coarse salt: good for use as toothpaste. Also used in washing newborn babies. (Wine was used to wash newborns as well.)

- Jasper stone: good for "diabolical dreams." Jasper stone was not ingested but used as an amulet.

- Valerian root: good for insomnia, especially when added to a cup of warm wine. (Valerian is still used today for insomnia. You can find it as the main ingredient in herbal sleep preparations.)

- Cinnamon: excellent all-around spice for balancing cold, wet humours. Wonderful for sinus infections. Today we know cinnamon is also good for supporting healthy blood-sugar levels.

- Onions: cut into slices and stuff down your stockings when you have a cold.

- Hyssop: good for those with liver disease.

- Fennel: a good all-purpose remedy. Fennel can be added, whole or crushed, into boiling water to make a tea. This tea is useful for digestive disorders, fevers, infections, and pain. (Modern herbalists swear by this remedy. Fennel tea is available at all major grocery stores.)

- Sage: if you have a "rotten stench" emanating from your body, snort some dried sage. If it doesn't work, you won't be able to smell yourself anyway. Sage, when boiled into a tea, is also good for arthritis.

- Thyme: wonderful when both eaten and applied to skin for skin ailments.

- Parsley: used for chest pain and fevers, when boiled. Made into a poultice (paste), parsley can be applied to joints afflicted with arthritis. It is also recommended for "menstrual derangement."

- Black tea: useful for curing diarrhea, especially when taken with cooked apples. (This remedy is still recommended today by natural healers, and many would attest that it works.)

Art Supplies

Many herbalists also collected raw materials to use in pigments for the great church paintings in progress all over Europe. So, as you collect your herbs, keep an eye out for supplies, including:

- Lapis lazuli and azurite: can be finely ground for blue pigment.

- Malachite: used for green/yellow pigments.

- Turmeric and cumin: to create gorgeous gold hues.

- Dirt: if the dirt has an interesting color, as the earth in Italy does, take some with you.

- Bones: when bones are burned for hours, you can scrape the black powder off them to make a rich black pigment.

Bibliography/ Suggested Reading

Images of Plague and Pestilence
By Christine M. Boeckl
2000, Truman State University Press
Kirksville, Missouri

The Great Mortality: An Intimate History of the Black Death, the Most Devasting Plague of All Time
By John Kelly
2006, Harper Perennial, New York

Medieval Sicily: The First Absolute State
By Henry Barbera
2000, Legas Publishing, New York

Return of the Black Death: The World's Greatest Serial Killer
By Susan Scott and Christopher Duncan
2005, John Wiley & Sons, Chichester, West Sussex, England

After the Black Death: A Social History of Early Modern Europe
By George Huppert
1998, Indiana University Press, Bloomington, Indiana

Medieval Art
By Marilyn Stokstad
2004, Westview Press, Boulder, Colorado

The Power to Heal: Ancient Arts and Modern Medicine
By Rick Smolan, Phillip Moffitt, Matthew Naythons
1990, Prentice Hall Press, New York

About the Author

Ginger Garrett is the critically acclaimed author of *Chosen: The Lost Diaries of Queen Esther*, which was recognized as one of the top five novels of 2006 by the ECPA; *Dark Hour;* and *Beauty Secrets of the Bible*. *In the Arms of Immortals* is book two of the historical fiction trilogy Chronicles of the Scribe.

Ginger creates novels and nonfiction resources that explore the lives of historical women. A frequent media guest and television host, Ginger has been interviewed by *The New York Times*, Fox News, National Public Radio, Billy Graham's *The Hour of Decision*, *The Harvest Show*, and many other outlets.

In 2007, Ginger was nominated for the Georgia Author of the Year Award for her novel *Dark Hour*. A graduate of Southern Methodist University with a degree in theater, she is passionate about creating art from history. You can learn more about Ginger and her work by visiting www.gingergarrett.com.

For more information about the Chronicles of the Scribe series, visit the Web site dedicated to the books and to the world of medievalists: www.ChroniclesoftheScribe.com.

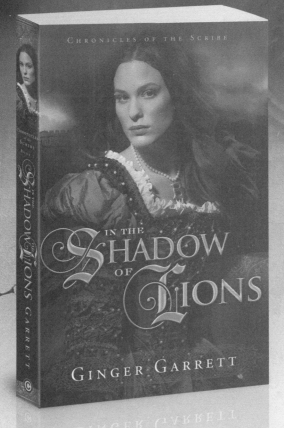

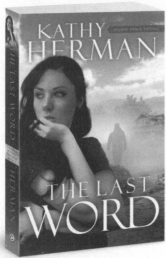